BRUISED

A novel by Azárel

 ®

A Life Changing Book *in conjunction with* Power Play Media
Published by Life Changing Books
P. O. Box 423 Brandywine, MD 20613

Cover design by Kevin Carr/photography by Carla McKenzie
Edited by Leslie German
Layout by Brian Holscher

Library of Congress Cataloging-in-Publication Data;

www.lifechangingbooks.net

ISBN *0-9741394-2-4*
Copyright ® *2005*

Dedication

This book is dedicated to the supportive group of family members and friends who have stood by my side. Thank you all for being a blessing in my life. I could not have accomplished this task without you. Your encouragement is greatly appreciated and will never be forgotten.

introducing
Power Play
Media

in conjunction with
Life Changing Books

Acknowledgements

Once again I've had to ask my Heavenly Father for guidance, direction and support while completing this novel. Without You, none of this would be possible. I truly learned that I can do all things through Christ who strengthens me. A special thanks to my husband for always having my back!!! 2005 has been an incredible and successful year for us both. Love you for life!!!!!!! P.S.- From the movie "Jerry Maguire" you complete me (smile).

Special thanks go out to all of the professionals who have worked diligently to make Bruised a success: Leslie German, as usual your professional editing skills are priceless. Kevin Carr of OCJ graphix.com, the cover has heads turning. Brian Holscher, thank you so much for the book layout. Shakira, can't get enough of your photography. Danielle Daniels, I told you that you'd make a great model for the book cover. Thanks for your poses, the many years of friendship and the crazy times we've spent together. Most will think the book is about us. But we know better (laugh). Schalette, thanks for coming aboard and bringing your level of professionalism to the organization. Most people wouldn't be able to jump in there and make things happen. Angela Jones, it has been such a pleasure knowing you. Congratulations on the start-up of Crystal Visuals Marketing Media Agency www.crystalvisualsmma.com.

Blessed is the only word that can be used to describe how I feel about the people who have been placed in my circle. I've been privileged enough to come across a fabulous group of test readers. Cheryl, (aka "Cel"), Emily, Catina, Danielle, Teresa, Leslie, (aka "Bean"), Ronnique, Shannon and Shaunda. I love each of you dearly. Believe me, I don't take your help lightly. Get ready for the next project. But don't breathe to long, Life Changing Books in conjunction with Power Play Media has several new projects coming your way (breathe). A special thanks again to my color purple sister, Cheryl (aka "Cel") for telling me that the ending of the first draft was "wack". Readers, thank her for the changes.

Lisa Williams, you're so wonderful you deserve your own paragraph. I can't thank you enough for the time and effort you've put into Life Changing Books. You wear many many hats and can't be thanked enough for all you do. I've watched you go from editing, to publicity, to delivery, to just plain nagging me to finish the book!!!! You've proven that you're down for life. A lot of great people have come from UMES and you're one of them.

A special shot out to the people who are always working the undercover publicity team ; Jeremiah, Don, Edna Swan, Jerri (aka. Stink), Kenya, Alaya, Janell, Wynetta, Saundra, Jackie and Jamila. Your support is greatly appreciated. I can't

Acknowledgements

go any further without mentioning my incredible group of young writers (Kwiecia, Khadijah, and Ashley). Not only have you been gearing up for Teenage Bluez, but you've worked overtime as sales reps, party planners, babysitters, hairstylist, and pool attendants (smile). I promise you it gets better.

Much much love goes out to my immediate family. There are way too many to name, but some that I must: Tam, what do I say? I am so lucky to have a sister like you. We have shared so much together and I thank you for the support. Even when I'm hard on you, it's only out of love. That's what big sisters are for.

Mommy, thanks for bringing me into this crazy world. You and Bill are truly loved. Thanks for looking out for all of us. Daddy, now that you've retired for the eighth time, get ready to write your story. Joyce, hopefully your pen is still moving. This is the year for your stories to shine. To my two grandmothers, Lover and Gram, the queens of grandmamas. I don't boast often in life, but when I speak about the two of you, I can't help myself. Words can never express the gratitude for the impact you've had and continue to have on my life. To Earnest 'Toot' Williams, what can I say? You breed hard working family members just like you. They call me lil' Toot.

Shout outs to the Fenners, Cookes, Williams, Newells, Vicks, Kinneys, Fords, Freemans, and the Woodruffs. When I wrote the last book, some people got crazy when I forgot to mention names. Just be proud of my accomplishments and forget about my bad memory. You know I love you.

Acknowledgements

Thanks so much to Darren Coleman (Do or Die, Don't Ever Wonder and Before I let Go) for being a true friend and business partner. It's amazing, you are really part of the family. Understand that Power Play Media is coming up!!!!!! Tyrone Wallace (Double Life) I'm so proud of your success. People are already asking about your new book. Zach Tate (Lost and Turned Out, No Way Out), you've outdone yourself this time, the book is hot. Much love to Shawan Lewis (Help Wanted), Natasha Gale Lewis(Men Cheat, Women Experiment) Danette Majette, (I Should'a Seen it Comin'), and Deborah Smith (Robbed Without a Gun) Jewell and Michelle, you're up next with Bliss.

Thanks to all of the distributors who have looked out for the success of Bruised. While I can't name them all, I'd like to especially thank: the entire A&B staff(Karen and Kwame thanks for looking out!) To Kevon and the Culture Plus crew, thanks for everything. Nati, at African World Books you are truly a man of character, thanks. Carol and Brenda at C&B, much love.

Even though my books are sold all over, I wanna especially thank the African American bookstores. Thanks for giving our readers a place to feel at home. Emilyn at Mejah Books in Delaware, you are a phenomenal lady. I admire what you're doing in your community. Keep up the good work. Karibu books in my hometown, you are awesome. Shot outs to Simba, Sunny, Yao, Tiffany, T Mac and the rest of the crew. Mr. Evans at Expressions, Masamba in Queens, Sepia Sand and Sable; much success to you all.

Whether you've given technical, moral, or emotional

Acknowledgements

support during this project, I want to thank you. If for some reason you're not mentioned, I still want to thank you.

And last, but certainly not least, to the two most beautiful little ladies in my life, all of this is for you. You are my inspiration and reason for living. I thank you for giving my life purpose and meaning. You have been patient in sharing me with so many people this year and for that I love you more than life itself.

Peace,

Azárel

Also by Azarel
A Life to Remember

Prologue

She jetted to her car shortly before dawn grasping her forearms. Carlie pressed the key alarm to unlock her Honda Accord Coupe. She placed her knee on the driver's seat to grab her cell phone from the charger. Chills draped her body when a suffocating spirit invaded her space. As she glimpsed over her right shoulder, a six foot shadow reached in her direction.

"Slap!" she was hit with an open hand. "No!" she screamed as her head hit the steering wheel. Not wasting any time, he grabbed hold of her wavy ponytail. Fearfully quiet, she kicked to escape his grip. His erratic behavior escalated when he noticed her look of sheer terror.

He whispered, "I can't believe you thought I'd fall for such bullshit! Bitch, you gon' pay for cheatin' on me." He pulled her, sending her body helplessly into the asphalt. Faced down like a criminal on an episode of *Cops,* warm blood dripped from her mouth.

Crouched in a fetal position, she anticipated his next move. "Uumph!" she bellowed as he kicked her multiple times in her torso. The final blow to her stomach nearly sent her unconscious. She didn't think she'd make it. The rage intensified. He continued to stomp his Timbs into her ribs. She tried to scream but nothing came out.

Chapter 1

Fool in Love

"Has the pain medication given you any comfort yet Ms. Stewart?" asked the nurse. The 200 pound woman began toiling with the covers to perform her hourly assessment. It had become perfectly clear to Carlie Stewart that her life had been turned upside down. Who would have thought she'd be lying in a hospital bed incapable of moving her arms and legs? Lately, she'd prided herself on learning to pacify Devon's temper. But nothing could calm him enough to stop the beating he had put on her this morning.

Although pain still surged through her body, the only thing she could think about was what her family would say. Especially Grandma Jean, whom she highly respected. While checking Carlie's bandages, the nurse mentioned that her Dad was in the hall talking to the doctor on duty. How could she explain to him that Devon was up to his old tricks again? After that last episode, Carlie had promised to stop seeing him. Maybe this was God's way of punishing her for sneaking around with Devon behind her Dad's back.

Carlie had thought deeply about her decision to continue seeing Devon. Deep down inside she felt that because she was twenty years old she shouldn't have to creep. Not to mention the fact that a sheltered life wasn't her idea of living. She wanted her Dad to let her learn from her own mistakes. This was one lesson she'd never forget.

Carlie lay curled up on the bed allowing her fingers to gently touch her bruised ribs. She slowly caressed her inner thigh. The pain she felt triggered a remembrance of the kicks and punches her legs had endured. The bruises that covered her legs brought back unwanted memories of all the brutal ass whippings in the past. Carlie wondered if this was what she deserved. If her fractured ribs didn't teach her to leave him alone, nothing would.

For Carlie, it started a year and a half ago when she met Devon at Club Nuevo, during the Christmas break from Lincoln University in Pennsylvania. Standing in line in 20 degree weather meant nothing knowing that she'd soon be inside shaking her ass to the beats of Jay Z. Devon fit the perfect description of what Carlie wanted in a man. His 320 pound frame stood six feet five inches tall, with a caramel complexion, hazel eyes and a distinct swagger in his walk. Draped in a Northface down coat, Roca Wear Jeans, and black suede Timbs, his attitude epitomized a true thug.

Before Carlie had a chance to move up in line, they made eye contact. A sexual attraction was obvious. Devon wasted no time. He grabbed her hand, snatched her out of line and walked towards his car, divinely parked in front of the club. Smiling the entire time, Carlie never protested. After moments of small talk, Devon assured her that his woman would never have to stand in line at any club in the Washington Metropolitan area. Carlie saw his domineering nature as a turn-on, not to mention she had always been a sucker for a bald head. The gun buried in his waist only added to the excitement when her new roughneck nearly suffocated her with a bear hug.

A knock at the door interrupted Carlie's thoughts. The dark-skinned female doctor could be seen from the slight opening in her left eye. While straining to focus on the other bodies behind the doctor, a lump formed in Carlie's throat.

"I'll come back after your visit Ms. Stewart," said the doctor.

"Okay," Carlie mumbled between the stitches in the side of her mouth.

Well dressed, standing six-foot three from the ground, Carlie's father Ricky Stewart, stood at the foot of the bed. Battered and speechless her heart stopped. Peering over his sunglasses, Ricky studied his baby girl's entire body like a coroner conducting an autopsy. His puckered brow demonstrated evidence of disapproval. Never saying one word, he slowly scanned the left side of the bed. Ricky gently lifted the hospital blanket to witness the damage beneath.

Although embarrassed, Carlie felt protected. She knew if her Dad had things his way she'd be locked in a bubble by now. She always wondered why there were so many do's and don'ts in life other than wanting to keep her away from any harm. At one point, Ricky could barely hold down a relationship due to his infatuation with Carlie. Fortunately for her, after she went off to college Ricky loosened up on the reigns a little.

Carlie watched her father guard her like the secret service. He had an air about him that resembled a black Tony Montana. It was a good feeling having him around until he decided to do something unusual. Mr. Stewart pulled the covers back to examine Carlie's body for a second time. He pulled out a digital camera and snapped away like a runway photographer as the proof of the brutal beating was being assembled. It shouldn't have shocked Carlie given her Dad's background as a successful criminal lawyer because this was step one in gathering the evidence.

Grandma Jean broke the silence with her swift entrance. Generally, she'd entertain the family with some of her slick, old-school slogans. But today was different. Her only focus was Carlie.

"Oh baby, you all right?" she whined. Tears welled in her eyes at the sight of her favorite grandchild lying in such a state. Grandma Jean leaned her frail, petite body over Carlie's upper torso. With her gray sleek bob resting on her grandbaby's chest she wept worse than she did at her husband's funeral.

Seeing her grandmother's face brought both pleasure and sorrow to Carlie's heart. Stroking her hand, Grandma Jean began to pray silently.

"Mama, she needs more than prayer," Ricky shouted. "She needs a gun!"

Grandma Jean continued to pray with raised voice while she squeezed Carlie's hand as tight as she possibly could.

"I have some other ways of dealing with this punk," Mr. Stewart retorted.

"And what is that?" Grandma Jean asked defiantly as she thought back to the unruly life her son once lead.

"You'll see," Ricky said.

"All I need is for you to backtrack and get yourself in some mess. You need drama like you need a damn hole in your head!"

"No… This is what Carlie wants!" Ricky yelled as he stared into Carlie's face. "Isn't it? Isn't it ?"

Tears streaming down the side of Carlie's cheek halted Mr. Stewart's words. He was now gazing into his daughter's brown eyes. It was almost as if he had forgotten about the situation at hand and just realized how beautiful his child was. Even with bumps, bruises, and bandages, Carlie was still gorgeous. Her jet black hair reminded him of his late wife, Catherine. In deep reflection, he thought about the resemblances of his two favorite girls. Carlie had taken on her mother's model figure, form-filled hips, and baby-doll face, but possessed her Father's Caribbean complexion. Undoubtedly, Carlie had her Dad wrapped around her finger.

Grandma Jean shook her head in disgust. "We might as well be livin' in the jungle wit the got damn animals she mumbled." Turning to Carlie she spoke with concern. "What a way to start your summer break," she said as she placed her hands on her hips.

"Carlie, listen to me, and listen good!" Ricky ordered, rubbing her hair. "I love you, but you're going to have to start loving yourself."

"I do," Carlie said mumbling each word.

"This is it. I'm not leaving this up to you this time. You *are* going to press charges and you *will* get a restraining order! Also. …"

The ringing of the phone brought silence to the room.

"Hello," Mr. Stewart said. "Hello… Hello…."

Dad glanced at Carlie mesmerized by his daughter's long eye lashes. Slamming down the phone, he continued. "Don't accept any phone calls from Devon," he ordered suspecting Devon was the phone stalker.

"Dad I can barely talk to you."

"That's not what I said."

"I know...," Carlie said frustrated.

"That's why we're in this situation now. You don't like to listen."

"Cut her some slack, Ricky," Grandma Jean interjected.

"Now Carlie, I know it hurts you to talk. But I need to know exactly what happened this morning," Dad said.

"Can we talk about it later?" Carlie whined waiting for her grandmother to halt the interrogation before it started.

"Carlie. ..."

"Well, last night, I left Devon's before the storm. I told him that I would call him once I got home. When I arrived it was clear that the electricity had gone out, killing the phone lines. I knew Devon would be furious if I didn't call. So thinking ahead, I plugged my cell phone into the car charger." Carlie slowed the pace of her speech. Her mouth ached from the constant movement of her jaw. She looked at her father and decided to endure the pain. "Unfortunate for me, I fell asleep and never went back outside to get my phone." Not sure if she could muster the right words to tell the rest of the story Carlie paused.

"I'm waiting," Dad shouted as he paced the floor.

She hesitated. "When I walked out to my car this morning, a figure appeared from nowhere. Without a word he grabbed me and asked where I had been. Looking into his bloodshot eyes I knew he was delirious. Nervousness took over as I attempted to tell him what I told you. Before I knew it, I was on the ground. My mouth felt as if the whole side of

my face had been split in half. Noticing the blood dripping
from my mouth, I became speechless. Devon had landed a
mean blow to my right chin.

I heard a voice yell, "I can't believe you think I would fall
for the bullshit! Bitch you gon' pay for cheatin' on me!" He
slung open my car door, grabbed my phone, and began
searching through my recent calls. "The battery looks charged
to me," he shouted as he threw the phone in the grass.

"Anticipating his next move, I balled up. He kicked me
over and over again in my side. When his complexion turned
colors, I knew that was it. After feeling the blow to my eye it
nearly sent me unconscious; I didn't think I would make it.
His rage intensified as he kept pumping his left foot into my
stomach. I tried to scream, but nothing came out. I just laid
on the ground lifeless. If it hadn't been for the newspaper
delivery truck driving up. ..."

Carlie couldn't even finish. The sound of the phone ringing diverted all attention in the room to Ricky. Only mini
huffs and puffs could be heard by the time Mr. Stewart
answered the phone. Carlie tried not to make eye contact,
but she knew what her Dad thought. As her father slammed
down the receiver, his lips twitched. He glared at the phone,
at his daughter, then turned back towards the phone as his
head dropped into the palms of his hands. A hush filled the
room for several minutes. All were at a lost for words.

"I could kill that bastard," Ricky shouted in anger. He
knew if he followed through he'd have a good chance of getting off if he got caught. Tired and drained he figured the situation called for serious planning and quick, discreet action.

"Okay Mama, let's go so Carlie can rest. That's what she
really needs right now."

Grandma Jean landed two wet kisses on Carlie's forehead. Tears flowed once again from Carlie's weak body, but these were tears of joy. Joy because she knew Grandma would stick with her through it all. Ricky with his hand on the door turned to say his goodbyes.

"Baby, I may be hard on you, but I love you." He paused briefly waiting for a response from his baby girl, but quickly exited behind Grandma Stewart after seeing that Carlie had turned slightly unwilling to look him in the eye.

Dad's eyes grew to the size of watermelons as he stepped into the hall. He could not believe the delivery boy stood there holding two dozen roses, sporting a smile as wide as the Atlantic ocean. Snatching the card from the vase, Dad read intensely. The boy stood in a quandary. He couldn't understand what could have provoked Mr. Stewart to block the door to the room. Finally, he choked up enough nerve to speak.

"Excuse me sir, I'm not here for any trouble. I'd like to deliver these to Ms. Carlie Stewart if you don't mind."

"I'll take those," Mr. Stewart said as he forced the flowers away from the young man's hand.

"I'll need a signature," the delivery guy replied shaking his head in disbelief.

Ricky removed the gold plated Marc Blanc pen from his Armani suit jacket. "It would be my pleasure." Mr. Stewart quickly signed in his fancy Stewart & Associates signature and sent the boy on his way.

Ricky and Grandma Jean stood stiff outside of Carlie's room as the delivery boy moved at a snail's pace down the corridor. With each step he glanced back over his shoulders watching Mr. Stewart as if he were some type of serial killer.

Ricky had perfected the art of intimidation and in return watched him like a hawk until the elevator doors closed completely.

"He'll pay for this," Ricky roared as he read the message to his mother. "You damn right it will never happen again," he shouted as he crumbled the card in his hand and walked off dumping the roses in the trash. Grandma Jean followed shaking her head.

Carlie's room was quiet at last. Twenty minutes later the obese nurse returned for routine stats and updates. She administered both pain and sleep medication, then turned to leave the room. Carlie signaled for her attention.

"Miss, when will I be able to go home?"

"Sweetie, I have no idea. Only your doctor can make that decision. But it shouldn't be anymore than a few days. Now get some rest," the nurse said as she dimmed the lights and shut the door.

The codeine was taking effect when the phone rang. Carlie contemplated not answering it, but figured if she didn't, her Dad would return to check on her.

"Yes Dad," she said answering the phone in a groggy tone.

"This is your Dad, but not Ricky."

Hearing his voice sent chills through her body. Carlie sat motionless unsure of how to respond.

"Carlie, I'm sorry baby. I'on know what came over me. I never meant for it to go this far. You hear me baby?"

Carlie didn't respond. No matter what he said, images of him striking her would not leave her mind. In her heart she wanted so badly to believe the words he was pleading to her. Letting her mind drift back to what he was saying, she decided to speak.

"Devon, you need a punching bag, not a woman. ... "

"Baby, you the best thing that ever happened to me," Devon interrupted.

Carlie began to cry. The phone fell from her ear to the floor as she sobbed for nearly ten minutes. When the nurse came back to check on her, she found the phone laying on the floor. When she picked the phone up, there was a strange look on Carlie's face as she heard someone talking. The nurse handed Carlie the phone and walked out.

"Hello."

"Hi baby, I'm still here. I figured we'd cry together."

"Yeah, but we aren't in this hospital together. I'm the one with the bumps and bruises," Carlie said with raised voice.

"C'mon Carlie, you hit me too."

"Devon you are three times my size."

"Carlie, I'on wanna argue wit'cha. I need to be makin' things right. Baby, you my queen and I love you," he sniffled.

Deep down inside Carlie wanted to say I love you too, like she had done so many times before, but she had to stay strong. Devon's love was powerful. Holding her ground she told him it was over. She ended with a plea for space and time to think about them ever being friends again. When she heard the sound of the phone disconnect, Carlie thought that maybe she'd pulled it off. Just maybe she could be released. But then the phone rang again.

"Hello," she said in an unwelcoming tone. Cries were heard. If Academy Awards were being issued for best performance by a lying dog, Devon would've won by a landslide. After thirty minutes of listening to Devon's love testimonies, a drowsy Carlie finally said "I love you, too."

Chapter 2

Stake Out

Devon pulled to the front of the Grand Hyatt Hotel just in time to be the center attraction. As usual, the Black Men's Coalition party was packed. While people drove up in their shiny whips prepared to showboat, Devon outshined them all. As he stepped proudly out his yellow 2004 Hummer, he embraced his supporters with a bump of the shoulder and a heavy pound. For the last two months he cared about nothing but pimpin' out his baby with spinners and getting his sweetie detailed on a regular basis.

Devon could easily be mistaken for someone famous by the way everyone greeted him. Standing curbside he and Kirk resembled two hefty bodyguards with whom no one in their right mind would want to tangle with. Devon's enormous build didn't stop him from wanting to be fashionable. For some reason he considered himself a trendsetter. So, it didn't surprise the partygoers to see him in a pin-striped button down shirt, dark tan khakis, and rockin' Gianni Versace sunshades. The lack of sun didn't matter, that was Devon's style. Kirk, his long time side-kick, on the other hand, was plainly dressed in unflattering attire as if he weren't on his way into the hottest party of the summer.

They could already hear the sounds of the self-proclaimed Pied Piper of R&B inside putting it down. As Devon made his way through the crowd, he stopped frequently repeating excuses as to why he hadn't returned any phone calls that day. It was evident that he was the man on the streets and a hot commodity with the ladies. Devon decided to wait by a concession stand for Kirk who was sent on an errand to park the truck. Although a street smart thug, Kirk was free spirited, and took a back seat to Devon's domineering personality. On far too many occasions, he had to stray from his low-keyed character to go to battle alongside Devon. He knew his boy was always wrong, but remained by his side and was prepared to kick ass whenever he needed him. At times, Kirk even tried to persuade Devon to see how foolish he behaved sometimes. But it never worked.

Still in all Kirk stayed loyal. He often thought about the time when he visited a female friend and thirty minutes into the visit, her boyfriend showed up with a gun. Kirk didn't know much about the girl, and wasn't sure how she'd play him. Naturally, he panicked. He tried to figure a way out of the house.

While the deranged man outside yelled and kicked at the door, Kirk called Devon just to let him know his whereabouts. He wasn't sure if he'd make it out alive. But Kirk was sure that Devon would retaliate. Within minutes, Devon made it to the neighborhood and shot up the whole block searching for Kirk. Needless to say, the young lady's boyfriend jetted and Devon became Kirk's hero. At times, Kirk gets sick of remembering Devon's rescue. But if playing

Mr. Belvedere for his buddy keeps him happy , then it's cool with Kirk.

While catching a hot second alone, Junior, a loyal customer, pimped toward Devon in an all white linen suit. With their fist meeting simultaneously Junior asked, "What's up, D?"

"Nothin' much," Devon replied dryly. He checked himself, then his surroundings.

"So you don't answer yo' phone no mo', huh?" Junior asked.

"Oh yeah…, yeah, you know I'm a busy man." Devon smiled rudely excusing himself. "I'll get at 'cha as soon as I'm straight."

After making a flavorful exit, Devon was greeted by several young ladies all of whom had shapes that caused his manhood to transform into rock hard candy. Zarria, one of Carlie's closest friends, was among the admirers. Although pretty and petite, Zarria was dressed like she was auditioning for a Girls Gone Wild video. They all talked trash as Kirk quietly approached the circle.

"What's up for tonight?" The young lady with the green contacts asked exerting her attention toward Devon.

"Ain't shit," he replied, checking to see how closely Zarria eyeballed him.

Devon's admirer closed in on him. "I love me a negro with a bald head," she said standing on the tip of her toes. She slid her hand across Devon's scalp.

"Aiight." Devon cleared his throat and looked around. "Watch what you say, you 'bout to get yoself into somethin' you can't get out of," he said half-laughing.

Zarria gave Devon the eye.

"What?" he asked as if he didn't care about anything.

Zarria, feeling the need to speak, pulled Devon to the side for privacy. "So, have you talked to Carlie?" she asked, popping her gum as hard as she could.

"Briefly," Devon said nonchalantly.

"Well, *this time* I think she overreacted."

"You do?" Devon replied changing his demeanor. He was happy to hear that Zarria was still his number one fan.

"Yeah, I mean you're the best thing that ever happened to her. Of course, she still thinks the sun rises and sets on her father's ass. But one day she'll come to her senses."

"You should holla at'er more often. She needs somebody smart like you to train her," Devon said eyeing Zarria as if she were the last piece of meat at the market. Devon had always thought about the possibility of getting with Zarria, but was unsure if she'd tell. One thing was for sure; she wasn't worthy to be his girl. He wanted a woman who's *wifey* material. Not someone who was capable of dancing on top of a bar at any given moment.

"I tried to call 'er. But, she be fakin' on a nigga lately. She's probably frontin' for her daddy, but checkin' the caller I.D. every five minutes." Devon looked to see exactly who he was performing for. He had Zarria's undivided attention.

"Ummm...huh," she co-signed.

"Oh, she'll come to 'er senses. She needs to know that her big time Daddy might be able to get 'er in law school, but she'll always need me," Devon said with confidence.

By now, the faces of the ladies remaining in the huddle with Kirk showed signs of boredom. "Come on y'all, this ain't Sunday Mass. Livin' up," Kirk shouted in a partying mood.

The young lady who two minutes ago, drooled over Devon was now attracted to Kirk. She licked her lips slowly and used her green contacts to stare at Kirk from the top of his head to the bottom of his shoes. His deep brown skin had her mesmerized. *Big Chief Burette got it going on,* she thought. "You got Indian in your family," she blurted out.

"Nah," Kirk answered half laughing.

"Well you remind me of an Indian," she said. Besides, "I like a man with curly hair."

"I thought you loved a bald head," Kirk said sarcastically. He began to back away bit by bit. The thought of laying up with the green-eyed monster, gave him a bad feeling. Kirk loved pussy, but people who understood him, knew that he chose his women carefully. He claimed to be searching for Mrs. Right. So he stuck with his motto, *dodge one-night stands, dodge HIV.*

Devon had seen enough. He signaled for Kirk to fall in line as they moved out, but Zarria yelled out one last statement; a statement that would change Devon's entire night.

"You better stay close, her Dad is tryna hook her up with this guy from one of those Ivy League schools."

"Fuck that nigga. That would be her loss," Devon said shrugging his shoulders.

Kirk quickly followed behind Devon like a toddler. Peeling off a few hundreds for Kirk's impending bar run, Devon stopped abruptly.

"Here, I need a drink."

Kirk snatched the money. "I know you're not letting Zarria's comment get to you?" he asked.

"Hell no. I'm the man," he laughed. "I just need a moth-afuckin' drink. Now handle it, nigga!" he yelled. Kirk was gone in a blink of an eye.

Devon caught the stares of a big black guy looking him dead in his face. It took him a few seconds to realize it was a man he'd pistol whipped at a club several months ago. They eye-balled each other for a few moments until the guy walked away with revenge in his eyes. Devon never worried at all. He knew between the gun he had stashed on his side and the one Kirk was packing, the guy didn't stand a chance. Besides, Devon was the mayor of the streets and there weren't too many people willing to go up against him.

The hours quickly passed. Devon and one of the members of the E. Street gang became intoxicated after several drinks. From smacking girls on the ass to making degrading and sexist comments, Kirk was the only sober body who could apologize for their sinful acts and remarks. For Devon's size most couldn't believe that he had a hard time handling his liquor; but with his crazy rationale, he thought that he functioned fine, and always appointed himself as the designated driver. This was simply another demonstration of his need to control.

For some odd reason, seeing Zarria pass by ignited a strange annoyance in Devon. On one hand, in his drunken state, images of Zarria passing by nude entered his mind. Suddenly switching gears, he had images of Carlie on her father's couch tongue-kissing a preppy guy wearing an argyle sweater. Enraged, Devon ordered Kirk to rap up his conversation. Without a doubt, it was time to go.

Devon walked swiftly as if there was an emergency. Kirk trailed, unaware that he was about to repeat an event he'd done many nights before. When the Hummer finally pulled onto Yorkshore Drive, Kirk let out a sigh. His nerves jumped the entire ride hoping Devon wouldn't hit and kill someone, or have them killed.

Under normal circumstances, Kirk loved looking at the million dollar homes in Carlie's neighborhood. It was his dream to one day live large, like the Stewarts. He had even visited a model home a few blocks from Carlie's house. But tonight was different. He was unenthused. *Kirk wanted to go home.*

"Man, why the fuck we doin' this tonight? I had plans."

"Well, change 'em. We got other thangs to worry 'bout," Devon said in his commanding tone.

"I mean the girl hasn't been seen anywhere. What's the point?" asked Kirk aggravated.

"The point is…bitches are tricky. I don't trust her as far as I can throw her." Devon grinned. " So… we're gonna park right here and see what lil' Ms.Goodie Two Shoes is doin'."

Slumping down in his seat, Kirk began to get comfortable for his usual nap. He knew in his heart this would be a long night. Sticking to the routine, Devon would watch like a lion guarding his prey until morning assuring himself that no other man went near his woman. What he didn't realize was that Ricky Stewart had ordered Carlie to file a restraining order on him several weeks ago after her hospital release. Carlie put up a good fight in an attempt not to go against Devon. But Ricky insisted.

"Man, how long you gonna force her to be with you?" Kirk asked breaking the silence.

"You call this force?" Devon responded chuckling. "I call it tough luv."

"You got it bad, partner.

"Nigga, didn't I tell you to stop callin' me yo damn partner."

"Well you need to give this shit up. She don't deserve it." Kirk said with concern.

Devon didn't take action nor did he look at Kirk. He bit his lip and counted silently. Deep down inside he wanted to crack Kirk's jaw wide open. Weighing only fifty pounds less than he, Devon knew he could do his man right there in the seat. He always had suspicions that everyone had their eyes on his possession, and Kirk Fenner was no exception. Not to mention that his boyz had always discretely cheered for Carlie's release, but as always Carlie's man had his antennas up. Falling into a relaxed state, thoughts of the many romantic times he shared with his girl filled his mind.

The thought of Carlie's voluptuous breast and soft nipples gave Devon an immediate hard on. Hair rose on his chest as he imagined Carlie's full lips licking every inch of his body. The explosive movements made by Devon's wood had to be restrained. Opening his eyes slightly to monitor Kirk, Devon imagined Carlie straddling his engorged penis with her ass smashed against the steering wheel. He was rescued from his own body heat when Kirk turned over to let in some air through the window. After several deep breaths and refocusing for a moment Devon managed to redress his baby.

Quickly, he dialed Carlie's cell number. He got no answer. He dialed the number again. Still, *no answer*. He wanted badly to call on her house phone, but didn't have the energy to disrespect Ricky.

Hours passed and before long the sun peeked through the trees of the well manicured estate road. The sound of a nearby utility truck startled the sleepy stalkers. Ms. Ellis, Carlie's next door neighbor was in stage one of having her electronic gate installed.

Although the noisy utility vehicle could get by with ease, Ms. Ellis watched the Hummer intensely from her window. Devon became edgy. Unbeknownst to him, he was already seen. His truck was parked directly under a huge oak. A small black pinto was parked eight to ten yards behind him. The men on stake out were on duty just as Devon and Kirk were.

Devon got his cue when the lights flickered in the house. The clock on the dashboard read 5:30 a.m. Movement was detected near the blinds. Raising up and adjusting the mirror, Devon slowly pulled off. As he passed Carlie's house, he saw someone slightly move the living room blinds before closing them completely. Devon smiled as he pulled into a neighbor's driveway. He U-turned and rode right pass the unseen pinto which contained two men with matching pistols aimed directly at Devon's forehead. Slumped down in their seats, the opportunity to blast Devon from here to eternity had vanished.

Chapter 3

<u>Doctor Feel Good</u>

"Ahh…, that feels so… goo…d," Courtney Cox moaned while Ricky allowed his lips to suck her neck. By now his bedroom had been ran-sacked from the beginning of another session. Things were really heating up and Ricky loved every moment. He knew Courtney had him going ballistic when he knocked over his precious shooting trophies he'd won over the years. No one had been allowed to touch his prized possessions. Not Ester the cleaning lady; not even Carlie.

As Courtney ran her fingers through Ricky's hair, she reached down to awaken his manhood. She ripped the buttons from his Versace shirt to expose his chiseled chest. The sight of his nipples turned her on. Hungry, she began to flick the left nibble with her tongue. The sensation excited Ricky so much that he let out a loud moan. This was always a turn-on for him, but Courtney possessed a special trait that turned him out every time. Ricky called it knowing how to satisfy her man. Grandma Jean called it being a freak.

As Courtney continued to lick his chest she began to

caress his shaft. The head was special to her and called for extra attention. Ricky began to make loud and strange noises. Courtney placed her fingers over his lips. Within moments, he had feasted on each of her long, tangy fingers. Just the way she liked it, his fingers slowly entered her womanhood. The couple had been seeing each other off and on for the last two years so it was no surprise to either of them when strange sexual escapades took place.

Suddenly, Courtney pushed Ricky away, and revealed the leanest body he had seen in a long time. People thought Ricky looked good to be 40. But at 41 years of age, Courtney resembled a thirty-year-old hottee. As she began to yank off her clothing and accessories piece by piece, Ricky admired her toned physique. Not many women her age could entice Ricky. He normally liked his women young and trainable.

Courtney was an exception, she kept her body tight, especially her boobs. Her 36 DD's were perky and round and screamed to escape her bra. Ricky could tell she was ready. He moved in closer. Courtney immediately turned her back still wearing the silver thong that had been swallowed by her gigantic, yet voluptuous ass.

Leaning over the mini bar Ricky knew what she wanted. Normal sex wasn't good enough for Courtney. She liked it hard and raw. He had often wondered if he could ever make her his wife. He was truly tired of being alone, but in the back of his mind he'd always have to wonder if he was satisfying her.

On top of her sex addiction, Courtney had filed bankruptcy less than three weeks ago and needed a sugar daddy to take up the slack. Working on her third marriage was nothing to be proud of so she kept the details of the nuptials a secret from Ricky. Unbeknownst to her, Ricky was much more clever than she thought. A week after their first date- which he assumed would be a one night stand- he did a thorough background investigation. Some said it was the most ridiculous thing they'd ever heard, but for Ricky it was necessary. Besides, he was the founder of a million dollar law firm and couldn't allow any woman to come in and take half of what he'd worked so hard for. No doubt, everything would be left to his only daughter Carlie.

Stewart &Associates was built from nothing and was basically a gift from Ricky's old boss Renaldo Estovan. It's hard for people who know Ricky to believe that he had once been a hired killer. He never backed down from a battle. Ricky had only one rule; he didn't kill women and children. Other than that, bodies were open game. But between Grandma Jean's prayers and Estovan's money Ricky attended the Harvard School of Law and graduated Magna Cum Laude seven years ago. He's a living testament that evil can be transformed.

"What are you waiting for," Courtney growled turning her head around like the exorcist. Waving a string of beads, she grinned. "Oh…. You're waiting for these."

"Not tonight," Ricky responded throwing the beads to the ground. His slim, muscular body pressed firmly against Courtney's. She stood in perfect stance waiting for him to give her what she had come for. Her French manicured nails scraped a scraggily line in the wood of the mini-bar as Ricky rammed his dick into her pleasure garden. Within seconds, the twosome panted uncontrollably. Ricky yelled as loud as he could. Between breaths he grabbed Courtney's hair and slammed her on the dresser. She arched her back and tightened her muscles to fit perfectly around his dick. They relocated to a chaise nearby so Courtney could assume her favorite position. She straddled Ricky and slowly lowered her hips.

Suddenly she took all of him. Together they began to move like two dogs in heat. She jumped up just as Ricky was ready to explode. *I'm not finished with you yet*, she thought. She slowly took him in her mouth. Ricky moaned uncontrollably.

Courtney's hands moved perfectly synchronized with her mouth. Faster and faster she worked her tongue. Ricky was on the verge of going into cardiac arrest when Courtney began the grand finale. Like a mad man Ricky tried to push Courtney away. Instead of loosing her grip, she grabbed his butt cheeks as Ricky released all of his tension from the past few weeks.

Courtney remained in a zone. "Oh…baby…," she hollered, as Ricky flipped her on her back. "Oh…That's it," she yelled. "That's the spot." Courtney roared when Ricky entered her. This only boosted his ego. Women had often told him he reminded them of a stallion. He figured either it was true or they were out to become Mrs. Ricky Stewart. Yes, Ricky was a hot commodity, but tonight he belonged to Courtney.

Sweating profusely, Ricky thrust harder and harder. "Not yet," Courtney screamed. Her walls tensed. "That's it," she yelled louder. The sound of the doorbell slowed Ricky's movement. "No…" Courtney cried. She jerked her body. "It can wait damn it," she said as she continued to move her ass back and forth.

Ricky had stopped all movement. He stood with his

wood in hand staring at her performance. Courtney was livid when he reached for his phone. "Who could be that fucking important ?" she asked.

"I'll be right down," Ricky said firmly into the receiver. "I'm sorry babe," he said. "This is extremely important. Otherwise, you know I wouldn't let anything ruin our time together. Give me a few moments, pleaseeeeeeee," he begged.

Courtney ignored him as she allowed her fingers to finish the job. Speechless, she stared him down as he cleaned himself and headed to the door. She sat on the edge of the bed feeling quite stupid. *What could be so important at 2 a.m.? Was it something she'd done? Wasn't her lovin' good enough? Was he screwing someone else? That's it,* she thought. "Another woman is downstairs right now trying to steal my man," she mumbled in a low tone. Courtney grabbed her clothes scattered around the room. She dressed quickly. Feeling like a used tramp, she headed for the door with her semi-weapon in hand.

Wanting to be certain before she attacked, she slowed each step she took. A part of her feared what she'd see once she got down stairs. Nonetheless, she was prepared to rumble if need be.

As she approached the door with her gun drawn, she fumed. Carefully she listened to Ricky talk inside his locked office. Two unfamiliar male voices spoke. The sound of Courtney's three inch pumps caught Ricky's attention as he excused himself to unlock the door.

Ricky slung open the door. "I asked you to wait until I returned," he said transforming from a sex craved maniac to a shady businessman.

"I thought you were down here being an adulterer," she

smiled glancing at the two suspicious men. The dark shades
and tightly fitted tees really had her going. Courtney wanted
to get a better look, but was stopped in her tracks.

"Do I look gay to you," Ricky said without cracking a
smile.

"Nooooooo. I just wanted us to spend some time together. But I'm sure you can't identify with that." Courtney folded her arms tightly. " Keep on, you might loose me," she
smirked.

"We're not even married. Now either wait upstairs or I'll
call you later." Before Ricky could slam the door Courtney
couldn't help but to notice the stern faces of the hushed men.
She knew it was in Ricky's system to hold business meetings
at odd hours, but tonight he was certainly grooming stone-
cold killers.

Eavesdropping outside the door, Courtney reflected on
Ricky's past. She'd heard the many rumors of his affiliation
with Renaldo Estovan, a well known Columbian Cartel dope
dealer. Supposedly, Ricky was the leader of a group of ruthless killers for the cartel. Not only did he carry out execu-
tions, but he was responsible for the deaths of several innocent people. In one particular case he was put on trial for first
degree murder.

The positive in all of Ricky's indecencies was that he
acquired his lust to practice criminal law. Estovan had hired
the cream of the crop for Ricky's defense. The Feds knew he
had murdered Nick Profaci, but had no hard evidence to
prove it. Ricky sat at the defense table week after week armed
with all the right answers to convict himself.

After being found not guilty, his desire to practice law
increased. He vowed never to allow incompetent, show-off

attorneys to convict criminals on bogus charges. After Ricky's case ended, Estovan wanted him to assume leadership. Estovan was fond of his ability to maintain his silence under pressure. Ricky's swift way of handling problems was impressive. Leaving his criminal life behind, Ricky became a retired soldier, and opted to attend law school.

The thought of sleeping with a murderer sent chills through Courtney's body. But Ricky's charming manner had her sprung. *So what if he was having a secret session with two mass murderers?* As she turned to creep up the stairs a particular word sparked her interest. She cringed at the phrase, *bury the waste.* Holding her breath Courtney behaved like most of the females Ricky dated in the past. She removed her coat and pretended to have patience. This was just a wake-up call letting her know that it would take more than sex to get him to the altar.

Chapter 4

Pissed

Shortly after 11 p.m. a Mazda MPV rolled into the parking lot known as *the hole*. Southern Garden apartments was a criminal's sanctuary. The most common drug deals and gun battles took place there. Not even the young had a curfew. They played in the wee hours of the night like it was two o'clock in the afternoon.

Thugs sat on cars dealing, while crack heads walked the cul-de-sac. As a known unsafe zone, there was one way in and one way out.

Feeling the stares, Devon stepped from the borrowed van. As usual, he made sure he switched his cars regularly especially when handling business. With his broad shoulders, he boldly strutted toward bldg, #29. Some watched him closely, while others moved aside. It was clear that Devon was the man in the hole and his presence commanded respect.

"What up, Big D?" a voice yelled from a third floor balcony.

"D, Kirk been lookin' for you," an elderly pipehead relayed as he passed by.

Devon nodded. When it came to business, he was a man of little words. He popped his thumb up and grinned.

"Le'me hold somethin'," a toothless woman asked bombarding Devon with her hand out.

"I ain't got shit," Devon smirked.

Walking inside the subdued building, Devon was met by Junnie a retired dime bag peddler. Devon promoted Junnie to the big times when he appointed him as the major supplier of the hole. Although he made more money, he continued to wear his played out low top fade and dark blue mechanics jumpsuit *regularly*. Junnie had no interest in faddish gear.

After he slapped a wad of cash in Devon's hand, Junnie provided an update on his workers. Devon listened intensely as he flipped through the wad. The expression on his face hardened.

"Where the fuck is my damn money?" Devon snapped.

"Hold up man," Junnie frowned as he took a step back. "Le'me explain. We better than this," he stated avoiding eye contact with Devon.

"Save ya stories, broke-ass nigga," Devon jerked pretending to charge Junnie.

Scared shitless, Junnie distanced himself as he began to ramble. "Whitey was holdin' the shit when 5-0 came around. Before we could get the signal, they had thrown him against the car and took the shit from 'em. All of it," he said lowering his head.

"This shit ain't a game," Devon yelled as he moved forward. "Whitey ain't responsible for my fuckin' loot!" Forcefully he gripped Junnie's neck with the thought of teaching him a lesson. Surveying the area, he thought carefully about how to handle his thievin' employee.

"C'mon man," Junnie pleaded with a twisted expression. "Stop actin' like a bitch!" Devon yelled as he stomped his foot loudly on the worn tile. "I take it personal when niggas try to play me like a fool."

By now Kirk and Ray-Ray were nearing the building. Opening the door they watched the brewing altercation. Not knowing how things would play itself out, Kirk blocked the door. Ray-Ray a lower man on the totem pole who looked like he'd just been released from the pen watched for incoming traffic. The sight of Ray-Ray's dreads swinging like baby snakes scared Junnie even more.

"Listen, man, I swear I'll get yo money..."

"Aiight." Devon smiled cutting Junnie off. "It's settled. That'll be 20 g's includin' my pain and sufferin'," he laughed releasing Junnie.

After catching his balance, Junnie shook his shoulders and twisted his jumper back into place. Although relieved he never once looked at Ray-Ray or Kirk. In his heart he felt like he represented all the guys who never had the opportunity to get over on Devon. "I'll get at'cha when I get yo loot," Junnie said glancing over his shoulder.

Devon turned away. He breathed slowly and dropped his head. Resembling Dr. Jekyll he bit his bottom lip. Kirk got the signal instantly. Standing their ground, Kirk and Ray-Ray prepared for the ultimate. They knew Junnie wouldn't leave the hallway alive. Raising to his toes, Devon snatched his gun from his side. The sound of the chamber clicking put fear in Junnie's soul. It was time. Devon's wild laugh filled the hallway. Mr. Hyde had been revealed. As weird and psychotic as it sounded Kirk and Ray-Ray naturally joined him. Junnie looked helplessly into Devon's eyes. His grin alone could've killed him.

Without delay, the sound of the gun barrel slamming into Junnie's head startled everyone but Devon. With each hit, he pounded harder and deeper into his face. Junnie's body lay limp on the cold floor failing at his attempt to block the blows. His body shook like he was having a seizure. The shock of being pistol whipped overwhelmed him.

In between the death defying screams, Junnie pleaded, "C'mon D, stop this man."

Devon paused. The torture came to a sudden stop. But, Devon continued to breathe heavily. He had Junnie cornered on the floor. Kirk turned away shocked at what had happened to his former co-worker. Devon lifted his leg across Junnie's small frame. He unzipped his pants pointing his dick in position.

Although Ray-Ray was known to commit ruthless acts, he could not believe his eyes. Devon pissed all over Junnie. The foul smell of urine sparked Kirk's attention again. After a few seconds of silence, they all laughed. With a flick of Devon's hand, Ray-Ray and Kirk stood directly above Junnie to finish the job.

"Daaammmm...," Ray-Ray slurred, amazed by the damage to Junnie's face.

Suddenly, a body appeared at the top of the stairs. "Leave dat boy lone," an older woman in her sixties yelled. Holding a small gun to her side she squeezed tightly.

Devon thought quickly. Although he'd murdered many, he'd never shot a woman. In addition, he thought about the fact that he'd have to kill Junnie as well, if he took the woman out. And he definitely wanted his money first.

Headed in the woman's direction, Devon was stopped by

Kirk's hand. "It's not worth it partner," he said. "Let's get outta here."

After deep thought Devon spoke. "Let's go boys," he said moving toward the door. The woman pointed her gun in his direction.

Devon's initial thought was to shoot granny at point blank range. Although angry, he was no fool. *The woman's gun might be loaded,* he thought. He'd been shot twice before. He knew exactly what it felt like to have a shell lodged in his body. The first time he was hit the bullet was intended to put him in the grave. Luckily, for him the assailant hit him two steps short of his temple. With blood gushing from the side of his face, Devon didn't care about dying. Rising to his feet he remembered giving chase behind the gunman who had already taken off in his car. Devon trailed the car like an Olympic runner going for the gold. After several minutes of loosing gain on the man, Devon slowed himself, still with the will of a stubborn mule. The only reason he gave up was because of the police officer who noticed him drenched in blood. Stopping Devon to see what the problem was, the officer was astonished and more concerned than Devon to see an injured man sprinting behind a car.

Although Devon never caught the gunman, he made sure he packed a pistol at all times. The next time he was confronted with a potential gun battle, he smoked the suspect without a second thought.

"Hey D," Kirk called refocusing Devon's attention. "We need to go, partner, our folks outside are giving the signal. The undercovers are paying us a visit."

Although no sirens were heard, Devon knew he had to think quick. Any opportunity to catch him red handed would bring the police satisfaction. A strange car pulled close to the front of the building. Two young undercover officers jumped from the car.

Their presence upset the mood in the hole instantly. While most criminal activities ceased, the black officer didn't startle them as much as his older white partner. The physical features of the black cop reminded them too much of their own. Sporting a fresh set of braids, he pimped just as hard as Devon.

Watching through the doorway Devon noticed the enormous black mole on the side of his cheek. He was certain he'd seen that mole before. But then again, he had many run-ins with the law and all the black officers were beginning to look alike.

For a moment the older white officer stood close to the car surveying the area with a frown. As soon as he moved away from the vehicle, everyone scattered with the exception of three teenage boys. They laughed at the thought of a police officer limping like Herman the Monster. "Nigga, how you gonna catch somebody with one leg longer than the other," a wavy haired boy joked. The officer continued to limp forward taking mental notes. When one of the teens made the comment about him having three strands of hair, it must have hit a nerve. The officer immediately went back to the car.

Watching the peculiar men closely, Devon knelt before Junnie.

"Listen carefully my man." Devon looked Junnie directly in the eye. "It looks like the Feds are outside. I'm sure they're not here to save you. They're probably here tryna catch us with something on us." Devon waited for his reaction, but

Junnie lay speechless. "Now if we walk outta here together, we'll be okay. Otherwise, they'll be able to question us if they think somethin' happened in this hallway. You wit' me?" Devon raised his brow.

Junnie nodded.

"Man, I hate that this had to happen, but you brought it on yoself," Devon alleged. "Let's get you cleaned up." Without hesitation, Devon turned to Ray-Ray. "Take off your t-shirt."

"What," Ray-Ray said puzzled.

"Nigga, don't question me. Take off your t-shirt. And keep your damn eyes on what's goin' on out that door."

"Looks like e'rybody gone. Even the police." Ray-Ray threw his shirt at Devon. Pissed, he hated that Devon gave Junnie his army print t-shirt. Ray-Ray took pride in his army fatigues that he rocked regularly. He was weird like that; and often referred to himself as G.I. Joe.

Although Junnie remained quiet, he was relieved that Devon was still speaking to him. Catching the shirt that was thrown to him by Devon, he wiped the blood from his head. Confusing thoughts bounced around in Junnie's head. He felt like a fool because of his boss' treatment. On one hand, if he continued to work for him he would be talked about in the hood. On the other hand, he figured he'd rather be an embarrassed fool than a broke one.

Devon's extended hand snapped Junnie back into the present.

Raising up from the floor, Junnie listened to one more of Devon's remorseful testimonies. Though he knew it was mostly bullshit, it felt good to see his heavy-set oppressor sweat.

"Let's go get somethin' to eat. I'm hungry," Devon said heading out the door. With his motorcade following, Devon and his crew walked as if nothing had transpired in building #29. Neighbors couldn't help but watch them closely. The stained blood and bruises on Junnie's body were evident. Under the spotlight they all knew a quick exit was necessary. With accelerated speed, Devon smoothly passed a few hundreds to each of his look outs. But before reaching the MPV Kirk noticed a flash. *A camera*, he thought?

"Did someone take a picture?" Kirk asked with concern.

"You know who it is," Devon said nonchalantly as he sped off. "Fuck it, *I'm untouchable*."

Junnie sat in absolute silence. His mind raced. *I might have just what the Feds need. Devon has destroyed my reputation for life. He needs to have more done to him than what the Feds will do. And I'm just the man to do it.*

Chapter 5

Lucky Lady

The next week seemed to move in slow motion. With only five days remaining before Devon had to appear in court, the love birds spent each day rekindling the flame that had died only a few weeks ago. While riding the love roller-coaster, Carlie couldn't figure out how she would maneuver her way out of appearing in court. There was no way she could bring herself to testify against the man who three days ago slid a three carat platinum ring on her finger. It was the same ring Carlie had admired while on the many Georgetown shopping sprees, compliments of Devon.

Over the past few days, Devon went overboard. He had finally given Carlie the combination to his safe and was paying extra attention to her every need. One afternoon while practicing his targets at the gun range Devon surprised Carlie with a pamphlet displaying a brand new 2004 SL 500 Mercedes Benz. Not saying one word, he quickly pushed the picture back down into his pocket.

Carlie blushed while trying to focus with her hand on the trigger guided by Devon's gentle touch. "Are you getting it?"

she asked looking in the direction of her freshly painted tattoo that read *Devon's Forever*.

"Nah, but somebody else is," he said rubbing his cheek against Carlie's, as she nestled herself against his teddy bear frame.

"Who?" Carlie asked, praying that he was talking about her.

Pow, Pow, Devon hit his target as he always did. Releasing Carlie's hand, he squeezed her frame tightly. She was a little woman with a lot of curves, just how Devon liked it. It was understood from the gate that his women had to stay under 120 pounds.

Devon gently guided his hands across her hips before giving his finger a sharp movement from right to left. It was the usual motion signaling Carlie to move. Under normal circumstances, she hated for Devon to expect her to move on the command of his finger, but the thought of the SL Benz had her hypnotized.

Pulling into the parking lot of the dealership twenty minutes later, a slender, Caucasian gentleman waved to Devon as if he were being paid to wait for his arrival.

"Yo, Devon," the sales agent said, slapping his hand. "Everything is all set and waiting for you in the finance office," he continued, resembling a servant as he shut the door to the Hummer.

"Aiight," Devon responded, rubbing his hands together in excitement preparing for the treat.

"So, this is the lucky lady," the sales agent said admiring Carlie and extending his hand in her direction.

"My man," Devon called making sure he had the salesman's undivided attention. "Worry 'bout the car," he said turning the man away from Carlie. Touching his shoulders, he continued. "I'll worry 'bout the lucky lady."

Carlie shook her head and followed Devon. She never wasted time trying to be cordial to strangers in front of Devon. She knew he'd intercede, so there was no need in wasting time by extending a hand. In addition, Devon didn't particularly care for white people. For years, he listened to his father come home from work, ranting and raving about the *white man.* Devon heard it so much that as he grew older, he found himself repeating the same racist comments his father had once made.

In the finance office, the mood was solemn. It was as if some secret deal were taking place. Carlie sat perplexed, but satisfied. She wondered if the car was going to be in her name, or if she'd at least be able to pick the color. Within minutes, the female finance officer handed Devon a pen for his signature. Carlie strained as much as she could trying to see the final sales price. The $90,000 figure had her adrenaline pumping so hard that she barely noticed the fake name Devon was using for the paperwork.

"Devon, why can't we put the car in my name?" Carlie interjected.

"Nah, baby I'll handle e'rything includin' the payments. Besides, how would you pay for somethin' like that?"

"I'll get a job," she shot back submissively.

"Absolutely not!" Devon banged his fist into the palm of his hand signaling that the decision was final. "You're not workin' anywhere. Your only job is to take care of me," he laughed.

"That's so sweet," the finance officer said. She waved a set of car keys in the air as she opened the door to her office.

It was nothing like Carlie had imagined. She wanted to shout but managed to keep her composure. The sleek, silver 500 SL was calling her name. Devon signaled for her to get in. Carlie looked like a kid with a new toy as she introduced herself to her new ride. Moments later, Devon kissed her on the cheek with instructions on where not to drive the car without him. As usual, he laced Carlie's palm with a wad of hundreds. Within seconds, he had gone off to take care of business leaving his woman caught between feeling spoiled and incarcerated. As she pulled off the lot, Carlie knew the first person she'd pick up, Zarria.

The two had been friends for nearly fifteen years, but fought like sisters. Their relationship started off rocky the first day they met at the recreation center in their old neighborhood. While both girls were trying out for cheerleading, Zarria talked loudly and was very outspoken. Her intent was to gain the attention of a newcomer to the hood. The young man had Zarria's heart, but wasn't at all interested in her. He wanted Carlie. Zarria accused Carlie of stealing her man which turned into their first verbal fight.

It was a surprise to everyone in the neighborhood when the girls became best friends. Even though they settled their differences, there was always a bit of envy in Zarria's heart. But at least Carlie couldn't see it. She hated the fact that Carlie had beautiful skin while she took on the looks of a pale red-bone. She also never had the family structure that the Stewarts possessed.

Zarria's mother and father ran out on her at an early age leaving her with a trifling aunt. Not only were they lacking as a family, but they were broke. Zarria worked hard for everything she got, while Carlie was given everything on a silver platter. Carlie's love for Zarria disguised the basis of their relationship. That was her girl and nobody could say anything bad about her.

By the time Carlie made it to Zarria's high rise complex her girlfriend was already out front ready to roll. Dressed in a form fitting outfit, Zarria admired the car. "Oh shit," she said articulating each word slowly. "This is what's up." Zarria made loud and crazy noises showing her excitement about Carlie's new ride. She ran her fingers alongside the paint of the car, then through her freshly permed hair. "Let's ride," she said.

The ladies zipped through town at high speeds. With enormous revs of the engine, Carlie felt unstoppable. Hollers and whistles came from every guy the ladies passed and the girls were enjoying every minute of it. As the night fell, Zarria had the perfect idea. It was the idea that Devon had already warned Carlie about earlier. Undoubtedly, the car was not to be driven to any clubs or hot spots.

"Let's ride past the club," Zarria shouted.

"Oh, no. Devon and I already agreed that I wouldn't anywhere without his approval. It's for my own safety."

"You believe that shit? Girl, you locked up with chains and you don't even know it."

"Zarria, that's enough. I'm doing exactly what Devon told me to do." Carlie checked her cell. Luckily, she hadn't missed any calls.

"You a loyal motherfucka." Zarria smacked her lips. "I tilt my tittie to ya," she said leaning back in the seat.

Zarria spent a few moments complaining to Carlie about the right to drive where she wanted to, but Carlie wasn't buying it. She and Devon had been getting along too good and she didn't want to mess that up.

All of a sudden, Carlie thought about the fact that she'd have to tell her Dad about the car. Immediately, she whipped a U-turn in route to Yorkshore Estates. The SL embraced the darkness and hugged each curve. Although Carlie was traveling at the speed of lighting, she did notice a black car trailing her. She had been trained by Devon to detect these types of situations. Carlie made a quick left. The car behind her speedily followed. As the SL slowed its speed, so did the car behind her. Carlie had to think quick and her road dog was no help at all. Throwing her cell phone to Zarria, Carlie said "Call Devon, he'll know what to do."

"Girl, are you crazy? We're closer to your Dad."

"I know, but he won't understand," Carlie said accelerating again.

"Fool, your Dad has won shooting awards!" Zarria shouted.

Carlie shot back. "Devon would want me to call him. Now call him!"

Within minutes the plan was in effect. Carlie was roughly ten minutes from Devon's neighborhood. The closer she got, the safer she felt. More people became visible, more street lights shined, and more police cars lined the roads. Carlie never thought once about stopping a police officer nor did the cops think about stopping a speeding car in Devon's neighborhood.

Pulling up into Devon's cul-de-sac, Carlie began to slow down. Without coming to a complete stop her eyes assessed the lot in search of Devon. She wasn't sure what to do next. At this point, Zarria was kneeling down in the seat unaware of what was about to happen. Carlie paused when she noticed that the black corvette had come to a complete stop. Waiting for the assailant's next move, Carlie could see a red dot in motion reflecting off the corvette. She knew Devon was near. As her eyes carefully followed the laser, she located her knight in shining armor. Only a true soldier would think of positioning himself in a tree.

The first warning shot that rang out sent the culprit backing up at 70 miles per hour. The second shot missed. As the corvette made its escape, Carlie was satisfied that she'd been saved by her superman. Nothing else mattered.

Although Devon scared the assailants away, he couldn't help but wonder who the two guys were. Why were they following Carlie? Carlie wasn't known to have many enemies but Devon was. Carlie had to be kept safe until he could figure out if anything was brewing in the streets.

Devon ordered Carlie and Zarria to spend the night at his apartment. "Carlie, call your father, and tell'em you stayin' with Zarria tonight."

"Who said we're staying here?" Zarria asked.

"Wholesome girls don't hang in the street," he said leading them into his place.

Zarria's twisted lips showed that she thought Devon was full of shit. "Nigga you hangin' out and you already taken," she snapped. "Now what?" she asked as if she'd won the dispute.

"I don't answer questions, I do the asking," he said nudging Zarria at the shoulder as he passed.

"Quit irritating my man," Carlie said. She was thankful for what Devon had done and wished her friend would show some gratitude.

"He didn't do anything special, Carlie." Zarria shook her

head in disbelief while following her friend around the room. "Even Tarzan can swing from a tree," she teased.

Carlie ceased all talking. There was no getting through Zarria's thick skull. After all, she was happy with the changes she'd seen in Devon. The only disappointment for the night was that Devon wouldn't be in the house with her. He had more unfinished business to take care of. Little did Carlie know that his first line of business was to pay off a telephone employee to view Carlie's monthly cell phone records.

Zarria couldn't believe she was stuck at Devon's on a Saturday night. She had envisioned being strung by a strong, handsome man by now. Instead she was being held hostage by someone who wasn't even there. Zarria contemplated on catching a cab, but as usual she'd used all her money on nails, hair, and feet. She even thought about calling a few guys to pick her up but she knew Devon would kill anyone who found out where he laid his head. At the thought of loosing the battle, Zarria became pissed and thought she'd use her ammo to upset things.

"You know, Mr. Stewart wouldn't have missed his target," she said.

"That's enough Zarria. You know the rule," Carlie said before falling off to sleep. "Nobody disrespects my man."

Chapter 6

Talk is Cheap

Yorkshore Drive buzzed with loud sounds humming from lawnmowers and hedge trimmers. Inside, Carlie sat in her quiet house, camped out at the window. After checking her brand new watch, compliments of Devon, she peeked through the bay window to make out the location of her neighbors. For a Saturday afternoon, she noticed far too many people who would be eyewitnesses for Ricky. Most of the yard work on her block was usually done by noon. Surely, this set-back would mess up her plan.

Carlie shrugged. She looked around the formal living room and checked over her shoulder for any sign of Ricky. Her first thought was to open the front door and jet down the hill. Then, reality hit. Ricky would be on her heels like Smokey on the Bandit. Carlie grabbed her phone and punched the numbers. "Hey," she whispered.

"Where you at?" Devon asked.

"Uhhh… I'm still in the house."

Devon was careful about his choice of words. He wanted to show Carlie that he could change and do right for more than a week. "I'on know why you whispering," he said in a loving tone. But I'll wait out here as long as it takes."

Carlie smiled as she paced the floor. "Which block are you on?"

"Come to the bottom of the hill. Turn right, and I'm two streets over. You'll see me sittin' here, unless yo Steven Siegal ass father finds out I'm here."

Carlie snickered softly. "I'm coming."

"Hurry up. Waitin' ain't my style. Plus, I'm horny," he said.

"I'm trying to figure out how to get this garment bag out of the house without looking like I'm moving."

"Leave it."

"What?" Carlie asked in her lowest pitch.

"Daddy got you. You can cop all new gear when we get to NY." Devon breathed. "That's if we ever hit the highway."

Carlie hung up. She couldn't wait to be in Devon's arms again. Over the last few days she'd been treated like a queen. Besides, from what Devon had broadcasted, the days to come would get even better. He had promised that today the two of them would drive to New York for a day of splurging and a night on the town. Carlie knew that aside from the fun, their lovemaking would be just what the doctor ordered. It was always that way. Carlie called it *make-up loving*.

At the thought of being with Devon intimately and the sound of Ricky turning on the shower, she made her escape. Carlie opened the door, dashed down the stairs, and ran like crazy. With one foot in front of the other, she sprinted as if she were runner at a track meet. Her long black hair bounced and brushed her shoulders with every move. A few neighbors waved while in return Carlie managed to shoot them a weak hand signal. When she reached the bottom of the hill, Carlie stopped to catch her breath. She glanced back toward her house, then toward where her knight and shining armor said he'd be waiting. At that moment she could see the yellow Hummer sitting on the corner. With Devon in sight, Carlie jogged slowly until she reached the vehicle.

Devon hopped out and ran to open the door for his princess. He kissed her slightly sweaty forehead, gently. "Let's go," he said lifting Carlie with ease into the truck. He watched her round backside closely. After all, it was Carlie's plump ass that originally captured his heart.

The touch of Devon's hands around her waist felt more than good. Carlie knew that this was the start of a new chapter in their relationship. What she didn't know was what to tell Ricky in terms of her whereabouts for the weekend. Carlie thought about it momentarily, as Devon surprisingly reached across her to buckle her seat belt. *Wow, that's a first*, Carlie thought.

"These are for you," he said reaching below to grab six long stem red roses.

"Thanks." Carlie leaned over the console between them and kissed Devon's cheek.

"Don't think your man is slippin'. I know you prefer pink. But the florist in your neighborhood was all out," he said spitefully. "And Ricky thinks he's doin' somethin'. Shit, he gotta step his game up. My woman should live where the neighborhood has the best to offer." Devon laughed for a split second, until he caught himself. He grabbed Carlie by her shoulders and pulled her close. "I gotta learn to love'em. He'll be my father- in- law some day."

Carlie smiled her approval. "Devon, I need to go past my

grandmother's house," she said half-blushing. My father will definitely call her, so I want her to know that I'm okay."

"Aiight. Whatever you say." Devon pretended to be cool with Carlie's plan. If this had been weeks ago, he would have checked his woman under the chin for trying to call the shots. It had been established, he was the *big boss*, but for now it was about getting out of the dog house.

On the way to Grandma Jean's house, Carlie thought more about Ricky. She wondered if he had realized her absence. *Would he be that crazy to come and look for me? Or will he think I just ran out for a while?* She could have kicked herself for not even leaving a note. *For what. It would've been a lie anyway,* she thought.

For the next twenty minutes, the couple listened to a CD Devon burned just for Carlie. When track #4 began, Devon gave his best impersonation of Levert's, *Baby I'm Ready.*

"Girl it's time for me to give you all the love you need. Now baby I know that you deserve the best, and I can't keep treatin' you like I treat the rest..." Devon's hands fondled Carlie's breast as he sang. In between the high notes he pulled her close massaging her ear with his tongue. Devon was like crack, he knew Carlie was hungry. "And not just a little bit, I wanna give you all of it," he continued singing his heart out. As he got deeper into the song, Carlie's body temperature rose. No doubt, Devon was a tease. She wanted him right there in the car; especially when he hit her favorite part. *Baby I'm ready, baby I'm ready, come on, baby I'm ready..."*

Carlie shook her head. Although Devon's voice sounded like an American Idol reject, she loved every minute of it. He had even gone as far as using his Pepsi bottle as a microphone. In between dips and interludes, and playing between

Carlie's legs, he finally pulled onto Grandma Jean's block. As soon as Devon stopped in front of the house, Carlie jumped out hoping the serenading would continue once they got back into the car.

"You coming?" Carlie turned to ask.

"I'ma hold things down right here."

"I think you better show your face. My grandmother will want to read through you." Carlie laughed.

Within seconds Devon had tucked his gun deep under the seat, locked the doors, and trailed Carlie with his hands behind his back. By the time Grandma Jean opened the door, Devon had reached the front porch.

"Well, what do I owe the pleasure?" Grandma Jean asked sarcastically. She placed her hands on her hips and assumed a fierce stance.

Devon removed one hand from his back and kissed Grandma Jean's hand. "The pleasure is mine," he stated pretending to have manners. Then, unexpectedly, he pulled the red roses which had been given to Carlie from behind his back.

"Umph." Come on in," she said surprised by Devon's behavior.

"We can't stay long," Devon responded following Grandma Jean into the kitchen. He grabbed Carlie's hand tightly like they were posing for a couple of the year photo. "I'm takin' your lovely granddaughter to New York. Anything she wants, it's hers." He looked deep into Carlie's eyes.

"Now, don't take her up there and beat her." Grandma Jean stared Devon in his face like she was ready to draw her piece. "I know how things go. You come around here actin' like Prince Charming, and pretending everything is okay. Then you get her alone and whip the crap outta my baby."

"No...that's behind us. Trust me."

"Trust you! Huh."

"She's in good hands," Devon stated confidently.

"And he's been going to anger management," Carlie interjected.

"More than that, I realize that Carlie is my everything," Devon said sincerely.

"Now Devon, I don't know what ya selling. It seems fake to me. But if Carlie loves ya, I'll try to like ya." Grandma pulled a vase from the bottom cabinet and filled it with water. "It's not me you gotta kiss up to." She shook her finger toward Devon going a mile a minute. "It's my son. And right now he's going through male menopause."

"We'll talk man to man," he said.

"I'on know. He already said you remind him of that Suge Knight fella, but not as cute. And if you act like him, he's gonna have to show ya something."

"I understand the concern. Hey...." He clapped his hands together resembling a politician, then opened his arms widely. "I made a mistake, but it ain't gonna happen again." Devon pulled his body up behind Carlie as she rested her butt tightly on his dick. Carlie leaned back, and allowed Devon to slip his tongue deep into her mouth.

Immediately Grandma Jean started her ranting and raving. She never paused between words. "And don't be going to New York, having sex and acting wild. "And you damn sure better not be having no oral sex." Grandma's head and finger moved simultaneously. "As a matter of fact, if I find out anybody in my family is doing that kinda crap, they'll never eat off my dishes again."

Carlie and Devon laughed all the way to the door. "We gotta go," Carlie said. Everyone could tell that she was extremely happy. She wanted badly for her grandmother to like Devon. She knew the word *love* was a stretch, but things were looking up. "Grandma, don't tell Dad that I left with Devon." Carlie pleaded with her eyes.

"Tellin' lies don't do nothin' for ya, but make ya burnnnnnnnn. I ain't burnin' wit'cha." She walked past Carlie and opened the front door.

"Pleaseeeeeee. At least tell him that I'm okay." Carlie hugged her grandmother. "I'll be back tomorrow."

"Bye Grandma," Devon smirked.

"Now, you don' gone too far. Boy, I ain't never said you could start calling me Grandma. Now, y'all get on off my damn porch." Grandma Jean smiled as she closed the door. There was something fishy with Devon. She knew he was still a dangerous thug, but she exhaled knowing that her granddaughter was happier than two pigs in slop.

***

Carlie was just waking up from a short nap when Devon tugged on the covers. The long ride to New York and the quick shopping on 5th Ave. called for some sleep. After checking into the Marriot Marquis in Times Square, the couple *handled business* as Devon would say, and fell off to sleep. Carlie yarned as she sat up slightly and threw one leg out of the bed.

"Why are you already dressed ?" she asked

"Good men don't lie in bed all night," Devon said. "Besides, I took care of my job." He rubbed Carlie's leg seductively like he was ready for round two. "Didn't I ?"

"Uh, well...," she joked. "What are we doing tonight?"

"We're gonna eat and hang out in Harlem?"

"Sounds good. I've never been to Harlem."

"That's why you with the sharpest nigga around." Devon looked at himself. He admired the Kevin Garnett jersey he wore and his fresh pair of Sean John jeans. "Stay close, I'ma put you on the map."

Carlie strolled past Devon ignoring his last comment. "Give me twenty minutes," she said turning on the shower. "What should I wear?"

"You know. Something sexy. But for my eyes only."

Carlie smiled awkwardly. "Well, we only bought three outfits so far. Which one do you want me to wear?"

"You pick." Devon squeezed Carlie on the ass. "I'll get the truck and wait for you out front."

"Wait..."

The door was shut. Choosing her own attire should have been wonderful news, but instead Carlie felt she was taking a chance on messing up. She wanted Devon to be happy. More importantly, she wanted their weekend to be a hit. Carlie showered, dressed, and was pushing the down button on the elevator within thirty minutes.

Walking out to the truck she could tell Devon was impressed with her mauve linen pants, and off white linen shirt that revealed a touch of cleavage. Her eyes followed Devon as he got out of the truck and opened the door. Carlie couldn't believe it. This gentleman stuff was becoming a habit. *Devon was really changing.*

Before long they had arrived at *Amy Ruth's* on 116th, famous for chicken and waffles. Although the restaurant wasn't fancy, it was well-known and obviously a hot spot. Most had to wait outside in line, while Devon of course slipped the host a $100 bill.

Once seated, Carlie and Devon surveyed the restaurant in hopes of narrowing down their dinner choices. For Devon, everything looked appetizing. After all, they hadn't eaten since earlier in the day; they were famished. While Devon's mouth was set on porkchops smothered in gravy and macaroni and cheese; Carlie chose fried chicken and waffles. After reviewing the menu for the third time and giving their orders, Carlie and Devon chit-chatted like it was their first date. This was the kind of relationship Carlie longed for. She just knew she'd feed him cheesecake from her fork after dinner and they'd make sweet love into the night. Everything seemed perfect, until Devon frowned.

Once Carlie caught a glimpse of his scowl, she turned to see the problem. A tall, old friend of Carlie's stood directly behind her. Although nothing serious had ever gone down between them, they had unfortunately dated once. That was a problem. *Bad timing,* she thought. Carlie couldn't believe her luck. Of all places, she had to see someone from D.C. while in New York. *And in the presence of Devon.*

The unannounced gentleman grinned widely showing his mouthful of gold teeth. "What up?" he said not even acknowledging Devon.

"Hello," Carlie said apprehensively. "This is Devon, my boyfriend." She pointed. "Devon this is Alex."

"You lookin' good," Alex said to Carlie.

Carlie's heart felt like it had dropped into her shoe. Devon's chair screeched as he stood up. For the first time since he approached the table, Alex looked at Devon. "Yeah,

I know you," he said. "I'm from around the way, just like you." He extended his hand. "Me and Junnie go way back."

Devon never shook Alex's hand nor did he intend to. In his mind it was disrespectful to speak to his woman. He didn't care where they knew each other from. His first thought was to body slam Alex into the brick wall to his right. Then, he thought about getting to the Hummer to grab his piece.

After that, four more guys walked up behind Alex, ready to take their seats. "I'm out," Alex said. He touched the back of Carlie's chair waiting for a response.

Carlie said nothing. She watched Devon watch Alex. Devon turned to the side, pulled out his wad, and counted off four twenties. *So much for eating,* she thought. He dropped the money on the table and gave Carlie the finger signal. As he walked off, Devon watched Alex and Alex watched Devon. Carlie trailed wondering how the night would end. Deep inside, she knew this was nothing major. Seeing someone she knew wasn't a crime. At least she knew she wouldn't get whipped. But, for the first time in over a week, the old Devon had resurfaced.

Chapter 7

Pink for Positive

"Carlie," Ricky yelled, as he banged on the bathroom door. "You've been in there a long time. We need to talk!"

"I'm not feeling well," she answered.

"Well, you've obviously been well enough to hang out late, night after night." Ricky paced the floor as if he were talking to a guarded prisoner.

"Dad, I'll be out in a minute."

Carlie removed the pregnancy test from the box. Chills exploded through her body as she sat nervously on the toilet. Like an addictive pill popper she downed three Advils. The headache she'd experienced over the past few days was definitely caused by the stress of her cycle being 15 days late. *Come on Mary...* she thought. Up until this point her cycle which she called *Mary* was pretty normal. Now, with the end of June approaching, Carlie had reason to worry. She knew better than to have unprotected sex with Devon. But bareback was customary for him and it was his way or the highway. He'd pretended a dozen times to pull out before having an orgasm...so many times that Carlie had stopped complaining about it.

The bathroom was quiet when the urine hit the little stick. Within seconds, a dark pink line appeared. Carlie's eyes opened wide, straining to certify the accuracy of the results.

"Ah...shit," she exclaimed, loud enough to be heard by her guard dog.

"What's wrong," Ricky asked with concern.

"Uh..." Carlie responded. She was annoyed that her Dad was close enough to hear her. Yet confused about what was happening to her life.

Slamming the toilet seat down, Carlie wrapped the applicator between a bunch of toilet tissue. After burying the evidence deep in the trash, she thought for a moment, then put on her game face. Carlie opened the bathroom door confidently, as if nothing happened. Walking down the stairs as quickly as he could, her father's footsteps trailed behind her. Step after step, Ricky followed Carlie like a hound.

"OK. What is it?" Carlie asked taking a seat in the kitchen. When the papers hit the table, Dad had already begun to stare his daughter dead in the face.

"So, now what?" he asked. Is this the type of hoodlum you want to be involved with? I worked damn near ten years to get our life on a different track. And your ass is gonna fuck that up!"

Carlie couldn't respond. She hated herself for disappointing her father. She also thought deeply about the rap sheet that laid in front of her. She knew Devon had lived a life of crime, but now his record was being revealed right before her eyes. Charges that ranged from conspiracy, carrying concealed weapons, and attempted murder covered the pages. All bearing the name Devon Donnovan McNeil.

"Did you know that Devon was on trial in 2001 for murder and all the witnesses were eventually murdered too?"

"He…"

"No. You need to listen!" Ricky refused to let Carlie get a word in.

"Who do you think killed those people?" Changing positions as if he were on trial, he continued. "Did you know that Devon has been locked up ten times over the last eight years? And get this… Five of those times have been for carrying stolen weapons. Did you know some of those guns have been dirty? Do you know what that means?"

Without giving Carlie time to answer, he continued. "They were used to kill people! I bet you ride around with him and his Glock on a regular! You do know why he won't register them, right? Do you hear me, or am I talking to a zombie?" he yelled.

"Huh?" Carlie asked in an elementary tone.

"Are you that in love, or did I raise a fool?"

Carlie held her breath when Ricky's coffee mug crashed against the wall. She couldn't believe her father had gotten so angry over Devon's past.

Ricky grabbed Carlie by the shoulders. "At some point this has to end. I'm responsible for your well being and I'll be damned if you're gonna fuck your life up." He shook her rapidly. "Do you understand?"

"Yes," Carlie answered. Her tone proved that she was worried. Rightfully so; Ricky had never behaved this way in her presence.

Ricky shook his head. "You and I have nothing in common." He looked at Carlie in a daze as if he was searching for more hurtful things to say. "Maybe you're not my daughter," he spat. Immediately he felt guilty. Ricky hollered, "Fuck, fuck, fuck," before heading back upstairs. Carlie listened as he mumbled other curse words under his breath both in English and Spanish. He only spoke both languages when he was fed up.

Embarrassed, Carlie never raised her head until her dad was completely out of sight. Images of what her life would be like flashed before her. She imagined visiting Devon at the Hagerstown Correctional Facility with little Devon crying on her hip. She couldn't believe she was madly in love with a hardcore criminal. Like now, Carlie had often had bad visions of miserable life-long experiences with no way out. If only she could see her fate waiting for her around the corner, she'd leave him now, before it's too late.

Ricky stormed downstairs only to stop right in front of Carlie's face again. "There are no surprises in this house," he yelled holding the pregnancy applicator tightly in his hand. Carlie couldn't believe the way her privacy had been violated. This was the final straw.

Yells were heard all through the house. It was hard to tell who was angrier. Although Ricky thought about slamming his fist through the wall, he tried to think rationally. His baby's life depended on him.

"So what are your plans," he asked.

"I don't know," Carlie answered in between the many sniffles.

"Now is not the time to cry. Crying won't help us."

"Us?" she asked. "It's my baby, and my life. I'll take care of it."

"Oh…so you want to have the devil's baby huh? "Let me ask you this." Ricky kneeled down looking Carlie directly in the face. "How do you think you're gonna take care of a baby by yourself? Because I can assure you Devon won't live to see twenty-five."

"I don't know...I don't know... I don't know..." Carlie spoke each word at a careful pace. Walking around the kitchen, she cried as her hands massaged her temples. "I know you don't want me to keep it," she said. Carlie avoiding making eye contact with her father. "But I thought we didn't believe in abortion!"

"If you want to continue living the way you do, I'd think long and hard if I were you. Besides, have you thrown your dreams of becoming a lawyer out the window? You better do some soul searching," Ricky said before leaving the room.

Carlie could see that all of the drama was taking its toll on her Dad. She knew he didn't want her to keep her unborn blessing. Her first thought was to pay Grandma Jean a visit. She knew she'd get some words of wisdom. Deep down inside, she knew she'd make a great mom. However, Devon's parenting skills were questionable. One thing was for sure... the pregnancy would have to be kept a secret from Devon or else it would turn out to be her worst nightmare.

Chapter 8

<u>Torn</u>

Tears flowed like the Nile, while Ricky zipped through town. Holding his composure, his heart went out to his daughter but he had to do what was in Carlie's best interest. Even Grandma Jean couldn't bare to see her precious granddaughter's life being thrown away. Considering Carlie's future, she put aside her long time Christian beliefs in order to momentarily favor abortion. Carlie clearly remembered her grandmother throwing up both of her hands looking toward the sky chanting, "Help me Father." She added, "Lord forgive me, but this child does not need to bring another Devon into this world."

As the money green Jaguar pulled up to the abortion clinic, Carlie's cries worsened. As soon as Ricky opened the door, the shouts started. One woman yelled, "Abortion is murder!" Moving quickly, Ricky pushed Carlie along. Another protester blocked the door prohibiting the two of them from entering the building. In a soft, warm tone she murmured, "Don't disappoint that precious gift inside your body. Your Father gave that to you."

Carlie held her stomach tightly. She refused to lift her head up. Ricky pushed the woman out of their path with ease. Once inside, he did all the talking.

"May I help you?" the slim receptionist asked in her southern accent.

"Sure, we have an appointment for Carlie Stewart."

The receptionist shot Carlie a strange look. She wondered why her father was taking control. "Ms. Stewart will have to sign her own consent at the bottom." She nodded in Carlie's direction.

The woman handed Ricky a pen and all the necessary paperwork that needed to be filled out. Ricky looked several yards away at his daughter who walked away and at this point was a basket case. He breathed, assuring himself that everything would be okay as he watched Carlie bite her nails neurotically on the sofa near the entrance. Ricky's mind wondered. He couldn't understand how someone with Carlie's intellect could get caught up into such bullshit.

Ricky had lost count over the years on how much he'd spent on Carlie's schooling. The enormous figure was now nearing $170,000. She had gone to the best private schools since kindergarten and consistently made the honor roll. A 4.0 became so easy, she rarely had to study. Book smarts, Carlie certainly had a lot of, but Ricky was starting to question her common sense. He figured anyone getting involved with Devon must be lacking in that department. Losing his concentration, Ricky began to interrogate a nurse about the required counseling session.

Startled, Carlie jumped in amazement. She couldn't believe her eyes! If looks could kill, Carlie would be dead by the inspection Devon was giving her. He stood at the entrance way allowing his fist to touch one another as he swung them back and forth.

The expression on Ricky's face said it all as he turned to see Devon standing there.

"Ah...shit," Ricky said in the lightest tone possible. The hue in his face now resembled a radish. On fire, he looked around the waiting room. Not wanting to draw any attention, he calmly said, "You were not asked to come here. Now leave!"

"I came to talk to Carlie," Devon said leaning in her direction.

Carlie flinched at the sight of Devon reaching across her path. She knew she had deceived him. Her reflexes assured her that a blow was on the way. Bending down Devon clinched her chin.

"Carlie, we leavin' this place. I know you been brainwashed, but I'm here now. Don't worry," he said wiping a falling tear from her eye.

"Call the police," Ricky instructed the receptionist.

"Sir, maybe ya'll need to take this outside, and come back when everything is clear. We don't need any additional problems. We have enough outside those doors," the receptionist responded coldly.

"You will be held responsible if something happens to my daughter."

The receptionist shook her head, "I'm sorry," and stepped away from the desk.

By the time Ricky turned around, Devon had reached for Carlie's hand as if he were an angel flown down from heaven. He appeared to be a different man. With a sad look, his mouth made a gesture as if he were going to speak.

"Don't touch her!" Ricky yelled losing patience.

Devon's face boiled with anger. Every bit of hate he had for Mr. Stewart came bursting through. "You don't fuckin' rule me Old Timer," Devon snapped.

"Oh…. But I do have the right to tell you what to do concerning my daughter," Ricky shot back.

"No, the hell you don't," Devon barked. He grew angrier by the second.

"Y'all will have to leave," the receptionist said appearing from the back of the room.

Devon completely ignored the lady. Shoving his body to block Carlie's view of her father, he pulled her close to him and held her hands softly. Expressing his need to be with Carlie and his unborn child, Devon's face revealed the pain he felt at the thought of her killing their baby.

Carlie's heart softened with every word spoken by the man her father was surely planning to attack. At the same time, she was torn between the only two men she'd ever loved. Accustomed to asking God for guidance, Carlie began to pray with her eyes looking deep into Devon's.

He asked, "Is this what you really want?" Devon never released her hand.

Carlie appeared confused when she responded. "I don't know."

"Ah…hell," Ricky shouted! "You're not thinking."

"But Daddy, I love him!" Carlie shouted hoping her plea would get a small piece of sympathy from her father. By now she had conjured up enough tears to fill a well. "I just need more time to think about all of this."

"I'm not giving you more time to talk to this thug." Ricky moved forward in their direction.

Immediately, Devon dropped Carlie's hand. He displayed his killer smile. Gripping his .45 automatic firmly, his evil look worsened. Carlie knew Devon was in a non-negotiable mode. For several seconds, no one made a move or sound. Devon finally burst into his usual psychotic laugh when Carlie surrendered. Frightened, she allowed Devon to guide her towards the door.

Ricky couldn't believe he was about to allow his daughter to be kidnapped by this maniac right in front of his own eyes. Feeling helpless without his cell phone, he surveyed the room for other options. Unfortunately for him, nothing would stand in the way of what was about to take place.

Devon grinned victoriously as he backed up with Carlie near his side. "Yeah." He nodded.

"Son, you're about to make me get 6 digits behind my name." Ricky paused, then continued as calmly as his soul would allow. "Think about this," he said. Ricky balled his fist and cracked his knuckles. He was careful in handling the overwhelming hate bottled inside of him. A nagging sense of guilt tugged at his skin. One option was to attack Devon and tussle it out in an old fashion fist fight. Reality hit. Ricky would have to shoot Devon if he wanted his daughter back badly enough.

"Whatever you say, Old Timer, whatever you say," Devon said repeatedly, pushing his back against the door. Once outside, Devon never took his eyes off Ricky, who continued to walk towards the couple.

"Dad this is best. We'll talk later," Carlie begged. She made eye contact with her father. "Please.........."

Ricky decided he would jet to his car for his ammunition. Sadly, he was outnumbered when the protesters began to clap and chant. They walked directly between Ricky and his daughter.

Without delay Devon took advantage of the opportunity. Together they moved quickly. Carlie and Devon successfully made it to the rented, silver Taurus. Ricky eyeballed the car as they fled the scene catching a glimpse of the tag number.

Virginia tag # PTR is all he caught. "Damn it," he yelled.

Speeding down Pennsylvania Ave., Devon turned cold never trying to console his crying woman. Anticipating the police, he drove like a dare devil in the Indianapolis 500. With each corner he took, skid marks and smoke were the only evidence of proof that he'd been there.

The long journey outside the city gave Carlie an opportunity to take a guilt trip. *Maybe if she'd been thinking she wouldn't have tried to kill their baby. Who wouldn't be mad,* she thought? *Maybe Devon isn't as bad as everyone thinks?* She tried hard to justify Devon's actions. *Maybe focusing on trying to be a better girlfriend would make more sense.*

Carlie began to relax a just a bit, after an hour into the trip. The pleasant scenery helped to somewhat ease her mind. But she couldn't help but to be nervous. Devon was way too unpredictable and she'd be a fool to think that she wouldn't pay for trying to kill his baby.

Driving along route 270 near Frederick, Maryland, gave her a chance to think more and more. She thought about popping three Advils and going to sleep. Then, going back to school popped into her mind. She even thought of Ricky. But when Carlie realized they were in the middle of nowhere, her alarm went off inside. She tried not to worry knowing that Devon really loved her. Yet something inside of her couldn't help but to be scared. Devon's demeanor had changed from cold to nothing at all.

The slowing pace of the car caught her attention. Devon turned quickly onto a trail that within the blink of an eye would cause anyone to pass by. A small cottage sat nestled at the end of the trail. Bile rose up in Carlie's stomach. Exactly what was Devon up to? Would the details of her death appear on the eleven o'clock news? The entire situation troubled her deeply.

"This is us, Baby," he finally spoke.

"What are we doing here?" Carlie asked.

"We need some time to sort thangs out... away from everyone else," he said. "Besides, I thought you liked bein' in the mountains." Devon rested his palm on Carlie's shoulder.

"I normally do," she responded afraid to let Devon know he seemed deranged at the moment.

The smell of potpourri hit the couple in the face as the door opened to the cabin. Surprisingly, everything in the cabin was neatly placed. It looked as though it had been pre-pared for visitors. When Devon walked out to the car and returned with a duffle bag, Carlie's mind raced again. *Would an oozy appear? Would he really kill her?* Carlie watched him closely. Her heart raced. Unzipping the bag, Devon pulled out a black, sexy, one–piece garment still dangling with tags.

"See, I been plannin' this for weeks. I just never thought I'd have to kidnap you for us to come here. I made sure I brought you a few thangs."

Carlie never responded. Once Devon began to take his clothes off, her mind began to settle a bit. Just maybe she wasn't about to become a statistic. Devon grabbed his lady by the hand leading her to the bed. With his lips, he stroked her face gently. While rubbing his nose back and forth across her belly, he began to speak.

"It should be illegal for me to love you this way. I can't imagine life without ya," Devon proclaimed. "Carlie, do you know what I would do if you left me?" Devon unbuttoned her form-fitting pants.

"What's that?" Carlie questioned, fighting the fire building inside her.

"I won't even discuss that right now. Just know that it wouldn't be good." The intensity of Devon's kiss became stronger. "You ever cheated on me?" he asked, halting all sexual activities. He waited for his love to respond.

Carlie was livid. She wanted Devon bad. He was the only one who had ever hit her special spot. By no means was she a virgin before she met Devon; but his loving was certainly the best she'd ever had. He always had a way of getting her worked up only to make her wait. *She hoped it wasn't intentional.* "No," Carlie snapped looking down into his face.

"Oh, because you know I'd have to kill you," he said nonchalantly. Devon's tongue reconnected to Carlie's stomach. He worked his way to her breast with gentle licks. At the same time, Devon massaged Carlie's moist inner thigh. "Ya my diamond," he said making sure every stitch of Carlie's clothes had been removed.

"What good is a diamond if nobody ever gets a chance to see it? I mean I don't even get to hang out with Zarria that often."

"I'on know if that's good or bad." Birds of a feather flock together, damn it! I want my woman to have a good reputation." Devon rubbed his hand against Carlie's vagina. "Enough of that. Let's put it all behind us. God said, Be kind and compassionate to one another, forgiving each other, just as Christ Jesus forgave you."

At that moment Carlie slipped into a state of shock. First of all, Devon had never stepped foot in a church and now here he was quoting the scriptures. *Maybe it was possible for people to change,* she thought? Secondly, the pleasure Devon was now giving her was unbelievable. Laying back Carlie's legs were spread wide apart like an eagle. Small quivers quaked up her spine with each light bite. Devon feasted on her body all the way down to her toes. He sucked intensely, giving special attention to her big toe, just the way she liked it. With his tongue tickling every inch below her knees she could take no more. Carlie was fully ready.

Devon turned her over onto her stomach. He began licking the small droplets of sweet sweat that had already begun to form on her supple skin. Carlie suddenly arched her back as she felt Devon reach her special spot. She knew she was at her weakest point. She craved his entrance.

Devon took pride in his foreplay. He knew exactly what to do to turn Carlie on and what would send her overboard. Carlie on the other hand was more concerned with feeling Devon inside of her. She was whipped and didn't even know it.

He entered her slowly, inserting just the head into her well lubed womanhood. Devon wanted to test '*his pussy*' just to see how much she wanted him. He teased as he moved away from Carlie and swiped his fingers softly over her clit. You would've thought his piece was made of gold, Carlie quickly yanked him back into position. As her grip tightened around his neck, she was ready for Devon's shock treatment.

Multiple organisms was his specialty, and Carlie went crazy at the thought of what was to come.

Calculating every inch of his entrance into the woman he planned to serve until she could take no more, Devon flipped Carlie over. He kissed her forcefully with every breath he took. Each moan heard from Carlie excited him even more.

Devon knew he couldn't breathe without Carlie in his life. He wanted to show her that no one could love her better than he- physically or mentally. Sweating and panting, Devon was now taking total control. He had her open like a gynecologist giving a pap smear and Carlie enjoyed every plunge. Devon exploded, but continued like a race horse. Carlie wanted more, so he gave his all.

Devon had something to prove and was doing a hell of a good job. As the minutes progressed, he became more and more energetic. Savoring every moment, they both looked each other in the eyes as they made love into the wee hours of the morning. Hours later, while Devon's sweat covered Carlie's body it was obvious that they'd be together forever.

"Devon, I need to call my Dad to let him know I'm okay."

"I'll take care of it for ya baby. I got whatever you need."

"No, I think I need to call him so he'll know I'm not showing up for court tomorrow." Carlie hugged Devon tightly.

"Whew! I was worried," he joked.

As Carlie dialed her Dad's number, fear of what he would say took over her body. The idea of telling him she wanted to be with Devon frightened her. She knew Ricky would go ballistic, but she had Devon by her side and little Devon inside of her. When Ricky answered the phone Carlie immediately developed confidence. While she spoke, Devon lay directly next to her. He smiled that smile that warmed her heart as she told Ricky she was going to be with Devon forever.

Bruised

Chapter 9

Shit Happens

Carlie couldn't help but to feel blessed as she thumbed through her new wardrobe. She knew there were hundreds of women who would kill to be in her place. Contemplating on what to wear was rough given the large quantity of clothing Devon had bought her over the last few weeks. Since pink was her favorite color, Devon topped everything when he accessorized her wardrobe with a pink diamond cut bracelet. She was starting to feel right at home considering the hurdles he had jumped to make her feel special.

Although she went from living in a prominent well kept neighborhood to a torn down garden apartment complex, she was more than pleased. Devon's apartment was nice considering the monthly rent of $800. It was located in a secluded area in the southern part of Prince Georges County, and was a cover up in case someone thought he was making big money. Although his place was laced with the finest furnishings and electronics on the inside, compared to her house it was a shack. However, not having Ricky on her back was a blessing in itself. Even though she missed him, life with

Devon was satisfying.

Carlie smiled when she held the fifth dress in front of her body looking into the full length mirror. Although undecided about what to wear, she was pleased with her petite shape. She turned slightly to the side to imagine her Janet Jackson abs with a tiny bulge. *Pregnancy won't ruin my shape that bad,* she thought. *I'll exercise and pop right back into shape just for Devon.*

Finally deciding on her gear, Carlie thought black and sexy would be appropriate. Devon hadn't revealed exactly where they where going but the Vera Wang crop pants and sheared tube top seemed perfect in Carlie's eyes. Fiddling through her shoes, she became slightly disappointed knowing that she couldn't sport her never worn three inch black stilettos. Devon had forbidden her from wearing high-heeled shoes. He had often said they were *fuck me pumps* and made for women who wanted to get done by all types of men. Besides, he had an excuse now. She was carrying his child.

Carlie knew that having a baby by Devon would be a challenge. His rules were far too crazy and would keep her and the baby from living a normal life. Besides, she was well aware that she'd be the primary care taker. Devon did not have a father figure in his life, nor was he cut out to be a father. As a matter of fact, Devon wasn't very family oriented at all. Carlie had met his mother on only two occasions since they'd been together. Both times, they had gone to his mother's house only to eat and run.

Devon mentioned having a sister, but always got quiet when she asked about her or other members of his family. Quite frankly, she didn't know much about Devon's past. He was truly a loner and expected Carlie to follow suit. After slipping her hand under her shirt she tried to smile. Carlie exhaled at the thought of bringing her baby into this crazy world.

The sound of the horn excited her. She grabbed her purse and headed out of the door. When Carlie ran down the stairs, her long ponytail bounced as she jumped in the car as if this was their first date. It was a strange feeling riding shotgun in the car belonging to her, which she barely got an opportunity to drive. While Devon spoke on the cell in his usual codes, Carlie chilled thinking about how she wanted to spend her last 3 weeks in D.C. before heading back to college. It had been a crazy summer in her eyes, but she could feel better days on the way.

Pulling up to the restaurant the valet attendants opened both of their doors simultaneously. Ending his phone call, Devon wrapped his arm around Carlie's waist as she grinned showing off her pearly whites. Carlie screamed when the double doors opened to Ripken's Place. Her eyes opened widely as she looked around the room. She noticed Kirk and a few of Devon's friends that she hadn't seen before.

Catching a glimpse of Zarria warmed her heart. "So, you knew about this. You are one sneaky bitch," Carlie joked.

"That's my job," Zarria said expecting a hug.

"Aaww! Thank you, thank you," she said looking around at all the balloons attached to the chairs. "What's this all about?" Carlie asked observing the décor of the quaint restaurant. She noticed that the plaques, memorabilia and frames that lined the walls were all dedicated to legendary baseball players like Babe Ruth, Satchell Page and Hank Aaron.

"This is a celebration for many reasons but most of all

just 'cause I wanted to honor you. I know I can be an asshole sometimes, but I'm puttin' that shit behind me." Devon squeezed her hand tightly.

Unbelievable looks were seen on the faces of all guests, except Zarria. She wasn't giving any rave reviews for Devon's performance. It was all a game in her opinion and one she had witnessed several times before. A part of Zarria didn't want Devon to do right. She felt that Carlie had already been given the world from her Dad. It would be a catastrophe for her to receive the best of both worlds while she had nothing.

"Plus your birthday is coming soon. I believe that's September 8th if I'm not mistaken," Zarria said jokingly. You know you'll be back in school, so we're celebrating e'rything tonight, girlfriend." She slapped Carlie a high five as hard as she could. "Somebody gave Devon some tickets to see Usher tonight at Constitution Hall," she said leaning back showing off her skimpy halter dress.

"Sounds good to me," said Carlie looking for confirmation from Devon.

Devon turned his head and joined in on the conversation with his invited guest. Carlie looked over to see Kirk pulling at the fringes on Devon's shirt jokingly.

"Where in the hell do you get all this shit, partner? Is the tailor comin' to your house?" Kirk asked sarcastically inciting others to laugh too. Corrupt, a business connection of Devon's was the loudest. He rarely got the chance to hang with Devon on a personal basis and certainly not with Carlie around. While he enjoyed Devon and Kirk's spat, his red-bone rental date kept her hand in his lap. For the entire evening, she nibbled on Corrupt's ear and played beneath the table. She was about as trashy as they came and barely spoke a word.

Aside from Corrupt's friend, the table was full of life. After downing the sixth bottle of champagne, and eight apple martinis, the conversation grew more hostile. Although everyone had their share of drinks, Kirk had knocked back at least three bottles on his own. This was rare for him, but would definitely explain his unusual behavior.

Hours had gone by and dinner had been a hit. After all the lobster tails, stuffed shrimp, and other succulent foods had been cleared from the table, the hostility increased. Kirk continued to joke and make comments about both Zarria and Devon.

"Kirk when the fuck you gonna get a girl," Devon said sipping a glass of Cristal. "Seriously," he added as his glass hit the table with a loud thump.

"When you give me some time off," Kirk laughed.

"Oh, so it's my fault yo ass ain't got no rap," Devon badgered.

"Nah nigga, if I wasn't always on stake out with you, maybe I'd have me a chick," Kirk said in a more stern tone.

"Hey, slow yo' road dog," Devon blasted helping Kirk to remember who was boss.

"No, slow your road, partner," Kirk shot back.

"Okay... I think we've all had enough to drink," Carlie said. She rubbed Devon's arm in an effort to calm him down.

"Stay in a woman's place," Devon snapped. He snatched his arm away and eyed Kirk.

He looked back to Carlie. "Do we understand one another?" he said firmly.

She nodded. Carlie rubbed his back just the way he liked it.

Devon snacked on the toothpick engaged between his teeth. He never took his eyes off Kirk. Carlie sensed that her fun-filled celebration wasn't going to have a happy ending. Staying as close to Devon as she possibly could, she whispered softly in his ear.

"Baby, let's go home. Don't mess up this night for us. Remember we only have three more weeks together."

"You checkin' for this nigga?" Devon asked waiting for a response.

Surprised, Carlie had a blank look on her face.

"Nigga, pick on somebody your own size! I'm feeling good, partner. Ain't nobody catering to your ass tonight," Kirk shouted bringing attention to the table. "This girl can't even say nothin' without you actin' like a watch dog." Kirk grinned trying to bring back a little laughter to the group.

Devon returned the smirk. When he raised slowly, the whole table watched his actions closely. Everything seemed normal as he asked the waiter pleasantly for the check. Biting his lip, Devon eyeballed everyone at the round table. His circling of the room inspired an uncomfortable feeling in everyone.

Aiight," Devon roared, swinging a baseball bat he'd snatched from a display on the wall. "So ya wanna defend my woman," he said looking straight into Kirk's eyes. Kirk's response was slow and well thought out. Scanning the room he looked to see who was watching. Out of the corner of his eye, Corrupt smiled at the thought of the duo ready to go at each others throat. There was about a 45 second moment of silence until the table came tumbling down from the impact of Devon's swing. Glass covered the floor while the linen tablecloth was drenched in champagne.

Walking within two feet of Kirk's evil frown, Devon grabbed him by the neck. His ability to take hold of a big guy like Kirk surprised everyone, but no surprise compared to Kirk yanking away exposing a nine-millimeter. Everyone scattered from the table with the exception of Carlie. Keeping her eyes lowered like a school girl in trouble she pretended this was not happening.

"Kirk, don't do this," Zarria yelled! "It's not worth it. You know they've already called the police, let's go," she shouted. At the sound of the word *police*, and with *warrants pending* Corrupt and his girl exited the restaurant swiftly.

Laughing, Devon put his bat slowly on the floor. "Oh, so this is how we do. You wanna use the piece I bought you, *to kill me*." Devon shook his head in disbelief. He wanted to teach Kirk what it felt like to be betrayed. "I thought we were boyz."

"You brought all of this on yourself," Kirk said lightning up a little bit. "Ya know you my nigga, save those bullets for somebody else," Devon said walking right up to his boy as if he knew Kirk didn't have the heart. "Let's go," Devon said, giving Carlie the signal with his finger.

Devon walked past the manager who waited by the door for the police.

"Sir, do you know what you've done?" the aged gentleman asked.

"Nah, everything is aiight though. Shit happens," he said shrugging his shoulders as if he'd done nothing wrong. Here's a little something for your trouble. He sneered, peeling twelve hundreds from the wad he carried in his pockets. Throwing the money carelessly, Devon walked out with his number one side-kick and his favorite girl right behind him.

"The night is young," he yelled. "Let's go have some fun!"

The mood was ruined, but with liquor stains on Kirk's shirt and a bad feeling on Carlie's mind, the three of them met up with Zarria and Corrupt only to party until the wee hours of the morning.

Chapter 10

All Bets Off

The commotion inside 729 Emerson Street in Northeast D.C. was normal for any Stewart gathering. If there was one thing that Grandma Jean knew how to do, it was throw a party. In honor of her 76th birthday, over thirty of her unruly off springs were in attendance.

The atmosphere was combined with wildness and good cheer. The Matriarch of the family enjoyed having a packed house, especially with all of her four children together, Ricky, Charles Luder, Angela and Calvin. Out of her three boys, Calvin was the exception to the family. His quietness didn't fit in. Charles Luder on the other hand was the exact opposite. His boisterous ways were normal and especially enjoyed by all the younger cousins who giggled at him often. Angela, Ms. Stewarts only daughter, always made her presence known. As a devoted social worker, her comments made the family's skin cringe at every function. Besides her lectures, she was the best cook in the house.

The kitchen counter was filled with all kinds of soul food resembling a Thanksgiving spread in August. The smell of the macaroni and cheese, collard greens and candied yams filled the room.

Charles Luder the eldest of the Stewart boys talked as loud as he could out talking everyone in the room. Making his way around the table he pushed people aside without saying excuse me. "What fool forgot da damn Hen Dog?" he asked at stage two of his drunken state.

"You already done bought up every bottle at the store," Grandma Jean replied. "I'on know what kinda fool I raised. Help me Father," she said waving her hands above her head. "Charles, sit your tail down, boy."

Charles Luder shot his mother a nasty look. He hated to be called Charles. Because he was named after his deceased father, the middle name *Luder* was very important to him. For Charles it was a sign of family respect; for others it was plain country.

Charles Luder had always been heavy-set, but after years of drinking and very little exercise he was now pushing 280 sloppy pounds. Most of that was carried in his belly. "Mama, I know it's ya birthday in all, but this is how we do," he said. Charles Luder raised his cup for a toast.

Grandma Jean shook her head and focused on Ricky, who had been silent the majority of the night. Ricky sat in a recliner like a sophisticated gentleman sipping on a glass of Remy Martin. Ms. Stewart knew from his demeanor that something was troubling him. She was used to him joining the rest of the family in their loud voices as they taunted one another. Strangely, Ricky ignored everyone as he glared at the pictures on the mantle. The photos reminded him of all the good times the Stewart family shared over the years. He also thought about the closeness of his kin that was fostered by his mother and respected by all. Only one thing was missing.

"Man, what da hell is wrong wit you?" asked Charles Luder sitting on a stool directly in front of him.

"I'm relaxing," Ricky replied giving a half-ass smile.

"And where da hell is Carlie?"

Ricky didn't respond. His thoughts drifted. His decision to cut Carlie off was now final. Cutting her ties with the family was the last straw. Carlie hadn't been to any family functions or even visited over the last few weeks, but missing her Grandmother's birthday was inexcusable. He knew it would be hard but it had to be done. He figured if Carlie had to rely totally on Devon, she'd soon realize the importance of family and the fact that Devon was no good for her.

As usual, Ricky's mother threw him a life vest. "Carlie had something important to do," Grandma Jean interjected. "I'm sure she'll try to make it."

"Sure she will," one of Carlie's cousins replied. "Devon ain't lettin' her come over here. He's got her on lock down," she said sucking her teeth.

"Dat pot belly lookin' moderfucker! What'cha wanna do 'bout dat boy, Ricky," Charles Luder asked waiting for an answer. "Mannnnnnn, you've gotten way toooooo soft. Dat suave, nonchalant role you playin' is gonna get yo damn daughter killed," he slurred.

Ricky sat with little emotion. "No, Carlie is gonna get herself killed." He enunciated each word with purpose. "And I have a date," he said raising from his seat.

"Fuck dat," Charles Luder exploded! "What's more important than my niece?"

"He's going to be with that heifer," Grandma Jean said walking towards the kitchen. Carlie's situation is much more important than Ms. Courtney or whatever the hell her name is." Talking to herself, she continued. "I'm not writing my baby off yet. She needs me," Grandma mumbled as she stopped to land a wet kiss on Carlie's picture sitting on a wooden table.

Although unhappy with Ricky's attitude, Grandma began to fix her son a to-go plate. She didn't want him relying on no woman to feed him. Besides, she was sure that the freakazoid her son was fornicating with wasn't feeding him nothing, other than what was between her legs. She was used to pacifying her family. That was her gift.

In the other room the noise level got higher and higher as Ricky, Charles Luder, and Angela debated over Carlie. At this point every family member had now flocked to the living room to be nosey. Most stuffed their faces and listened while Ricky was being interrogated in front of everyone.

"I can't understand how you can just leave her to fail?" Angela asked with her hands on her hips. Her tall frame stood just as high as her brothers. Angela had always been told she resembled Tyra Banks and should consider modeling. But for Angela there was nothing more important than helping others. Social work wasn't a job, it was her passion. "So you're not going to do anything?" she questioned.

"Oh, she hasn't seen nothing yet!" Ricky paced the floor. "I'm not paying for college this coming semester and she's not coming back home until I know she's completely done with that thug!"

"Shiiiiid, yo ass was a thug too," Charles Luder interjected.

"But, I didn't beat my women," Ricky shouted. The room became silent. Ricky clinched his teeth. He couldn't believe that everyone knew his daughter was living in fear with Devon and he was doing nothing about it. He was supposed to be the strong arm in the family. Everyone was aware of his history, even the younger nieces and nephews.

"First of all, Carlie needs someone to talk to," Angela said sincerely. "She's definitely not going to be honest or come clean if she thinks Devon will be able to get to her. I'll invite her over to spend the night with me."

"She won't come. Besides, he won't let her," Ricky snapped.

"I just want her to know that she has help and that we're here for her. It's worth a try. I'll call her." Angela looked at her mother and brother. "What's the number?"

"We only have a cell number for her," Grandma finally answered.

"Is this Devon guy going to answer her phone," she asked agitated.

"He might, but he'll be nice. He's always nice around us," Grandma explained. "He waits until he gets her by herself to act like a damn fool." Grandma's finger moved back and forth at full speed as she fussed. "God knows, I'd kick Devon right in his scrawny ass penis. I'm 76 but don't let the numbers fool you," she continued. "The C in Christian don't stand for chicken, 'cause I'll whip his ass like he stole somethin'.

The entire room keeled over in laughter. Grandma Jean was known for being feisty in her day. It was just thrilling to see her still ready to fight weighing 120 pounds soaking wet. With Grandma on a rampage, Angela tried to calm things down.

In between her lecture she filled the trash with the empty

plates that lined the table. Angela was considered to be a clean fanatic. As soon as she hit the door, people knew she'd either start cleaning or either giving another '*How to*' sermon.

"Listen, what is important right now is getting Carlie away from him. Even just for a while. We must talk some sense into her. She probably thinks what he's doing is okay." Angela looked at Ricky searching for some reaction. "Is it just mental abuse or physical too?" she asked.

"Both," Grandma quickly spat.

"Oh, no. Why didn't anyone tell us. You all are just as much to blame. You can't keep this a secret!" Angela yelled as she looked around the room. The mood grew somber. "Look, Carlie has no self-esteem and is living with Lucifer who is stealing her joy day by day! We have to do something. What's the number?" Angela began dialing. She frowned when she got the answering service. "Carlie, it's your Aunt Angela. Call me. I want us to go to that new Spa on 18th street, my treat," she said hanging up the phone.

"Bro, I say let's go get her," the youngest of the Stewart brothers spoke. He hadn't said two words all night until now. "Word on the street is that he has one of his goons watching the house when he's not at home. And when she leaves out, he has her followed."

"Dat cock sucker got my niece livin' like a hostage!" Charles Luder was furious. He had heard enough. He stood like an army soldier ready for battle. "You ready Ricky," he shouted.

"It depends on what you call ready," he said heading towards the door. "I'm gonna rid myself of all this mess. I'm not ruining my life or yours because Carlie wants to be shacked up with a controlling gangster."

Grandma Jean rushed to hand Ricky his food. Looking into his eyes she could see his pain. "It'll all blow over and she'll come back to us," she said. "Trust me, prayers work."

Outside the door Ricky thought about Charles' comments. His plan to retaliate sounded noble, but not clever enough. *What if Carlie is happy this way? If he had Devon killed would she hate him for life?* He wasn't willing to chance that. Within seconds, Ricky had dialed a number on his cell. "It's off," he said into the receiver. The person on the other line verified. After hanging up Ricky felt better. His only hope was that everything would work out in Carlie's favor. Ricky's watchdogs had been called off. She was now on her own.

Bruised

Chapter 11

Sleepless Nights

Mildred McNeil darted away from the window pretending to clear the dishes from the table. As usual the clock striking 6 p.m. was a nightmare for all living in the McNeil household. After several minutes of peeping through the blinds and anticipating the arrival of the tyrant, the moment had arrived. The entire family knew to be on their best behavior. Hearing the drunken footsteps of her husband of fifteen years, Mildred let out a sigh.

The sound of the door swinging open would make one think the police were on the scene. Wiping the sweat from his forehead, Darnell McNeil surveyed the room when he entered the small but well kept efficiency. He froze in the middle of the floor as did everyone else in the house. Suddenly, he was on the move as he spoke in a crazed voice.

"Woman, where's my damn food?" he screamed.

"It'll be on the table in a few minutes," Mildred replied softly.

Avoiding eye-contact she began opening pots and slapping food onto the plate as quickly as possible.

Darnell turned his forty-two year old body in the direction of his two children sitting silently on the area rug. Since their father's arrival the volume in the house changed from the high note of twelve to complete silence.

"All I do is work hard all day for my family. And this is the thanks I get!" Saliva dripped from Darnell's mouth as he waited for a response. "Am I appreciated around here?" he garbled.

Mildred moved faster. As usual he was in the blind. Mildred did appreciate what Darnell had done for their family over the years. He had been on the same job as a custodian for the last twenty-five years and had been up for a promotion twice in a row. Unfortunately, due to his drinking problem he was passed over each time.

Mildred nervously bent down to set the plate on the table when a terrible stench hit her nostrils. The familiar smell of gin forced her to take a step back.

"What, you too good for gin? That's what's wrong with you now. You're too up tight." Raising from his chair the children scattered. "Here, take a sip," Darnell said trailing his wife with a flask.

"I don't want it," Mildred said with raised voice. "Besides, the children are watching us."

"Maybe they need some too," he said eyeing his son and daughter.

Mildred held her head high. "That's enough! We're not doing this in front of the kids," she said crisply.

Darnell, stunned by his wife's response stood still while his eyes grew the size of golf balls. "Whore, don't you ever speak to me like that in my house." Darnell staggered towards Mildred at full speed.

Mildred took cover behind the kitchen table. Her eyes watered and welled up from fear. On many occasions, Mildred wanted to stand up to Darnell. It just wasn't in her. She paid close attention to her son, Devon who began to move toward her in a robotic manner.

I'ma teach ya to respect me," Darnell yelled.

Mildred was focused on little Devon, when the expected blow

knocked her off balance. Although the pain was excruciating, Mildred could see the knife that noticeably rested in her son's hand.

Bending over, Darnell positioned his face an inch from his wife's bruised cheek. "Do you understand who the Daddy of this house is?"

Little Devon raised his hand high above his head. His hand began to shake and a sick feeling took over his body. With Darnell's back to his son, he continued to rant and rave. Mildred's eyes opened wide when her husband turned around. With a strong force Darnell reached for the knife. When the blood splattered Devon McNeil woke up screaming.

"It's okay," Carlie said rubbing Devon's back in circular motion. "Calm down baby. You must've had a bad dream."

Devon sat up in bed sweating like he'd run a marathon. His thoughts flipped back to his childhood. Breathing heavily, his eyes met Carlie's.

"You know, I have dreams too," Carlie smiled. Grandma Jean always talks to me in my dreams. Sometimes they're sad, but mostly good."

"If I can help it, I don't ever wanna dream about my *no good* -father again," Devon said.

Carlie kissed his forehead. "You wanna talk about it?"

"Naw… I'd rather go back ta sleep."

Carlie nestled Devon in her arms and they drifted off to sleep.

***

Carlie woke up to a delightful smell. Exhausted from the interrupted sleep, she had to pry herself out of bed in an effort to relieve her bloated bladder. This had recently become a pattern since Carlie was nearly eight weeks pregnant. Opening the bedroom door, she was met with a smile and a breakfast tray.

"Just fa my baby," Devon said as he kissed Carlie on the cheek.

"I'll be right back," she blushed as she rushed past Devon into the bathroom.

When Carlie returned, Devon had creatively surrounded the tray with fresh pink roses. He served up home fries, pancakes, sausage, and biscuits.

"What brought all of this on?" Carlie asked.

Devon slid the tray across her lap. "Can't I treat my woman like a queen whenever I feel like it?" An imposter had taken over Devon's body. He continued to lay it on thick. "What do ya wanna do today?" he asked cheesin'.

"Whatever you wanna do," Carlie quickly responded.

"It's all 'bout you," Devon said as he leaned to shower her forehead with kisses. "Why don't we go furniture shopping?"

"Furniture shopping?" Carlie asked perplexed. "We already have furniture."

"I'm not talking 'bout furniture for this place. I can't allow you to move off campus without any furniture. I know you didn't think I'd send my baby and my woman back to

Pennsylvania without a decent place to lay ya head."

Shocked, Carlie's face lit up like fireworks on the fourth of July. She jumped into Devon's arms. In the back of her mind she had often wondered how she would weather financially once she got back to college. Knowing she could get help from Devon was different from being totally dependent upon him. Carlie had never relied completely on anyone in her life other than Ricky Stewart. And now she was well on her way to being a tax write-off for Devon. This would be a big move, but one she was willing to take. She'd always wanted to move off campus but knew that Ricky would never go for it.

"An agent has already found the perfect spot for us... I mean you," Devon said watching Carlie's reaction. "It's in Kennett Square, not far from campus."

"If possible, can I get a two bedroom? I want Tamia to move in with me. Please. ...," Carlie said like a school girl.

"Sure," Devon said as if he didn't have to think twice. But deep down inside he wasn't sure if this would be a good idea. Tamia was Carlie's mixed girlfriend from school who was known to be on the wild side. Her idea of commitment was far from what Devon demanded of Carlie. Tamia's independence and strength fascinated Carlie and troubled Devon. However, with the thought of showing Carlie he could change, he agreed to let her girl move in.

Tossing the tray to the side Carlie straddled Devon with excitement and drenched him with her sweet saliva just the way he liked it. She had been instructed frequently on how to keep her man. Devon's erotic zones yearned attention. Carlie began with wet pecks as she slid his boxers off exposing his "8" inch dick which was already at attention and armed. Carlie's tongue massaged Devon's inner thigh and prepped him for his favorite position. His temperature neared 100 degrees and detonated when she began rapidly licking him as if he were a blowpop. He laid there sweating wildly as if he couldn't control himself anymore.

Carlie remained calm while she thoroughly thought about every sensual move she made. It was an important day for her to drive him wild. After all, he was now her everything.

Devon had managed to slip his fingers in between Carlie's panties to feel the wetness. Since her pregnancy, he had noticed she stayed nice and moist. Quickly, he flipped her beneath him as he pressed his moist body against hers. Carlie yearned for more foreplay but felt Devon's manhood growing to massive proportions. Beginning to lick his upper chest area she wanted the moment to last forever. Wildly, Devon grabbed the headboard and entered Carlie with a powerful thrust. Holding on for dear life like a seasoned bull rider, Carlie moaned as Devon worked every wall of her warm vagina.

Suddenly, Devon got up. "Ask for it!" he said.

Carlie was shocked. *Was this something new? Surely, he doesn't think this is a turn on,* she thought. "You can't be serious," she whined.

"Ask for it," he repeated in a more serious tone.

Carlie did as she was told. Instantly, Devon picked up where he left off. At that moment, Carlie felt like there could be nothing better in life. She wanted their lovemaking to last all night long. Devon felt the same way, but uncontrollably his body began to jerk. Knowing what that meant Carlie pressed harder and changed positions just in time for a dual explosion. They both cuddled for hours with looks of happiness until they fell off to sleep.

***

The next few days were filled with joy, laughter, and healthy spending habits. Carlie and Devon became the Bonnie & Clyde of Washington, D.C. They shopped for furnishings for Carlie's new apartment by day and dined by night. Price tags meant nothing. At times Carlie had even snuck in a few baby outfits not even knowing if she was carrying a boy or a girl.

Strangely, Devon hadn't left Carlie's side. All of his calls had been put on hold and all life was clearly all about Carlie. She had no idea Devon had been seriously thinking about marriage. He wondered if he could truly give up his player card. Although he didn't have the desire to cheat on her, at least he was still able to maintain his playboy image around town.

Devon marveled at the fact that being married would give him a tighter reign on Carlie. *Mrs. Carlie McNeil has a nice ring to it,* he thought. The visions of her giving birth to his children and taking care of his home excited him. Even though he respected Carlie's dreams of wanting to become a lawyer, he didn't care. Devon wanted his woman to be attached to two things; an apron and a cookbook.

School wasn't really important to him and definitely wasn't considered a priority. After all, he dropped out in the eleventh grade following a two-day suspension. For Devon, the time off was more of a treat than punishment. He used that opportunity to roam the streets and build his clientele. Even though that was 10 years ago, Devon's mentality hadn't changed. At twenty-seven he still could care less about education.

Devon wanted badly for Carlie to put her schooling on hold and stay home with him. His plan was that after she had the baby Carlie would take a few classes each semester. He knew she wouldn't want to go for it, and deep down inside he wanted her to be happy. He thought that by getting Carlie an apartment in his name he'd at least be able to supervise her while he was away; not to mention the electronic tapping piece he'd secretly placed on her phone to monitor her phone conversations.

The ringing of the phone snapped Devon from his thoughts. "What's crackin'," he answered cheerfully.

"What's crackin'," Zarria asked. "Now why on earth would you answer the phone like that? That's beyond ghetto."

"I see you're still on the phone," Devon responded.

"Have you been giving Carlie my messages?" she asked.

"I forgot. We been busy." Devon pulled Carlie close to him as he smiled broadly. Carlie returned the gesture with a fake grin as she listened to the conversation. "If you find yoself a man, you'd be busy too," he joked.

"I tell you what, nigga, if he's anythang like you, I'll pass. Besides, I love 'em, fuck'em, and leave 'em."

Carlie can't hang with hookers," he said seriously.

"Look, she's leaving the day after tomorrow. I'm throwing her a small party at *Dream* tomorrow night in the VIP lounge," Zarria revealed.

"*Dream!*" Devon yelled slightly pushing Carlie away. Rethinking his reaction he silenced himself and handed Carlie the phone. He'd come so far and didn't want to blow it. Rubbing Carlie's shoulder he calmed himself and listened carefully.

"I had no idea you called," Carlie answered Zarria turning to confront Devon.

Girl, you might as well have your apron engraved now, before its too late." Zarria laughed at her own sarcasm. She continued to blow bubbles in between her words. "Anyway, we're giving you a going away party."

"Ahh..., I don't know about that, let me check with Devon." Before she could speak, Devon applied his index finger to Carlie's lips.

Zarria yelled through the phone. "I didn't say ask him, damn it! We grown ass women."

He smiled. "Of course I don't mind."

Removing the phone from her ear, Carlie cheerfully said, "Zarria said make sure you're there early so you can pay the bill." She laughed.

"I'll be there," Devon smiled like a counterfeit bill.

"Bet. We're on," Carlie said. "I guess a little bit of fun before I leave won't hurt."

By now Devon had made his way to the bathroom. Slamming the door behind him he banged his fist on the wall as hard as he could. *What kind of man would allow his pregnant girl to go to a club*, he thought? Why didn't he share his true feelings with Carlie? This was exactly why he kept home-wrecker Zarria as far away as he could. Just like he learned from anger management, Devon took 10 deep breaths and regained his composure. He remembered his vow to make things right forever. Consistency was the key. *Besides, what harm could come from one night out?*

Opening the door, he rushed near Carlie and wrapped his arms around her as tight as he could. She blushed within seconds at the thought of having him all to herself. *What more could a girl ask for?* she thought.

Chapter 12

No Way Out

Carlie threw objects at top speed across the cluttered room. She wondered if she had become senile over the last few hours. She'd just driven her car earlier that morning, so she knew the key to her Benz was there. "Where could it be?" she said scratching her head. She didn't want to call Devon considering how distant he had been over the last few days. With no other choice, Carlie grabbed the phone to call him. Then it hit her. She remembered the spare key she'd put in his safe when she first got the car. Her eyes widened. Darting to the safe, she quickly remembered the combination. Carlie let out a sigh after shuffling through the stacks of bills. To her surprise Devon had way more money than she expected. Without actually counting, she knew there had to be over $500,000. Suddenly, she spotted the extra key.

Although happy about finding the key, she couldn't help but wonder why it was missing from her ring. *Had Devon removed it? Or had it simply fallen off?* In either case, Carlie was ready to roll. Jetting to her car the neighborhood boys slyly admired her when she emerged from the apartment in her low heels, conservative linen dress, and chanel poncho. She felt good about not wearing anything against Devon's wishes. He had told her earlier that he'd meet her at the club. Carlie was sure he'd be impressed with her outfit.

After flying at top speed through town Carlie arrived at Zarria's shortly after ten.

"Girl, we late," Zarria yelled jumping into the convertible.

"Fresh weave, huh," Carlie boasted.

"You know I had to look good for the fellas tonight." she responded.

"You not doing so bad yoself." Zarria smacked her glossy lips. "Girl put that top up. You know this ain't my hair."

The girls laughed as they blasted *Drop it like it's hot*, by Snoop all the way to Dream Nightclub. As Carlie approached the club she dialed Devon's number to see where he thought she should park the car. After getting no response she headed straight for the valet. Carlie felt like a queen. As soon as she pulled up, her door was opened by a handsome young man who studied her every move. Marveling at the extra attention, she switched harder. The poles were moved aside as Carlie entered the packed club.

Zarria pushed their way through to the reserved section. Carlie searched for Devon. He was no where to be found. Immediately she reached for her phone to check for missed calls. Her attention was distracted by the waiting guest in the area sectioned off just for her. Zarria invited friends Carlie hadn't seen in years. Of course they all wondered where she'd been hiding.

The table was spread with spiced shrimp, boneless chicken, shrimp kabobs, jerk wings, and bottles of Don Perion.

Carlie did her best to speak to everyone as she stopped to give hugs and kisses randomly. Suddenly out of the corner of her eye she focused on the side view of someone resembling Devon. He sat without emotion at the end of the reserved area. Carlie kept him in sight as she made her way near him. After briefly chatting with an old friend, she made her move but the guy was not Devon.

She couldn't understand why Devon wasn't there. *Why had he been so distant? What was his problem?* she thought. Then it hit Carlie. This was her chance to let loose a bit.

Feeling a palm on her shoulder, Carlie turned to find Zarria.

"Let's have some fun young lady," she said handing Carlie a glass of Moet. "You never drink."

"Oh, I definitely can't drink tonight."

"You always say that," Zarria said putting the glass to Carlie's lips.

"Okay, I guess one drink won't hurt."

"Besides you need to loosen up a bit. Devon ain't here."

"Yeah. Remind me why I'm still with him?" They both laughed.

"Must be the sex?" Carlie slightly turned her head. "Or is it the money?" Zarria teased.

Carlie's dimples grew deep. The girls toasted at the thought of the benefits involved with being Devon's girl. Carlie agreed, as if she were getting the best of Devon, but deep inside she wasn't sure about the benefits.

The house lights dimmed as the entertainment of the evening began. Rayheim DeVaughn, the hottest sultry singer of the year prepared to take the stage. Carlie grabbed a half empty bottle of Moet and helped herself to a second glass.

Zarria was feeling real good and had found a nice bun to snuggle with on the dance floor. Men all around the club gawked secretly at Carlie for most knew she belonged to Devon. An outta town brotha obviously didn't care; he never took his eyes off of her.

"Sing it," Carlie yelled as soon as the music came blasting through the speakers. Rayheim was a new artist on the scene who welcomed the sounds of Carlie's cheers. Everyone could tell that she was starting to feel good. Totally out of character she began dancing alone. Slowly, her body started to grind with the beat of the music. The dark-skinned new-comer continued to stare. He stood in his iced out jewelry and watched Carlie closely. Tamia watched her guest, who kept Carlie under surveillance. She realized it was a bad idea to invite him.

Suddenly, Devon invaded Carlie's space. Their voices competed with the sounds of the music but were not heard by others. Everyone watched as their body language proved there was a problem. As usual Kirk stood by his side. The softness she had seen in Devon over the past few weeks had totally disappeared. Devon stopped to purposely look at everyone around him. His business was his concern *only* and anybody out of place would get dealt with. As Devon glanced back, Carlie already had her purse in hand. Zarria smacked her lips as she followed her girl.

Once outside, Carlie and Zarria talked in the car parked in front of the club. They felt safe knowing that Devon was still inside. Carlie was thinking of dropping Zarria off and heading home when a noticeably handsome guy approached the vehicle. Carlie smiled. It was the same guy who had admired her inside.

"Hello beautiful. I see you had some problems inside."

"Oh, nothing I can't handle." Carlie blushed.

"Oh word, Ma!"

I didn't catch your name," Carlie said. Her buzz had intensified since sitting in the car. She popped the glove box in search of her Advils.

"Yeah, Tamia forgot to introduce us inside. I'm Mike." He held out his hand and licked his full lips. "And your name, Ma," he said to Zarria.

"Zarria." She hunched Carlie in the back. "Ooh la la," she whispered.

"Just like a chocolate piece of candy," Zarria mumbled under her breath. She had visions of Mike's body that resembled a deep black Mandingo. "Sorry we had to run out," Zarria said taking control of the conversation. "I'm Zarria," she said to Mike.

Mike's presence was a complete turn on for Carlie. His above average height made her feel safe. His tender nature and unusual accent brought a strange sense of peace to Carlie. She returned the smile.

"Yo, I'm from New York and I would love to show you ladies a good time tonight. Can you suggest a good place for us to get something to eat?"

"No way," Carlie said. "I'm taken."

"Word," Mike snickered. "I'm not trying to marry you. I just wanna grab something to eat."

Carlie raised her hand cutting his rap short. His game was strong but not strong enough to ignore Devon strutting viciously toward her car. Without thinking, the smile erased from Carlie's face as she slammed the gas pedal, blowing dust on Mike.

"Why'd you do that," Zarria yelled protecting her hair from the wind.

"Devon was headed toward us stupid. And he didn't look happy either." Carlie stumbled over her words. She wasn't thinking clearly. She couldn't believe she had the guts to pull off on Devon. She thought about going back but figured she was already in deep trouble.

Zarria looked back, but Devon was nowhere in sight. The streets were lined with cars and made it difficult to pass through the slow moving traffic. Carlie became paranoid. Frightened as hell, was more like it. She knew Devon was either whooping up on Mike or coming for her. She knew that if she could just make it to New York Ave. she'd be safe.

As she sat in the bumper to bumper traffic on Kendall Street, she bit her nails deep into the skin. Looking back and forth nervously, her foot hovered over the pedal. Obviously the light had changed far ahead. A few cars moved up gradually, then stopped. Carlie tried to calm herself a bit. But the noise of loud honking horns and screeching breaks made her uneasy. She looked through her rear view mirror only to notice Devon driving like a maniac down the wrong side of the street. His bold attempt to catch her sent Carlie into a panic. Forgetting about the cars moving slowly toward New York Avenue, Carlie slammed on the accelerator. She darted right in the middle of moving traffic. Cars honked and swerved to prevent a pile up. Carlie turned right down the first street she saw. It didn't matter that it was a one-way.

She glanced over at Zarria unable to read her face. Zarria turned away from Carlie pointing her finger ahead. A sign in front of them read *Dead End*. Not able to speak, Zarria turned around to see the headlights from Devon's car. Carlie had given up. She had nowhere to run. The sirens heard in the distance didn't even give her hope. Zarria locked the doors for safety. Carlie knew better.

Devon pounded on the driver's side of the door with his fist. It sounded as if stones were being banged against the window. Carlie held her composure while Zarria screamed to the top of her lungs.

"Get out my fuckin' car," Devon yelled pounding on the front windshield.

Carlie lowered her eyes. She reached for the door handle but Zarria yanked her arm.

"Unless you wanna go to the hospital again, don't open that door!"

"Just let me talk to him. I'll calm him down," Carlie said in cat-like tone. Her heart thumped faster than before.

As the sound of the sirens got closer Devon's anger intensified. His size 12 foot came crashing through the window. Glass shattered everywhere. Grabbing Carlie at full strength, Devon cupped her face. No remorse was felt from the tears that drenched his hands. Tightening his grip, hurt filled his face.

"How could you embarrass me that way?"

"Wha...t do you mea...n," Carlie whimpered.

"What. What do I mean!" Devon pretended to strike.

Carlie flinched.

Although Devon had considered himself untouchable, jail was not on his agenda for the night. Carlie would have to pay for her disloyal behavior, but getting locked up wouldn't be smart. When the flashing lights entered the dead end street, he scurried to safety. Devon darted through several backyards eluding the police.

Carlie stood dumbfounded and her thoughts froze. Even the police pulling onto the scene didn't move her. Zarria jumped from the car prepared to spill the beans. Immediately a small crowd of neighbors appeared as they encircled the girls. Suddenly the area was covered with cops.

A scrawny police officer began asking Carlie information about her chaser. Zarria sung like a snitch in the pen. Leaving nothing untold, she freely made public all of Devon's information.

"His name is Devon Mc Neil. He lives at 11215 Parkdale ave, Apartment # 12..."

"Slow down," the officer stated with a raised brow. "Tell me what just happened."

Zarria began to give a detailed account of the chase. She started from the club to the present.

"He didn't do it. That wasn't him," Carlie blurted out. "She's mistaken officer."

"Are you sure about that Ms. Stewart," the shorter officer asked in disbelief.

"I'm positive," Carlie stated as if nothing happened. She began moving her hair back into place and brushed the glass from her seat. Zarria stood amazed. She wanted Carlie to look her in the face.

"He's gonna kill you fool. I'm not dying for you or with you!"

"Miss, let's all go down to the station. Give everybody a chance to calm down. We can help you. The car is registered to J. R. Cooper. Do either of you know who that is?"

"Hell no," Zarria answered.

"Yes, that's a family friend," Carlie said confidently. "Let's go, Zarria."

"Oh, hell no," Zarria stated with one hand on her hip and pumps in the other. I'm riding outta here with 5.0. This is one time you're on your own!"

Leaving the D.C. area and headed into Maryland, Carlie knew she couldn't go back to Devon. This was the last straw as far as she was concerned. With her cell to her ear, she waited for Ricky to answer. Carlie called back to back several times only to get his answering service. Finally, as a long shot, Carlie called Grandma Jean, who was known to turn her ringer off at 9 p.m. every night for the past thirty years. With no answer, Carlie pulled into the parking lot of a gas station and cut off the engine.

She lifted her steering wheel in an attempt to get comfortable. Curled up in fetal position she closed her eyes and prayed for better days.

Bruised

Chapter 13

The Exchange

Devon crept several blocks away from where his weekly rental was parked. The carryout on 7th and H in D.C. was the only store with lights on. Quickly, Devon stopped to check his surroundings. Knowing that the black duffel bag strapped around his shoulder contained $80,000 he continued to move. In his heart, he knew something wasn't quite right. Not sure about what his next move would be, his hand rested on his Desert Eagle for reassurance.

He stopped short in front of Hung Chung Lees to wait anxiously for his ride. Devon was somewhat startled by two loud drunks stumbling from the carryout. He shook his head as he thought of his own father. "Worthless," he said in a low voice.

Minutes later, two masked men appeared from nowhere. Devon could make out nothing but their blue attire and Glocks that had been pulled. Without warning, one of the perpetrators ran up behind Devon and rammed the tip of his gun to the back of his neck.

Devon gripped his gun tightly. His eyes focused on the

pant leg of the gunman behind him. The shoes and the texture of his pants was so familiar. He couldn't place it. Devon found himself in deep thought.

"Bust that nigga, he's got a piece," the shorter of the two said.

Devon moved his neck slightly. The tall gunman standing behind him spoke. "Nigga, don't move."

Just then, it all crystallized. The voice, the shoes, and the pants. He knew exactly who it was! Within a split second, Devon snatched his Eagle from his waist, spun at the speed of lighting, and knocked the assailant behind him to the ground.

Devon's eyes focused on a mechanic's jumpsuit. He couldn't believe Junnie was on the ground. He began shooting immediately, with the duffel bag still wrapped around his shoulder. Several gunshots fired back. He couldn't tell where the shots were coming from, but the war was on. Although it was two against one, Devon was prepared to handle his business.

Bullets sprayed the block. Some shattered the windows of Chung Lees, sending the few customers dodging for cover. Suddenly, the lights went out in the carryout, as Devon began to chase the shorter gunman. With only the street lights as a guide, Devon lost sight of Junnie.

He ran for nearly a half of a block at top speed trailing his accomplice. Although he became tired quickly, Devon would not give up. He had the opportunity to let off a few shots, but was determined to shoot him at point blank range. His dreams came true when an unlucky fall occurred.

The man on the ground lay with his face still covered. Without making a move, he protected his face. Devon took two steps forward. Without emotion he raised his gun and shot him in the head. Devon turned to his right, then left. The enemy was surely dead. Showing no remorse, he kicked him in his side. "That's for gettin' blood on my pants," he said.

Hearing a sound, Devon crossed the street to make his escape. He hoped that he had enough ammunition left to protect himself. Just then, a dark green Escalade screeched in front of him. Devon raised his piece but stopped after he identified the voice.

"What's up?" Ray asked between his cracked window. He sensed that something was wrong. Ray-Ray opened the compartment under his right elbow. He checked for his weapon.

"Let's go," Devon ordered.

Obeying his boss' finger motion, Ray sped off as soon as Devon had both feet in the vehicle. This type of action was just what Ray lived for. Wearing his black cargo pants and an oversized tee, he resembled a soldier ready for war. As the truck hit 80mph, Devon looked back only to notice two police cars scurrying in front of the Chinese carryout.

"Where does Junnie live?" Devon questioned.

"Aah… I don't know," Ray responded curtly. "Why?"

"I got business to handle, so it's not important right now. But, I got a bad feeling about somethin'," Devon answered. "The last time I had a bad feeling, six people died." Although Devon seemed tensed, he still managed to smirk.

"Man, I forgot to tell you about my man Dre from uptown," Ray said anxiously. "He said he has something to tell you about Carlie."

"My Carlie," Devon asked placing the palm of his hand on his heart.

"Yeah," Ray responded.

"What does it have to do with?"

"He wouldn't tell me. He said you'd want to know about it."

Devon didn't need any additional drama. He'd just been shot at and nearly killed. He wasn't even sure if the intent was to rob him or to simply take him out.

His attention was diverted when the truck rolled up on two SUV's sitting side by side. Although Devon knew that Rico, his Columbian connection occupied one of the vehicles, the dark tint on the windows kept him from knowing his exact location.

He knew Rico had a very good reason for being so secretive. Word on the street was that his Columbian connection had cops on his payroll and moved over 300 keys of cocaine monthly. Devon didn't consider himself a slouch, but he knew he was no match for Rico. Devon was both the boss and the enforcer in his camp. But for Rico, all he'd have to do is say the word for somebody to get done. Still in all, Devon didn't fear him, but he had to respect him.

He only had the pleasure of meeting Rico directly on three occasions. Normally he'd meet with Big Frank who was now walking his way. Resembling a 300 pound wrestler Frank motioned for Devon to hand him the bag. An unmarked car pulled up just then, but Devon didn't notice because it was out of view. Two men watched the transaction thoroughly. The younger of the two wore a bandana camouflaging his braids, while the older man loaded his camera. The duo had been on stake-out many times before. But today was considered a good day. The evidence mounted and the investigation was near the end. As soon as Devon handed over the money, the snapshots began. Devon froze at the sound of a car pulling up. Catching his breath, he sighed at the sight of Kirk, who was 20 minutes late. Little did he know there'd be a penalty to pay later. For Devon, when it came to business, *tardiness was not tolerated.*

Without any instructions, Kirk, and Ray began to approach Big Frank. Frank never budged. Holding on to the duffel bag, Devon spoke. "I need to speak to Rico. Personally," he added with a more sincere look.

Big Frank turned slightly for approval. Rico was already exiting one of the vehicles.

"What can I do for you, my man?" Rico asked in his Columbian accent. He reached upward to pat Devon's shoulder. Rico's complexion caught Devon's attention momentarily. If he didn't know better he would've thought Rico had just left a tanning salon. Devon hated to see people outside of his race trying to look black, but now was not the time to voice his opinion. Although Rico resembled a midget; he was clearly in his early forties. After giving Devon the once over, he continued. "You got something for me?"

"No doubt," Devon said.

"Who's that with you?" Rico asked referring to Ray.

"That's my man Ray-Ray. Some call him Ray." Devon patted Ray on the back. "He's a good dude. Trust me, he's aiight," Devon assured.

After several minutes of power talks, Rico and Devon shook hands. It was agreed that the $80,000 was the first payment on the 400,000 bill owed to Rico. Devon was now $320,000 in the hole.

By the time Frank returned to the semi-circle, hands had been shaken. Frank threw the bag full of cocaine and simultaneously caught the bag of money like a back catcher catching a home-run ball.

"Hey Devon," Rico said stopping in his tracks. "I'm a low-key kinda guy, you know man?" Rico watched for Devon's reaction. "Some guys were asking around about you."

"What guys?" Devon asked with raised eyebrows.

"I don't want to get in the middle of no mess. I'm about making money," Rico said shaking his head. Just watch yourself out there. You know you owe me too much money to be locked up or dead," he joked. "I get paid regardless," he said in a harsher tone.

Devon didn't answer. Turning to leave, he gave Ray-Ray instructions for the night and leaving with Kirk had already been a part of the plan. Gazing out of the window, Devon looked puzzled. Kirk knew that intense look meant trouble.

"So, what's going on?" Kirk asked.

Devon remained silent.

Kirk watched Devon hit his fist into the palm of his hand. He knew that meant something had either gone wrong or was about to pop off. "You okay, partner?"

"I'm straight," Devon finally said. "But we got plenty of business to handle."

"It'll work out," Kirk responded . "Let's get it done," he said in his normal supportive tone.

"Yeah, but in who's favor."

"Ours, of course."

Devon looked at Kirk. "Yeah." He nodded. "'Cause somebody's 'bout to be six feet under."

Chapter 14

New Beginnings

Carlie's distraught face matched her cries. Leaning against the steering wheel, she hollered. "Lord, why is this happening to me? What did I ever do to deserve this?" Each word was laced with a mixture of anger and tears. For hours she sat crouched in the seat of her car while guilt tormented her thoughts. In her heart she knew she'd be punished later. But what was she to do? Have a baby boy by a maniac who would eventually kill them both?

Although her stomach still cramped from the procedure, her heart ached like an eight inch stab wound. Dazed, Carlie managed to pull slowly away from the curb. The pharmacy was her last stop before heading back to school.

Tamia had agreed to drive her back to Lincoln considering her lack of strength. Tamia had even convinced one of her male friends to accompany them just in case of a run-in with Devon. But she failed to tell him what he'd be up against. Unless she was bringing Mike Tyson, it wasn't worth the trouble.

Nearly ten days had passed since the night of the chase.

After many days of talking to Tamia, Carlie decided she'd hibernated long enough. Besides, sleeping from couch to couch had taken its toll on her back. Eventually, the girls decided to move in together as agreed, despite the long list of cons.

Tamia's strong personality was an asset to Carlie. Although she'd calmed down a lot during her first three years at college, she couldn't hide that she was originally from the hood. Tamia did her best to stay far away from Devon. She had seen his kind before and by no means wanted to deal with his drama. She didn't even want Carlie to move in the furniture he'd bought for her. But Carlie kept it all, including the car. She felt that she'd earned it.

Strangely, she was elated that she hadn't heard from Devon since that frightful night at the club. Carlie reached out to her Dad for help. But to no avail, he never returned any phone calls. Carlie's heart was split in half. For the first time in her life her father deserted her. Grandma of course came to her rescue. Carlie accepted all of her Grandmother's support except for the offer to stay at her house. She didn't want Devon to find her there and create an unsafe place for Grandma Jean.

Pulling in front of the row houses on Florida Ave., Carlie was greeted by Tamia running towards her at full speed.

"Guess who's on the phone?" she whispered covering the receiver.

"Who?" Carlie asked with a puzzled expression.

"Mike." Tamia smiled handing her the phone.

Reluctantly Carlie grabbed the phone. "Hello."

"Hi beautiful," Mike said in a cheerful voice. "I've been trying to contact you for over a week now."

"Oh," Carlie said making facial expressions to Tamia.

"Yo, that's all I get for my hard work," he joked. "I have something for you. Can I bring it to you now?"

"Now isn't really a good time." Carlie looked to her left and right. She waved her hands signaling Tamia to hurry. "I'm on my way back to school."

"Come on now. I'm less than five minutes away. Besides I've been riding around with this stuff in my car for over a week."

Carlie agreed to wait and hung up the phone. The thought of another man coming to see her sent butterflies to her stomach. Then, a slight smile slipped through her lips. *What was this guy's intention?*

Without a doubt, she needed some quality time spent without a man. She needed a chance to get to know Carlie. *No Devon and certainly no one else with a dick*, she thought.

The sound of the gold Yukon broke her train of thought. Preparing to raise from her seat, Carlie was stopped.

"Don't get up, Ma. You look tired," Mike stated making a speedy entrance. "These are for you." From behind his back, emerged twelve, pink long stem roses.

"And… this," he said exposing a small rectangular box.

Carlie's reaction surprised Mike. "I can't accept that," she said avoiding his face.

"Word. And why not?" he asked.

"Because. You shouldn't buy me things." Carlie blushed. "You barely even know me."

"I know. But I wanna get to know you. So open it, before I open it for you." Mike's demeanor was warm and soothing. Just the few moments of joy he'd brought to Carlie's life meant a lot.

Amazed at his taste, Carlie nodded as she held the pink and black, quarter length teddy in the air. "Victoria Secret, huh," she asked.

"Listen, I know you have to go, but can I call you sometime?"

"Uhhh, I don't know, I know you mean well, but I've got a lot of negativity going on right now." Carlie paused and for once made eye contact. "And you're too sweet to be dragged into my mess."

"Let me be the judge of that," Mike said leaning forward.

Carlie jerked back. "What are you doing?" she asked uneasily.

"Don't worry, Ma. The last thing I would do is hurt you. I wanted to put this around your neck."

Carlie looked down to notice the diamond necklace Mike draped around her neck. "Call me when you're ready to talk," he said raising to his feet. "Get some beauty rest," he yelled. "Your eyes are way too puffy."

"I will," Carlie shouted bewildered by what had just happened.

***

The next few days dragged on. Hours seemed like days and days seemed like months. Carlie sat on the floor of her newly furnished bedroom gripping the half empty bottle of Boone's. She had hoped to drown away the pain deep inside. Instead she birthed a headache that wouldn't go away.

Thinking about her two-bedroom apartment made Carlie assess her current state. Yes, she appeared to be living well for a college student. *But was she really*, she thought to herself. Considering that Lincoln was located over an hour outside of P.A., all of the available housing was moderate.

Nevertheless, the three story apartment unit Devon had chosen was one of the best that the surrounding area of Lincoln had to offer. Besides, beyond the material things in her life, *she was a mess.*

As the mellow sounds of gospel singer Fred Hammond played in the background, once again Carlie was saddened. She had hoped the lyrics would cleanse her soul. A nagging sense of guilt pinched at her skin daily. Her life had taken an unwanted path and she didn't know how to make things right. From the loss of her baby, to the non-payment letter from the registrar's office, Carlie was stressed. She lay face down on the floor as she took one last swig before falling off to sleep.

The gentle taps on Carlie's shoulder could not awaken her. Assuming it was another dream she changed positions. Smiling momentarily she could hear grandma's voice. "Help me Father," she said. "That darn hooligan done turned my baby into an alcoholic." Carlie visualized her grandmother with her hands in the air and shaking her finger at 20 miles per hour.

"Wake up Carlie," Angela said shaking her shoulders. "It's three o'clock in the afternoon. Shouldn't you be in class? And why was your door unlocked? " At that moment Carlie realized it wasn't a dream. She stretched and surveyed the room. Grandma's aged hand held a sweet potato pie and small bags of groceries.

"Child, you need to clean this mess up. And yourself I might add," Grandma said leaning back with her hand on her hips. "When is the last time you had a bath?"

"Last night Grandma," Carlie said taking offense.

"Well take another one, a bird bath, ho bath, or whatever you wanna call it." Grandma sniffed Carlie. "Well I guess you don't smell too bad. You just don't look right."

Carlie couldn't help but to smile. Grandma Jean was on a roll.

Picking up the bottle from the floor she shook her head. "When is the last time you ate, child?"

"This morning," Carlie lied.

Angela could sense Carlie's depressed state. "So how are things going?" she asked cheerfully. Angela had already seized a bottle of cleanser from beneath the cabinet. Spraying the counter top, she repeated herself. "So, how are things going?"

"I'm fine, Aunt Angie," Carlie said quickly.

She was saved when the phone rang. They all knew the interrogation was about to begin. "Hello," she said.

For the first time in days, Carlie's spirits were lifted. "It's good to hear your voice too," she said. Knowing that Angela and Grandma Jean were watching her like a hawk, she turned her back. "Tamia shouldn't have given you this number," she smirked into the receiver. "I'll call you back. I have company right now."

Before Carlie could sit the phone down, Grandma was all over it. "That nigga is going to hell with gasoline drawers on." Assuming her normal fussing position she continued. "When are you gonna leave that boy alone?" She waited for a response. "Imagine you being a successful lawyer and showing up at court with America's Most Wanted on your arm."

Angela's laugh eased Carlie's mind.

Grandma, that wasn't Devon. That was Mike. "Thank you Jesus," she said throwing her hands up. "And why haven't I met this fella."

"Because he's just an associate." *A persistent associate*, she thought.

"Well, even if he's just an associate, it's better than that damn Devon. He just doesn't seem right for you." She kneeled to look into Carlie's face. "Besides, you're too smart for him. He's not the sharpest knife in the drawer." Disgusted, Grandma Jean shook her head.

Once again Angela laughed. "In all seriousness Carlie, I think what Mama is trying to say is that you deserve better. You gotta demand respect from guys now days."

"I do," Carlie spoke in a whiny voice.

"Oh no, I meet young women like you at work everyday who don't have a clue as to what self-respect is. If you clapping your hands at the club singing to the lyrics of '*Put it in yo mouth*' and '*Bitch move out the way*,' is your idea of respect, then you don't understand self-respect.

Carlie laughed at her aunt's outdated dance step. While Angela preached she pretended to grove to the imaginary music. She stopped short in front of Carlie. "In all seriousness, I'm glad our young brothers are doing big things in the music industry, but we've gotta start making the fellas respect us a little more, especially those sleeping next to us. "At work we deal with young women just like you who are stagnant in violent relationships. Some make it out. Some don't. Devon has a serious problem."

Carlie leaped from her seat. "He loves me Aunt Angela. He just has a temper. Nobody is perfect. Not even me. Right Grandma?" Carlie looked for support from Grandma Jean. She cringed at the thought of her Aunt being right.

In her most calm voice Angela spoke. "Nobody deserves to get beat."

Carlie's mouth dropped. She had no idea her aunt knew

about her past whippings. "One time it was my fault," she said defensively.

"It has never been your fault," she said talking to Carlie as if she were a toddler. "You are a beautiful young woman and can do better than Devon." Angela rubbed Carlie's cheek slightly. "Tell me one positive factor in your relationship." Angela stood and placed her hands on her hips.

Carlie quickly jogged her memory. While she flipped the pages from her past only crazy events surfaced. Then, out of the blue, it came to her. "Remember when he sent a limo to pick me up on Valentine's Day?"

"And," Angela said switching positions.

"Well that was thoughtful," Carlie said folding her arms. "The limo took me around the whole day, while I got pampered." Carlie talked as if that was the best gift she'd ever gotten. "I got my nails and feet done, I met Devon for lunch, and got my hair done."

"Yeah, I remember that day all right," Angela said with a frown. "That's the day he locked your butt in his bedroom while he went out for the night!"

Carlie couldn't argue with her aunt. She had tried to erase that night out of her mind for good. At first she was upset with Devon for having her take a shower alone after her Valentine treat. She just knew the two of them would have a great night together once she got out. To her surprise, he was gone. Not only did he leave her at his place but the door was locked from outside the bedroom with padlocks he had bolted to the door.

Carlie remembered calling him to find out why he left and she'd been locked in. He told her some phony story about an unexpected beef between some of his runners.

Devon said he feared for her safety and wanted her at his place. Carlie knew it wasn't true, but in her heart she wanted to believe Devon. Instead of getting mad, she cried until the wee hours of the morning wanting to go home.

By the time Carlie made it home, Ricky was furious. He had no idea why she hadn't answered his calls but he found out weeks later when he overheard Zarria and Carlie talking about it. Soon, the entire family knew about her Valentine lockdown. Carlie had nothing to say, but the embarrassment stuck for a long time.

"Carlie," Angela said with raised voice. I'm talking to you. I'm still waiting for you to tell me something positive about your relationship."

"He gives me money and buys me things…," Carlie said faintly.

"But you pay for it dearly. Do you really think you're happy?" Angela waited for a response. "A real man would never put his hands on you, and definitely wouldn't try to control your every move." Angela shifted her eyes toward Grandma Jean who sat shaking her finger at Carlie.

"Stop seeing him Carlie," Angela said. "Break away from him while you still have a chance. Cut off all contact," she added in a more demanding voice. "Have your cell phone disconnected."

Carlie gave her aunt a look that said "that's out of the question'. "Nobody else will be able to get in contact with me if I do that."

"Then change the number," Angela said sternly. "I can't bear to think about what might happen next. I've seen bad situations get worse everyday at my job. We're here for you," she said touching her shoulder.

"He told me once he'd never let me be with anyone else, but I think it's really over. He hasn't called and he hasn't paid my school bill." Carlie pressed her face into the palm of her hands.

"Don't worry about that," Grandma Jean said standing. If I have to use my retirement check, I will. This is your last year of school and you *will* graduate. Your dream has always been to follow in your father's footsteps and you *will* become a lawyer.

"Okay, group hug," Angela said grabbing Carlie and Grandma Jean. Carlie felt so much comfort from their strong embrace. "Let's keep in touch more." Angela squeezed Carlie again. "I love you. And if you need me for anything, call me. You'll be all right as soon as he's completely outta your life."

"I'm fine already," Carlie said raising her head high.

The door shut and a tear fell from Carlie's eye. This time, not from her woes but from joy. Her Aunt Angela was absolutely right. It was time to break free from Devon's bondage.

Carlie grabbed a brush and decided to take her Grandmother's advice. She had always been a kept young lady and looked good even at the most inopportune times. Today she was making a vow to become a better Carlie. No more troubles. No more Devon.

She felt confident as she grabbed the phone to call Zarria. She missed her wild friend and had both good and bad news to share.

Chapter 15

The Unexpected

It was near dawn when the car sped through the parking lot at 60mph. Draped in sparkling diamonds and the brand new Chanel bag she toted, Carlie was beginning to look like herself again. The Mac make-up hid what she really felt inside. Beneath the passenger seat laid a brown paper bag filled with her usual afternoon drink. Before removing the key from the ignition, Carlie was sure to grab her shades and her Boones.

Carlie strutted toward her building when she noticed movement from behind the bushes. Startled, she stopped. Thinking that she'd seen a shadow flash before her eyes, she watched the bushes intensely. She slowed her pace and turned to survey the lot. The majority of the cars were familiar with the exception of a U-haul truck. Angry at herself for still living in fear of Devon, she proceeded to her apartment. *Just an animal,* she thought. *I've got to stop stressing myself out.*

Once inside, Carlie grabbed the phone in her final attempt to get things right. Though difficult, she knew she had to try. She quickly punched the numbers into her phone.

"Stewart &Associates, May I help you?" the cheerful voice answered.

"Sure, Loretta. Is my Dad there?" Carlie asked.

"Oh, Carlie, how are you?" Loretta asked a bit concerned.

"I'm fine," Carlie said. "May I speak to my Dad."

"Aahh… I think he's in a meeting."

"Tell him it's important."

"Hold on honey," Loretta said as if she pitied Carlie. After several seconds, she returned to the line. "Carlie, he's not in at the moment. I'll have him call you." Loretta rushed off the phone.

With the receiver in hand, Carlie stared at the phone. Before a tear could fall a light knock pounded the door. "Coming," she yelled. The thought of Tamia leaving her key again annoyed her. Carlie thought about the speech she would give her irresponsible roommate as soon as she let her in.

As soon as Carlie opened the door, she lost her composure. Shocked, she took a deep breath and stepped slightly forward in preparation to slam the door if need be. With twelve identical roses and the same pink and black teddie she received last week, Devon stood before her. He grinned devilishly. "Ain't you gonna invite me in?"

"Of course," Carlie said. She didn't move. She stood stiff as a board. As her crazed thoughts bounced back and forth, she refused to make eye contact with Devon. She wondered if his gifts were *sincere?* Who was she fooling?

As Devon moved his foot forward to invite himself in, Carlie's heart stopped. "You've fixed it up nice," he said looking around. "You did it all by yourself?" he asked suspiciously.

"Sure did."

Devon sat the teddie on the chair. He began to take small steps around the kitchen in a circular motion. In between the mean looks shot to Carlie, he flipped through the mail on the glass table, while continuing to hold the flowers in the other hand. He turned to look at Carlie every so often, but remained quiet. His next step in the investigation was the opening of the refrigerator. Still he found nothing.

This was the first time Carlie had ever seen Devon so unkempt. He was in bad need of a shave and smelled like he hadn't bathed in days. Devon slowly sat the vase on the kitchen table and reached for Carlie's face. She jumped.

"Why you so jittery?" he asked in a peaceful voice.

"I just haven't had much sleep."

"I'm sure you haven't," he said turning to grab the lingerie. "I want you to put this on," he said in a demented voice.

"No Devon, sex won't cure our problems," Carlie said softly. She backed away from him.

"Would you rather wear the one you got last week?"

Carlie's eyeballs tripled in size. "Devon, I think you should go," she said. By now her body trembled at the thought of what was to come. *Had he seen Mike give her the gifts? Or did someone tell him?*

Devon grabbed her by the neck. "Put it on bitch," he said. Devon gazed at the extension cord plugged in the socket. He looked back at Carlie. "I said put it on."

Carlie began undressing. "Devon, I do love you. But I *can't* be with you anymore." The rage in Devon's face intensified as she spoke each word. Carlie slid the slinky piece over her head and continued. "I don't know what this will prove, but I want out."

"Oh, you want out," he said bending to snatch the extension cord from the wall.

Carlie's entire body shut down. Goose bumps covered her arms. Trembling, she begged. "No... Devon, No...." Her heart pounded faster. She clinched her teeth when the cord tightened around her neck.

"Put the shit on!" he ordered.

Carlie leaned back onto Devon while the cord squeezed her even more. "O...kay." She paused between syllables.

As soon as Devon let her go, he pushed her body into the table. Carlie caught the teddie thrown her way and gave it a nasty look. As she slid into the outfit, she realized there was a need to worry. Devon was crazy but this was his craziest behavior yet. Fully dressed, Carlie looked at him pitifully.

Devon pulled the Italian, leather-back chair he'd purchased to the center of the floor. Carlie stood there shaking. "Dance," he said calmly.

Carlie couldn't believe it. She stripped for Devon thousands of times to arouse him in the past, and was no stranger to giving him lap dances either. But today, something wasn't right. "Devon, we need to talk," she pleaded.

"Talk!" he yelled. "You better dance now, Bitch!"

Carlie closed her eyes immediately, praying it would all end. She stood half-naked in the middle of the floor as her hips began moving from left to right. Carlie danced with a straight face pretending to be okay. Inside, she cried. The man who was supposed to love her was now violating in the worst way.

Carlie turned around slightly stopping for various weak poses. Clearly she was giving a pathetic performance on purpose and Devon knew she could do better. "So, you'on wanna be here?" he barked.

Carlie hated having to open her eyes to look at him. Standing not even a foot from Devon's grip, she extended her leg a bit to keep from answering his question. Instantly, he grabbed hold of her leg and slid his arm up her thigh. Rubbing her seductively gave him an instant hard-on. Devon raised from the chair and attempted to ram his tongue down her throat. Carlie responded by turning away. A loud slap was given in return.

Devon's eyes now resembled a shot of Bloody Mary. "Oh, did you think you were gonna fuck oh boy and get away with it? You're an investment," he said crisply. Carlie's sniffles caused him to increase his tone. "You gonna pay for lettin' some nigga bang my baby in the head."

"What are you talking about?" she cried.

"You ain't thinkin' 'bout havin' sex with me 'cause you bangin' somebody else!"

"Devon, I haven't been with anyone but you...."

"I'on believe shit you say!" he yelled.

"I can't even have sex right now. I had an abortion!" Carlie screamed.

The powerful hit sent uncontrollable fear through her veins. Devon went ballistic. Carlie knew her end was near. He pulled tighter and tighter as he tried to choke every bit of air from her body. A knock came from the door. Carlie managed to yell!

"Nobody is here to help you, Freak," he snapped. Her body slumped to the floor when Devon ran to answer the door. Carlie prayed that it would be Tamia or a nosey neighbor. Coughing and barely breathing, she saw visions of Kirk and Ray-Ray standing before her. "Put all of this shit in the U-haul," he ordered. "I'll take care of her."

Kirk moved hesitantly. He felt for Carlie as he looked back at her. "Get movin' nigga," Devon repeated following Kirk through the hall. Stopping in front of the lined mirrors Devon looked at himself. He knew he wouldn't normally be seen looking this way. He hit each mirror with full force. The sound of the glass breaking gave Carlie a surge of strength to move.

As soon as she thought of escaping, Devon had kneeled before her. He reached above him to grab the knife off the sink. "We forgot to cut your tags," he said.

Carlie shouted, "no...," at the top of her lungs. Instantly, she curled into a tight ball clutching her shoulders. The blood that gushed from the side of her chin had no effect on Devon. He thought about cutting her again, but figured one slice on the face would always make her remember him. "Get up," he roared pulling her from the floor.

This can't be the same man that said he loved me, she thought. Before exiting the apartment Devon yelled to Kirk giving more orders about what to pack and what to leave behind. The moment Carlie's body hit the outside air, thoughts of what the neighbors might think entered her mind. Then she thought of Ricky. *If he only knew the pain she was suffering, surely he'd be here. Stabbing his daughter was going far beyond limits.*

The chilly September air stung her face like killer bees. Devon swiftly yanked Carlie down the stairs. Although an elderly neighbor did not know Carlie, she thought it was strange to see a woman barefoot and dressed in lingerie. "How are you," Devon smiled to the woman. It was then that the woman noticed the blood oozing down the right side of her face.

After not getting a response he continued to the parked Acura station wagon. With his arms interlocked between Carlie's, he reached for the door handle. Her small arms managed to slip through. She took off. Carlie ran several yards until she felt a yank on the back of her shoulder. Grabbing her by her hair, Devon dragged her several yards back to the vehicle. Once again, Carlie escaped. Without hesitation Devon reached inside for his 9mm.

"So, she thinks this shit is a game," he mumbled to himself.

Carlie, hadn't gotten far when she heard the first shot. Several bystanders had pulled into the parking lot. But all scattered at the sound of the gun fire. Although concerned, none were brave enough to lend a hand. "Help me somebody," she screamed in the front yard of a neighboring building. Barefoot and barely clothed she called out for help again. No one came to lend a hand. Devon walked boldly toward her with his gun by his side.

Kirk had just hit the bottom step when he saw Devon headed toward Carlie. With Carlie's flat screen in hand he yelled, "Let's go, partner."

"I'm waiting on Carlie," he laughed.

"We've got everything you need. It ain't worth ...."

Four headlights flashed simultaneously. Devon turned behind him when the siren sounded. Two more police cars speedily invaded the lot. Carlie still did not feel at ease. She had never seen or imagined Devon in this state but knew nothing would keep him from putting a bullet through her head.

"Drop your weapon," the chubby officer yelled at the top of his voice.

"Y'all don't know what this bitch did to me," he hollered turning in a circle.

"Drop your weapon," the chubby officer repeated, articulating every word.

Devon raised his gun and pointed in Carlie's direction. The sound of several guns clicked. Preparing to shoot, the youngest of the officers moved in Devon's direction.

"Ray-Ray yelled. "Man, put the gun down."

"Throw your weapon on the ground," another officer yelled. The younger officer had a close up on Devon. "I've got a shot," he said into his ear piece.

Devon threw his gun to the ground. He smiled. Backing up he stared at Carlie. Leaning on the hood of his car he followed instructions and placed his hands behind his head. The cops swarmed Devon within seconds. While two officers cuffed him, another checked the car for additional weapons.

"That bitch is a freak," Devon yelled.

"Shut up," the younger officer said. He pushed Devon's head toward the hood of the car.

Devon continued to snicker. "It's not my fault that I tried to treat her like a woman. She was born a prostitute," he yelled. A blow hit him directly in the stomach causing him to settle down momentarily.

Carlie was escorted with care to a squad car. The jacket thrown over her shoulders was an attempt to both warm and comfort her from Devon's words. *Neither worked.* She shivered as if she were having multiple convulsions. The blood continued to stream and the officers continued to panic. Carlie's body became weaker as she waited for the ambulance to arrive. Alarmed, a third officer grabbed a towel from his patrol car, and applied it to her face.

"Was he with anyone else?" the concerned rookie asked.

"Yeah." Carlie turned to her left. At a distant she could see Kirk's figure through the window of the U-haul. Her heart pounded once more. She wasn't about to let Kirk go down from Devon's actions. As a matter of fact, with Devon locked up maybe she could convince Kirk and Ray to return her belongings. "That guy was with him," she stated pointing to Ray. But he didn't do anything."

Vaguely she could see Ray-Ray's dreads shaking from afar. She had been watching him closely when he asked for permission to speak to Devon who was now restrained in the back of the police car. The first response was no, until Ray-Ray lied to the officer about his medication. Ray-Ray had two seconds to hear what Devon had to say. Clearly it had nothing to do with medication. Devon was up to something, but for now he was going to jail.

The sirens diverted all attention to the ambulance. Within seconds, Carlie was on the gurney. Surrounded by officers, they threw questions like darts. Carlie flinched at every hand that neared her face.

"We're here to help you," the curly-head paramedic explained with a kind voice. "What's your name?"

Carlie's eyes rolled to the back of her head. She prayed she had been saved. Grandma's voice entered her mind. "I swear if someone gave me the chance, I'd kick his ass like he stole something." A smirk appeared on Carlie's face. The paramedic smiled.

"I think she's gonna be okay," he yelled.

"I need to ask her a few questions," a handsome detective

asked. "Hello, I'm Detective Dawson. The gentleman who held you at gunpoint doesn't have any identification. Can you tell us his name?"

Carlie closed her eyes pretending to be asleep. *She wondered if Devon was watching from the squad car.*

"She can't answer questions right now," the paramedic said in her defense.

"Well this guy has 7 kilos of cocaine in his car. We need some information on him. And we need it now."

"I'm sure you'll figure it out," the curly head man said sarcastically as he shut the ambulance doors.

Chapter 16

Now in Session

It was nearly 3 a.m. when Tamia sprinted down the hall. Out of breath she asked the gentleman at the desk if Carlie Stewart had been brought in. "Visiting hours ended at 9 p.m.," the man said with a frown.

"I'm her sister," Tamia lied.

"Like I said, visiting hours end at 9 p.m."

"Like I said, I'm her sister." She rolled her eyes and darted past the desk. Tamia was in search of someone who would tell her what floor she could find Carlie on. Tears filled her eyes as she thought about the rumors going around town. Some had claimed Carlie had been beaten, dragged and shot three times. Others said that Carlie stabbed Devon after getting beat in front of the police. Tamia wanted the truth.

She roamed the halls and dodged several nurses on duty. Tamia finally ran into a young man who looked close to her age. The hospital was exceptionally quiet so she spoke softly. "How are you?" she asked.

No, how are you?" the handsome guy said, looking Tamia up and down.

Tamia put on her sour face. "I'm gonna be perfectly honest. You are a cutie, but I need to find my girl. I saw you with your scrubs on and figured you'd help a sistah out."

He laughed. "Oh, let me guess, Otis at the front desk wouldn't give you any information.

Hearing the several footsteps headed their way, Tamia paused. She turned to find Otis and three other guards standing behind her. Tamia focused on the stance of the guards. They stood as if they came with an official arrest warrant.

"Oh, she's with you Dr. Grayson," the shorter of the guards said.

"Yes. She's with me." He nodded and crossed his arms.

Within seconds, the goofy trio had departed. Tamia looked away from Dr. Grayson but her embarrassment still showed.

"Now, who is it that you need to find," he said.

"My girl, Carlie."

"I'm going to need a last name," he snickered.

"You have to excuse me. I'm not really in a joyful mood. My roommate was hurt really bad earlier tonight."

Obviously Dr. Grayson had clout. Moments later, they had searched Carlie's whereabouts and was now walking quickly down the third floor hall. The head nurse on the floor was just about finished with her routine when Tamia was noticed standing outside Carlie's door.

"May I help you?" the nurse asked sarcastically. She looked at her watch.

"Yes, you may," Dr. Grayson said as he positioned himself within the nurse's view. "This young lady is the patient's only family in this area. I know it's late but give her a few minutes."

He nodded and waved goodbye to Tamia.

Tamia smiled at the possibility of seeing Dr. Grayson again. But her mind-set quickly changed as Carlie's body was in full view. "Ohhhh… No…No…" Tamia couldn't believe her eyes. The side of Carlie's face had been stitched up. She shook her head over and over. *Not again,* she thought.

Carlie lay sleeping while Tamia wept at the sight of her friend. The nurse returned with a strange look on her face. "I'm leaving," Tamia sniveled.

"Oh, no sweetie, you stay. Here's a blanket for you and there's the chair." The nurse smiled and shut the door.

***

Ricky sat quietly in the back of the courtroom at Devon's arraignment. His alert look disguised the fact that he was exhausted from the drive to Pennsylvania in rush hour traffic. Dressed in an Italian tailored suit, he resembled a brotha in a GQ ad. With his legs crossed, he mentally recorded every word being said.

Seeing Devon enter the courtroom in a bright orange jumpsuit thrilled Ricky. In his opinion, Devon was right where he needed to be. *All animals should be caged,* he thought.

Taking his seat, Devon faced forward. For moments, he stared the judge directly in the eye. With his hands cuffed, his gaze switched focus when Ms. Duckett began to speak.

"Your Honor, in light of this man's constant run-ins with the law, I am opposed to bail."

Lisa Duckett a well-known prosecutor in the State of Pennsylvania had a reputation for winning. Her tough girl image, and thorough work caused most defense attorneys to feel inferior when going against her. The slender African

American woman was photographed regularly during high-profile cases and was easy on the eye. At thirty-two, Lisa Duckett was well on her way to a promising career.

Ms. Duckett rambled on about Devon's charges and reasons for not granting bail. "He's got charges ranging from assault with a deadly weapon, handgun possession, taking property without. ..."

"Honestly. You don't expect me to deny bail because Mr. McNeil took property without permission." The judge peered down at Lisa.

"It's against the law, Sir." She stood with one hand on her hip and a silver plated pen in the other.

Judge Blake cleared his throat. "I'll need some time," he said. While Mr. McNeil does possess a lengthy rap sheet, it by no means makes me believe he will not show up for court."

"Your Honor," this man has been identified by several witnesses as the man who tried to kill his girlfriend in broad daylight." Lisa breathed deeply. "If he is released, he may try to kill her again."

Judge Blake held his head downward scribbling on a legal pad.

"That is a possibility. However, I must uphold the law for every citizen."

Sure...Lets wait until she's on the seven o'clock news to do something about it, she thought. Lisa gave one hundred and ten percent to prosecute all wrongdoers, but there was a special determination to rid the world of abusive men. On numerous occasions she'd come across cases were the victim had cried out for help, called the police to the scene several times, and had even testified in court, but to no avail; the system put the abuser back on the streets only to repeat the same crime against their women.

Even though Lisa was known to have more courage than required, she stood silently. While she waited for Judge Blake to speak, her body shifted to the left only to meet Devon's malicious stare. Lisa bit her lip. "The state believes he should remain in custody," she said firmly.

Once again, Judge Blake cleared his throat. "I'd like to hear from the girl. I believe her name is Ms. Carlie Stewart." The judge peered over his glasses at the prosecution table. "I'll need to see her in my chambers as soon as possible."

Lisa's voice was now thin. "Sir, she's not willing to testify."

"The judge gazed at Ms. Duckett. "How do you know that when I just told you I want to see her?"

"My team was already on that task even before you asked, Sir."

"You're good, Ms. Duckett. I'll give you twenty four hours to get me Ms. Stewart. This hearing will recess until tomorrow at 11:00 a.m."

At the sound of the gavel, Ricky picked up his briefcase to head for the door. He waited with one hand in his pocket while he checked his palm pilot. When Lisa Duckett burst through the doors, he signaled to get her attention. "Do I know you?" she asked with a crinkled brow. Lisa continued to speed walk down the hall.

"No, I haven't had the pleasure. I'm a defense attorney," he said waiting for a reaction. "I've heard a lot about you."

"What's this all about?" Lisa asked irritated. She stopped to give Ricky a moment.

"I'm looking for a female to join my team," he said hand-

ing her his linen business card. "I'll be following the case
you're working on, but I already know you're about winning.
I'm prepared to offer you a $350,000 a year salary with my
firm."

Lisa's mouth dropped. "Are you serious?"

"I sure am." Ricky smiled widely. "Of course you'll have
to move to Maryland," he said. "And you still have to win
this case. I only want people who go for the kill on my team."

"That's me," Lisa laughed. Her teeth glistened as she
smiled.

"So you're not as hard as you appear to be in there, huh?"

"It's a tough career. So, I have to be tough at all times,"
she said. "You know the drill."

By now Ricky had tuned Lisa's words out. His mind and
body focused on her small frame and shapely legs. Although
Lisa was suited up in her Sunday's best, Ricky imagined what
lay beneath. Besides, Lisa already had one point over
Courtney. She didn't have a weave. Lisa's short sleek hairstyle
was just right.

Ricky finally snapped from his daze. "I've been in this
business much longer than you. So if you need any help, call
me." He took hold of her soft hand and kissed it. Noticing
the absence of a ring, he smiled.

Chapter 17

__Showdown__

" I can't believe this shit," Ricky blurted out.

"Oh, we'll get 'em," Charles Luder responded as he took a swig from the flask.

"Put that poison down and stay alert," Ricky yelled to his older brother.

The two men waited in a Bronco outside the courthouse to catch a glimpse of Devon. The news was out. Devon McNeil would be released momentarily. Ricky couldn't figure out what judge in his right mind would send a psychotic abuser back to the streets the very next day. He knew that Lisa had been unsuccessful in getting Carlie to speak against Devon. But in his heart he knew Mr. McNeil would be held without bond until his trial.

Main Street was relatively quiet for a Tuesday morning. From time to time a pedestrian was seen walking into, or from the courthouse. Although several empty cars lined the block and meter attendants pounded the pavement giving tickets, nothing would stop Ricky from blasting Devon's ass.

"Come on...Baby," Ricky said to himself over and over

again. He watched the swinging doors to the front of the courthouse intensely. No sign of Devon anywhere. Ricky polished his nine millimeter with an Armani handkerchief. In a trans-like state he continued. "Come on…Baby."

Charles Luder watched his brother closely. He knew he'd reached his limit. Charles' intent was to rid Carlie of Devon forever, but he wanted to make sure he didn't go to jail while trying. At this point, nothing seemed to matter to Ricky. He'd do it in broad daylight, right on Main Street if he had to.

A black SUV unexpectedly whipped past Charles' Bronco. The tinted vehicle stopped directly in front of the courthouse. Suspicious, Ricky sat up straight.

Several minutes passed without a sole in sight. Suddenly, a figure emerged. Ricky's heart pounded. Dressed conservatively, he rolled the sleeves on his custom made shirt. "It's time," he said looking at his brother intently.

Charles pressed the gas pedal slowly. Inching like a private investigator the Bronco moved under 20mph. They both watched the body approaching the SUV. The thin frame looked like he was on guard but never caught Ricky's stare. A mean look surfaced as he strutted to the passenger side. Charles continued past the truck without being noticed. Before he could swallow the disappointment his eyes received a treat. In his rear view mirror, he saw Devon exiting the courthouse. His path headed directly to the SUV.

"Turn around. Quick!" Ricky yelled.

Charles whipped the truck around. "I got dis baby boy," he shouted like a drunken cowboy.

Devon walked slowly as if he were on tour. As soon as he hopped in the back seat, the truck sped off. The Bronco trailed closely behind.

"Slow up a little." Ricky motioned with his hand. "I just need the right moment.

"Yeah, be careful, those young boys always packin'. You gotta come correct with them young niggas." Charles laughed. "I got somethin' fo they ass," he said raising his flask.

"Keep your eyes on that truck," Ricky ordered.

Within minutes both trucks were on I-95 headed south. Ricky didn't want to follow Devon for hours but knew he'd eventually be in familiar territory. *The truck would have to stop at some point,* Ricky thought. *Would it be at a rest area? Maybe he could get his shot off then? Not in broad daylight around hundreds of people.* Ricky brainstormed.

Unfortunately for Ricky, the truck never stopped. After getting on 295 the alcohol had started to wear on Charles' momentum. Tired from the stake-out, the brother's conversation lessened. Hours later when the truck exited the ramp at Benning Road, Ricky's body finally perked up. Previous reports from his guys confirmed that he knew where Devon was headed. This would be Ricky's first visit to *the hole.*

Ricky's thoughts about Devon were beginning to change. He'd always considered him as a guy with plenty of street smarts. But to allow an unknown vehicle to follow him for over two hours wasn't too bright in Ricky's book. Devon was all talk. And definitely ranked #1 as a punk ass woman beater. Ricky was determined to teach him a lesson.

Charles' words broke Ricky's concentration. "Turn in here?" he asked.

"No. Stop here. Let's see if they get out."

"Man, we can't stop right here in the middle of the hood.

There's a dead end straight ahead. Or we can follow them down there." Charles pointed to the Southern Gardens Apartment Complex below. "Everyone is looking at us."

"Okay move up some. There's a car behind us," Ricky stated.

Charles inched to the right, closer to the entrance of the hole. He waited for the car to pass. "You got enough room nigga, now what you gon' do," he shouted in his rear view mirror.

At that moment Ricky knew something wasn't right. He had to make a decision. Devon was smarter than he thought. Ricky checked his mirror watching an old model Capri behind him. No one got out. The young drivers wore do-rags and sat without emotion. Immediately another car pulled to Charles' left. The Bronco was now blocked in.

Devon emerged from the back of the SUV. He waved his hand inviting Ricky into the parking lot below. Movement in the area slowed.

"I'on know about dis man," Charles trembled. "Dis is definitely a set up."

"It's okay. You got your piece?"

"Yeah, but I misplaced my heart."

"This is for Carlie," Ricky said encouraging Charles. "Pull down there."

Charles moved forward into the cul-de-sac. The silver Capri moved directly behind them. Before the Bronco could come to a complete stop, a light tap on the bumper startled them both. Ricky knew it was time. He'd allowed Devon to get the best of him once before. *But not this time.*

"I can't believe you've been following me," Devon said approaching the passenger window. "You got life insurance?"

he asked while his hands remained under his Hobo hoodie.

Ricky's trigger finger itched. Leaning against the window, he held his nine millimeter down low. He could see the crazed fixation on Devon's face. He would never give up easy. Most importantly, Carlie would never have a chance to be free if he didn't do something about Devon. Now was his chance.

Ricky looked to his front and back. He looked back at Devon, then to Charles. Devon could sense that Ricky wanted to do more than talk.

"You want me to be Carlie's only Daddy, huh?" Devon joked.

Ricky's eyes look sideways. "If you had stayed away from my daughter, we wouldn't be here now," he snapped.

"I don't take orders. I give 'em," Devon said in a more serious tone.

"I got something to give you all right."

"Oh, now you threatening a nigga?" Devon questioned. Devon reached slow and deep into his waist. "How about this? You just fucked yourself dog." Spit landed on the tip of Ricky's nose.

Ricky grasped his nine even tighter. Devon was unpredictable, but Ricky was in for the long haul. He knew that blastin' Devon came with a lot of consequences. A decision had to be made whether it was it worth it or not. Ricky sat quietly looking for the right words to say.

The sound of the first bullet rang out. Charles hit the pedal only to ram into the SUV. Panicking, he switched to reverse. The bullet whipped past Charles' head at record speed. He closed his eyes lowering his body toward the floor.

"Charles, get out of the car!" Ricky yelled.

"For what. We're in da middle of a gun battle," Charles responded.

"They have us blocked in," Ricky yelled. Plus, I don't know who's shooting who. But I definitely didn't shoot at Devon."

"Then who did?" Charles asked.

"The guy in the mechanics jumpsuit did."

As Ricky pointed to Junnie hiding behind a car, a bullet meant for Ricky hit the side of the car door. Charles rammed the SUV again. He wasn't about to get out and run in the middle of a gun fight. Charles was beginning to have second thoughts about helping Carlie. For all he knew, she deserved exactly what she was getting.

After several attempts, the Bronco finally made its escape. Hitting every car nearby, Charles broke out. From the corner of his eye, Ricky saw Devon taking off in a Monte Carlo.

Devon stopped directly in front of Junnie who still hid behind the car. He jumped out the car and dashed to his left just enough to spot Junnie kneeling on the ground. Holding his hand steadily, his aim was stiff.

"Never bite the hand that feeds you," he said releasing the trigger. Junnie's head snapped sideways. The blood caused bile to rise up in Charles' stomach. "Did you see that shit," Charles screamed.

"It's all a part of the game." Ricky shook his head. He never took one eye off of Devon.

The engine of the Monte Carlo revved as soon as Devon was back in the car. Hanging from the window, he smiled with his pistol in hand. Ricky sat calmly concealing his weapon. The sounds of the sirens prompted both vehicles to take off. Even with the speed, Devon stared at Ricky. The

Monte Carlo and the Bronco battled to exit the narrow driveway of the hole. Suddenly Ricky raised his pistol. With only two feet away from Devon's head his finger pulled back. It was almost as if he'd received an instant order. The gun shot sound was all too familiar. People scattered about. As the police rolled on the scene, the residents of Southern Garden Apartments knew exactly what to do.

Bruised

Chapter 18

Flashbacks

The season was beginning to change. The days grew shorter, but not for Carlie. She sat lost in the center of the worn twin bed. Besides the aged desk and the wooden mirror that hung directly in front of her, there was nothing else to see. Staring at her reflection, she couldn't believe the dark circles that recently claimed a new home underneath her eyes. Dressed in a velour used sweat suit, she wished for peace.

She hoped that her stillness would settle her nerves. Just moments ago she'd awaken from a terrible nightmare that she was still in the process of making sense of. Flashbacks continued to occupy her thoughts. Carlie could see many people filing into the sanctuary. Most were dressed in black attire. Some people she recognized, most she did not.

Ricky sat on the front row crying his heart out, while his brothers sat in silence. Angela stood proudly to receive condolences. "She accomplished so much in her lifetime," a chubby woman stated. "If there is anything I can do, let me know," another woman said.

Carlie shook her head to erase the thoughts. A funeral was not something she wanted to think about at the moment; and certainly not her death. *It was only a dream,* she tried to convince herself. *I don't even know who died.* Yet, *I can't understand why I'm not able to erase it from my mind.*

Carlie instantly painted a mental picture of the coffin. As she envisioned Zarria approaching to pay her respects, she trembled. *Is that me in the casket?* Her mind raced as she did a virtual tour of the church. She couldn't remember seeing herself anywhere and for that matter, Grandma Jean either.

"Dear God," she began to pray. "I don't know if this is a sign. Maybe you're trying to tell me I'm gonna die. Or maybe you're trying to save me. Whatever your intent, help me. I don't know what else to do. I'm going crazy. I'm having dreams I don't understand and I don't know how long I'll be able to hide out."

Within minutes Carlie's mind settled. All visions of the funeral had ceased. Carlie decided to take a different approach. She wanted her thoughts to only focus on her present state and what she needed to do to fix the problem.

Carlie wrapped her arms around her legs and allowed her face to flop down into her knees. She couldn't believe her life had turned out this way. For the first time since grade school she only had $27.00 to her name. Her thoughts continued to explode in her mind until the ringing of her cell phone startled her.

She reached for the phone, then hesitated. She knew she'd been ordered not to answer her cell phone by the authorities at the Greenbriar Home for Battered Women. Carlie's counselor made the rules perfectly clear. For the safety of all of the women, no one was to know their whereabouts. Carlie was new to the program and most likely vulnerable. Answering her cell phone was not allowed for the first two weeks.

After the fourth ring, Carlie pressed the answer button. "Hello," she said with a soft voice.

"Girl, where the hell you been?" Zarria asked. "I've been calling you for weeks."

It felt good to hear Zarria's voice. "Oh, I've been around," Carlie replied.

"Bitch, please." Around where? First of all you haven't called me since you went back to school. Oh, so you got a new roommate and now you actin' brand new." Zarria smacked her lips several times between words. "Tell me where you at, we need to talk."

"Uhh...," Carlie hesitated.

"Tell me where you at crazy," Zarria yelled into the receiver.

" Have you talked to Devon?" Carlie blurted out.

"No. Have you?" Zarria lowered her voice.

"Nah. Let me call you back." Carlie hung up.

Carlie tried not to think of Devon, but there were sudden moments where she couldn't help herself. She sat nervously, because she knew Devon was trying his best to find her. She also knew he'd use any means necessary, even if it meant paying Zarria off. "No, no, no, no," she blurted. *What am I thinking? Zarria is my girl.*

With so many issues needing to be addressed, Carlie felt as if her next home would be the crazy house if she didn't get it together. She had gone from living well to residing in a shelter. Whether temporary or permanent, for her it felt more like lockdown. She felt so out of place.

The well-to-do Carlie Stewart now had nothing. Most of

her personal possessions had been seen leaving in a U-haul truck right before her eyes. What wasn't taken from the apartment had been left weeks ago at Devon's place. The thought of the U-haul jogged her memory. She thought of Kirk.

Carlie had always had a soft spot in her heart for Kirk. Although he rolled with Devon when doing his dirty work, there was something special about him. She truly believed he wanted the best for her. And somehow she liked him more than she should. After dialing the number to Kirk's cell, Carlie waited for an answer.

Three knocks diverted Carlie's attention to the door. Before she could speak, Angela walked in with her hands on her hips.

"May I ask who you're calling?" Angela gave Carlie a look that said, '*You must be crazy*'. Holding a tote bag in her hand, she waited for a response.

Carlie's mouth hung open. She dropped the phone on the bed. "Uh, I was trying to find out if my car is still in front of my apartment at school."

"For what?" Angela snapped.

"Because I want it. In case you haven't noticed, I have nothing." Carlie spread her palm and moved it slowly around the room in a circular motion.

"Material things aren't everything," Angela said pulling a linen handkerchief from her bag. She spread the cloth on the bed before sitting on it."

Carlie shook her head at the thought of her aunt's obsessive cleanliness habits. "The bedspread probably isn't clean anyway," Carlie smirked.

"But at least it's safe here," Angela shot back. In her most

articulate voice she explained. "Your safety is what is important. The beauty of this place and that car of yours should be
the least of your worries." Angela sighed. "I've been talking
to Dean Thomas at Lincoln. You've already missed three
weeks of school." Angela pulled out a stack of papers from
her bag.

"I was hoping you'd have something good in there for
me," Carlie said.

"This is good for you." Angela looked puzzled. "This is
your make-up work so far. We're hoping you can work from
here until Devon is locked up for good. I really don't think a
restraining order will keep him away from you."

"He's out!"

"I'm not sure. But don't worry. He won't find you here.
Just stay off the phone young lady!" Angela shook her finger
like Grandma Jean. They both laughed. "Well, it's nice to see
you laugh for a change," Angela said.

Carlie grew nervous. She pretended to be happy in front
of her aunt. "They don't give out any information in this
place do they?"

"Absolutely not." Angela stroked her niece's face. "This is
the best place for you. Your father wants you to come home."
Angela's brow crumpled. "Speaking of your father, has he
called here for you or been here?"

"No. I didn't think he knew I was here."

"Oh, he knows. We haven't been able to get in touch with
him for the last two days." Angela twitched her lips. "It's just
strange. He's probably with that Courtney lady."

"I think he's fed up with me," Carlie said looking for
sympathy.

"No he's not. You're his baby. We all love you," Angela

said wrapping her arms around Carlie. This is just one of many stumbling blocks you have to cross in your life. Hopefully most of them won't be this difficult." Angela let out a smile.

"Thanks for everything," Carlie whispered.

"Don't thank me yet. You have to do as they say around here. Go to the classes. Do your school work. And stay off the phone!"

"I understand," Carlie moaned.

"It won't be long before we can resolve all of this. Until then, we've got to make sure you graduate."

"I don't know that I really care about graduating this year."

"You've got to be kidding! You've always been excited about graduating and going on to law school. Honey, you are allowing Devon to steal everything from you."

"No, I'm not." Carlie tried to defend herself, but had no words to throw back.

Angela stood from the bed. She thought carefully before she spoke. "If you think about it, he took you away from your family a long time ago." She pointed to each finger and continued. "You've been physically and mentally abused. Now he has taken your freedom. Are you going to allow him to take your dreams too?"

Carlie didn't respond. But when her phone rang, the ladies looked at one another.

"Who is that?" Angela shouted reaching for the phone.

"It's just Zarria," Carlie said racing her aunt to the call. "Hello."

"Hello, my ass. You know it's me."

"Tell her you'll call her later," Angela yelled.

"Who dat?" I know you ain't staying which yo boring ass aunt?" Zarria popped gum between her sentences.

"Zarria, please... Let me call you later."

"Okay, but you better. I' been hearing some crazy shit in the streets."

"I promise Zarria."

"I'm leaving," Angela said slightly rolling her eyes. "Stay off the phone and do your work or you can expect to be taking orders at Wendy's soon. Also, if your father calls, be nice. He loves you." Angela blew kisses as she shut the door. She felt bad about not telling her niece about Grandma Jean's recent chest pains. Right now it was too much for her to bear.

Carlie lay back on the flat pillow wishing she were able to live a normal life again. She rubbed the scar on her left cheek remembering her latest assault. She tried to fight off the flashbacks displaying Devon's grip around her neck. Every attempt to keep her mind off of Devon wasn't working. She tried to remember some fun times with Zarria. But out of the blue, she thought about what Zarria had said about Devon. Every thought that entered her mind related to Devon McNeil.

She thought about what Angela had said. Then suddenly she thought about Kirk. *Had she left him a message? More importantly, had she even hung up the phone when Angela walked in?*

Bruised

Chapter 19

__Murder for Hire__

Courtney raced down Constitution Ave. headed towards the D.C. Courthouse. The thought of being with her man built a puddle of sweat between her three inch miniskirt. Minutes away she applied the last layer of lip gloss. As soon as she turned the corner onto 3rd Street, Ricky stood waiting patiently on the corner.

It seemed odd to see him looking scruffy. Courtney ignored his appearance. After all, he had spent the night in a holding cell and had just been released on his own recognizance.

Ricky blew through his mouth as he entered the car. "Man, I don't believe this."

"What is it?" Courtney asked with concern.

"They really thought I was the murderer." Courtney slammed on breaks. "You were locked up for murdering someone?" She glared into Ricky's face as she tugged to lengthen her skirt.

"Something like that," Ricky replied. Noticing the change in Courtney's demeanor he knew he'd have to tell her something. "Listen, somebody in Devon's crew got killed last night and I was there."

"Who?"

"You wouldn't know if I told you," he replied irritated. "His name was Junnie," Ricky stated without emotion. "The officers thought I did it at first. But somehow they were persuaded that it was Devon." Ricky had a sinister grin plastered over his face.

"Ricky, baby, what have you gotten yourself into?"

"Nothing I can't handle," he boasted rolling up his sleeve. "Head toward my house," he ordered. "I've gotta get some things straight and get a bondsman for Charles. He's got a stack of back child support charges."

"Back child support?"

"Yeah. As a matter of fact, it's for a child I didn't even know he had." Ricky sighed in disbelief.

"Okay, this is getting crazier by the minute." Courtney shook her head as they headed toward Bowie. During the entire drive Ricky talked in codes on the phone putting his plan into action. Courtney eavesdropped harder than the KGB. Although she was unable to make out exactly what was going down, she smelled trouble. And she could possibly be dead in the middle of it.

Even though Courtney worked as a bounty hunter and carried a gun, she wasn't cut out for street life. Her position was all but handed to her by a friend as a favor to help her financially. In Courtney's eight and a half months of working, she had hunted down only one person who jumped bail. Luckily for her, a fellow bounty hunter captured the man for her.

"Ricky I've been thinking about us a lot lately," Courtney

said. "We need to talk."

"About what?" Ricky asked. He stared into his side view mirror.

"You're not even listening," she whined.

"Courtney look, I don't have time to baby sit at the moment! My life could be in danger."

"Well my life is in danger 'cause a sistah's clock is ticking."

"Do what you gotta do," Ricky blurted out. He turned all the way around to look at the jeep behind them. "I'm not making any matrimony moves knowing I'm not ready. And as far as being a father, I can't keep up with the daughter I have now."

Courtney smacked her lips. "Um….."

"Make a quick turn here," Ricky said out of the blue. He looked in his rear view mirror. "Turn again," he said.

Courtney's heart beat faster with each turn. The car behind them passed swiftly. "You scared the shit outta me," Courtney yelled.

"I'm just being cautious," Ricky warned. "Devon is ruthless. I'm not sure how far he'll go at this point. Then again I do," he said pointing to his house as they pulled in front of the garage. His front door was spray painted and left wide open.

"Ms. Lilly, Ricky's nosey neighbor came running toward the car. "Mr. Stewart, I can't believe this has happened on our street! I called the police as soon as the alarm company called me..." She ranted a mile a minute.

"Calm down. At least no one was home." Ricky looked carefully up and down the street. He turned to look at the writing on the door.

"The police said they tried all of your contact numbers.

They couldn't get anyone but me. ..."

Ricky was beginning to drown out Ms. Lily's voice. He entered the house slowly after telling Courtney to wait outside. Without his firearm that had been taken the night before, he inched down the living room hall.

Nothing seemed to be missing but everything was out of place. *We're watching you* was not only sprayed on the front door but on the bathroom mirrors as well. Ricky had no fear. He checked every level of the house leaving Carlie's room last.

Upon entering her room, he wanted to scream. The panties spread out on the dresser and floor had him at a loss for words. Anger took over as he began to beat his fist forcefully on the wall.

Ricky's temperament continued to change. Headed back down the hall, he thought of his next plan. Entering his room he noticed the red light flashing on his dresser.

Beep... Ricky listened. "Boy, where in the hell have you been. I know you out with somebody's damn daughter. I ain't stupid. Do I look like Jane from the first reader? You better call your mama back, boy. I need a ride to the doctor."

Beep... "There is no escaping me. You are nothin' without me. WE WILL BE TOGETHER. You're mine! Face it! And tell yo whack ass father, he's gotta be dealt with. I won't ask you to choose. I'll make the choice for you. Look for me when I get out this joint."

***

Ricky jetted to the small safe in his walk-in closet. With bloodshot eyes he kneeled and fumbled with the dial. The sound of a screeching car prompted him to jump up. As he approached the window, he breathed seeing that it was only

Courtney having a temper tantrum as she pulled off. Getting back to business, he headed toward the safe again. The combination containing the digits of Carlie's birthday had once been quite easy to remember. Even in his state of instability, Ricky was strategically mapping out his plan. As soon as the lock clicked he grinned wickedly and removed his .357.

***

Carlie's heart warmed as she listened to the message on her phone.

"Hello beautiful. I just thought I'd call to see how you're doing. I guess I got tired of waiting for your call." Carlie blushed slightly at the sound of Mike's voice. Then a sense of guilt built inside. *Was this considered cheating?*

"Call me when you're free, Ma. I'd like to see your pretty face again." As Carlie pressed nine to save the message she couldn't help but to think of Mike's sexy voice.

It had been nearly two months since she'd been held or felt a strong sense of love. Carlie's life had always revolved around a man being there to protect and nurture her. With the absence of Devon, Ricky, and her personal possessions, she felt naked.

After pressing one to retrieve the next message, Carlie was shocked. She couldn't believe what she heard. "Carlie, it's important. Get up wit' me at 240-808-9910," Kirk said with a sense of urgency. "Don't tell nobody you're calling me."

Chill bumps spread over Carlie's arms. She was slightly thrown by the message. *Why would Kirk call me,* she thought. *Did Devon have him call me? No, what am I thinking. He'd never want him to call me.*

The recording repeated, "To delete this message and go to the next, press 7." Carlie saved the message. She knew she'd want to listen to it again.

Carlie hung up to dial his number. Thinking like Devon had taught her, she pressed *67 to block her phone number. "What's up?" she said when Kirk answered.

"Uh… We really need to talk." Kirk spoke in a desperate tone. "Devon is on some ol' crazy shit. I think you need to go away for a while."

"Is he locked up?" Carlie asked.

"For now. But that don't mean shit. He's already sent a few fellas to your house to look for you. Where are you?" he asked with concern.

"Ah… I can't say at the moment."

"Yeah. I understand. You're learning quick."

"Oh it's no offense to you," Carlie said defending herself.

"It's all good. Whether you know it or not, I care a lot about you." The conversation went silent. Kirk paused for several seconds which felt like minutes. "I always knew you were too good for that nigga anyway... Are you there, Carlie?"

"I'm here."

"Listen, word on the street is that Devon hired some people to go at your dad. He wants him done. For you he has ordered light punishment."

Carlie's became nauseous. She tried to put on a front for Kirk. "He doesn't know where I am, so I ain't worried. Plus, my dad can handle himself."

"Well keep in mind that Devon is ruthless," Kirk said as he schooled Carlie on Devon 101. "I'm sorta watching my back too. I'm on his list right now, but I can handle mine. You know it's either Devon's way or the morgue. Frankly, I'm tired of it."

"You and Devon always have issues. I bet y'all will be

okay by tomorrow." Carlie tried to understand Kirk's feelings, but she could only focus on thoughts of her dad. She had to warn him! "Kirk, thanks for the warning. I've gotta go."

"If you need me, call me. I'm outta town right now."

"Cool," she said. "By the way, do you know if my car is still at the school?"

"I'm sure it is." Kirk's demeanor changed. "But leave the car alone. It's not worth it."

"Okay," she replied quickly. Carlie hung up and called Tamia. She knew her aunt Angela would be mad, but it was time to leave the shelter.

Bruised

Chapter 20

The Trick

Zarria pranced through the metal detectors at the Federal holding center where her new found friend had been transferred. Wearing the tightest jean skirt she could find, her hips moved in rhythm. Gaining the attention of several male correctional officers, she switched harder. "Cleared," the muscular officer said in a seductive tone. He nodded for Zarria to head toward the hallway.

As she entered the visitor's hall she searched for Devon. Tilting her dark shades slightly, she spotted him. "All the way down !" a female officer yelled. Zarria strutted boldly in her 3 inch pumps. As she passed through the row of chairs, her Barbie doll jean skirt became a distraction for several inmates. A petite woman shouted to her man, "Turn your damn head around." Zarria knew she was receiving too much attention, but was flattered nonetheless.

Devon sat in the far left hand corner of the room alone. As Zarria neared him, a bony C.O. walked away as if he'd been in a secret meeting with Devon. "Good lookin' out," Devon ended when Zarria stood before him.

Grabbing her by the back of her leg he studied her thick thighs. "Sit down," he said pointing to the chair.

Zarria moved the chair away slightly. Devon yanked it closer to him.

"Look Devon, I really don't wanna be here." Zarria looked around the room. She hoped no one would recognize her.

"So why did you come?" he asked waiting for a response.

"Cause you asked me to nigga!" Zarria rolled her eyes as hard as she possibly could.

"Lets not play games," Devon said rubbing his hands together. "We're gonna help each other just like we discussed on the phone. I'm da man. And remember, there are privileges that come wit' bein' down with the man."

"Pleaaaaase… like what?" she asked sarcastically.

"For one, I treat you better than I treat most hoes, 'cause if you'd been anybody else I would'a slapped the shit outta ya by now for bein' disrespectful."

Zarria snapped her head back. "Excuse me." The thought of getting into Devon's pockets prompted her to carefully watch how she handled his comment. Devon had briefly told her on the phone that she may have to handle some money issues for him. Little did she know that all of his money was either in his safe or on the streets.

"Aiight, this is the deal," he said moving closer, lowering his voice. "Carlie's father took Junnie out!" He grinned. "But since I was on the scene and the police didn't witness nothing so they locked me up. I guess I looked like the usual suspect."

"Why was Carlie's father there?" Zarria asked.

"That's another story. But 5'0 locked his ass up too."

Devon began punching his fist into the palm of his hand. "The problem is once I got to D.C. jail, the Feds came and got me on some other charges."

"But, what about Carlie's father?" Zarria asked again.

"Oh, he's a problem. He's out and I'm still in." His face tightened.

"Have you been charged?"

"Naw… They're holdin' me on all kinda bullshit charges: assault from Carlie's case, suspected murder, and now the FEDS wanna question me about drug activity."

"Dammmmmn…," Zarria slurred. "So what do you need from me?"

"You got two jobs. First locate Carlie and let me know where she is. Don't tell her I need her yet. I need her to do some administrative thangs for me." Devon watched closely to see if Zarria was falling for it.

"If you use Carlie to help you, then why do you need me," she snapped.

Devon slipped his hand near Zarria's skirt. She slowly crossed her arms and twitched her lips. "I need you to pick up some money for me." As his hand moved further Zarria's mind raced. With a tight squeeze of the thigh he said, "I can't trust Ray. And Kirk is nowhere to be found. I need you."

Zarria smiled inside. *Devon needs me?* she thought. *The pay better be worth it.* She leaned forward with interest as she exposed the black thong peeking from the top of her skirt.

"Call Ray from a pay phone," he ordered. Tell Ray to meet you in person. Don't talk on the phone. I'm telling you Zarria, don't fuck this up," he pointed as if she were a child. "Hav'em contact Rico and let'em know that I ran into a little trouble. I need about two more weeks to pay him. You got it."

"I got it !"

"Tell Ray I said to hit you off wit a little somethin' 'til I get out. My lawyer is on the case, so I'll be out soon."

Zarria took notes in her mind. It would be easy to find out Carlie's location. *But why does Devon wanna know her location if she can't tell Carlie right now?* Her second task would be slightly harder. Finding secretive Ray would require work.

When Zarria raised from her seat to leave, she heard the officer yell. "Visiting hours are almost over!"

"Where's my hug?" Devon questioned with a devilish look.

Zarria hesitated, then moved forward. The moment Devon wrapped his arms around her body, guilt formed inside of her. *It's just a hug,* she thought. Feeling his plush grasp of her butt cheek gave her a sudden change of heart. *Oh well, what Carlie doesn't know won't hurt her?*

Chapter 21

Concrete ain't cute

Tamia rolled up in her tan Solara shortly after 4 p.m. Carlie knew she was a true friend when she agreed to pick her up. What person would leave Pennsylvania, drive to Maryland, and then directly back to Pennsylvania? Carlie also thought about the fact that Tamia was missing an important test just to take her back to Lincoln University in Oxford.

Reaching to give Carlie a hug Tamia slyly examined her friend. Carlie had indeed changed. But Tamia wouldn't dare mention it. Strangely, she wasn't iced out in jewels and didn't rock any of the latest gear.

"So, what's up girl?" Tamia asked. "I wanna know why you're so pressed to pick up your car? I told you it was still in the parking lot."

"Yeah, but since you decided to move, I'd feel better if the car was with me," Carlie said as if her mind were already made up.

"With you where?" Tamia stopped the car and rolled her eyes. "Have you forgotten that you just moved out of a shel-

171

ter today? You haven't had a home in over four weeks. Why don't you stay with me for a while," she said with concern. "Devon's stupid ass would never think of looking for you at my new place."

Carlie moaned as if she were thinking. "We'll see."

"Now my place is not what you're used to." Tamia chuckled thinking about her new apartment in the hood. "But it's better than staying at the other place waiting to be in Devon's version of the Texas Chainsaw Massacre." She laughed at her own joke. "But it is safe," Tamia said in a more serious tone.

"I said I'll think about it," Carlie snapped as she checked her side view mirror.

The girls rode with the music blasting so loud for the next hour and a half. While Tamia jammed to her old school CD mimicking the lyrics to Slick Rick's *Hey Young World,* Carlie sat in silence.

"Remember this," Tamia screamed as she moved her body from side to side.

"Yeah, I remember," Carlie said dryly. Tamia could tell she didn't want to be bothered. Her interest was into checking out the cars that passed by.

Although traffic was heavy, Carlie was able to keep her eyes on the black SUV nearing the car. The truck moved in and out of traffic swiftly. Unable to see through the tinted windows, Carlie's fear intensified.

"Switch lanes!" she yelled to Tamia. Carlie smiled inside priding herself on a tactic she'd learned from Devon.

"Why?" Tamia asked.

"I think someone is following us."

Tamia adjusted her rear view mirror. "I don't see anybody." Irritated she gave Carlie an *'are you trippin' look'*. "You are paranoid to the 5th power," Tamia teased.

The SUV pulled beside the girls on the left side of the vehicle. The window rolled down slowly. Gold teeth covered the entire mouth of the passenger when he smiled. Signaling the girls to roll the window down, Carlie's fear was eased. It was obvious this was not a hit but they were being hit on.

They both searched for the appropriate response. Then without hesitation Tamia whipped into the right lane and sped off the exit. Tamia looked over only to see her girl laughing about the bamma with the gold teeth. It felt like old times again.

Crossing over the 896 over path reminded Carlie of all the good times she had over the last few years. Oxford, P.A. may not have been home but it was a place filled with many memories. It had actually been the only place where Carlie could be free from both Devon and Ricky.

Passing the side entrance to the campus, she began to remember several events. She laughed to herself thinking about the time when Tamia was so drunk she ran all the way across campus from Hansberry Hall screaming about how she had to pee. The students in the area thought she was crazy. They couldn't believe that at two o'clock in the afternoon somebody would be that drunk. Tamia really shocked everyone when she pulled her pants down only to pee right in front of the Frederick Douglass statue.

Carlie's mood changed when she rolled pass Dickey hall. All she could think about was when Devon showed up at her Business Law class with a box of baby wipes. "What's that for?" she remembered asking.

"For you to remove that shit off your face," he said harshly.

Carlie's look resembled the look of a one year old. She had no idea what he was talking about.

"I watched you put that mess on your damn face before you left the spot. I'on want my woman lookin' like she just joined the damn circus."

Carlie snapped from her daze. She yanked the visor down to check her make-up in the mirror. As usual it was lightly applied. Second guessing herself had become a habit over the last few years and self-esteem was definitely an issue.

Shocked, Tamia let out a loud sigh. "Oh, my God!"

Carlie's face tightened while tears welled in her eyes. "Awe…awe…," she moaned crouching to grab hold of her stomach. One, two, three, her eyes counted. Then, when the fourth cement block was counted, it all registered. Carlie's heart was crushed. "How could he?" she screamed.

"He took the tires?" Tamia asked in disbelief.

No response was needed. The once glitzy 550 Sl sat destroyed on top of the cement blocks. Carlie turned to focus closely on the brick that still remained on the dashboard.

Although she fought back the tears, Carlie was determined never to cry again about anything related to Devon. She jumped from the car to evaluate the damage. Rubbing her fingers along the scraped horizontal key mark, she shook her head.

Emerging at a fast pace, Ms. Simmons a petite neighbor rushed to Carlie's side. Wearing her floral pink quilted robe and jellybean shoes, she held her heart. "I called the police when it first happened. But it didn't do no darn good," she said walking around the car.

"It's okay, Ms. Simmons," Carlie said in a firm voice. "Thank you for looking out for me."

"Oh, honey you're fine. I should'a told you the first time I saw that black bear sitting out here three and four o'clock in the morning."

Carlie shot her a surprised look. "It doesn't even matter," she said. "Even if I had known, I don't think anything could've prevented this."

Ms. Simmons leaned way back preparing to hold a lengthy conversation when one of her sponge rollers fell to the ground. As she put it back on, Tamia interrupted.

"Carlie," she yelled from the car. "I think we should get going."

"I'm coming,"she said thankful that Tamia called her name.

Truthfully, Tamia was afraid to even get out of the car. Her fear was that one of Devon's goons were watching. *Maybe Carlie wasn't so paranoid after all?*

Tamia checked her surroundings. "Let's go now," she shouted with a deeper tone.

Carlie slammed the door when she got back in the car. "That's it," she said. "I've spent the last three years catering to that nigga and this is the thanks I get!" Carlie's nostrils flared as she continued to fuss.

Tamia wasn't sure if Carlie was talking to her or herself. She wondered what was next for her girl. In her opinion, things looked real fucked up and didn't seem like it would get any better in the near future. Carlie staying at her place was starting to be more dangerous by the minute. Tamia thought about taking back her offer, but knew she wouldn't be a true friend if she did. She turned toward Carlie and noticed her demeanor had changed instantly. She no longer looked like a helpless college student. She took on a devilish look that had never been seen before. It was as if she had transformed into a demon.

"You okay?" Tamia asked.

"Oh, I'm fine," she said without hesitation. *I won't continue to be the weakest link,* she thought. *Devon has gone too far. If this is his idea of love, I'll show him mine. I just hope he can handle it.*

Chapter 22

Another Stake-Out

Kirk paced the floor of Room #207 at the Ritz Carlton. Pentagon City was the perfect location considering what he had to accomplish. Dressed in tight black sporting gear he packed his bag.

Kirk had recently begun to travel with everything he owned, from his jewelry down to his socks. His plan was not to leave anything behind. Nothing was certain in his life at the moment, and surely not where he'd lay his head at night.

Ready to go, Kirk slid a weird black biker cap on his head and a large backpack on his back. He dialed a number on his cell and waited for an answer.

"Yo, you ready to do this," he said to the person on the other end. "That's right. E'rything is the same as we talked about, partner." Kirk checked his Rolex. "Meet me at the same spot. I'll be in a grey Chevy."

Kirk hung up with a million things on his mind. The last few weeks had been super stressful. From making drastic decisions to ducking the FEDS, Kirk was on his last leg.

Luckily he had been warned that the drug agents had

Devon under surveillance and had been trailing him for quite some time. The only reason the surveillance stopped was because he'd gotten locked up. That meant trouble for Kirk. He was quite sure that just as they had Devon followed and his phone's tapped, somehow they were on to him too. Although Kirk wasn't the target, he would be implicated as well.

Kirk thought back to the day he pulled into his driveway and a white van pulled in behind him. He initially thought he was being robbed. Suddenly men dressed in black jackets jumped from the van to surround his car. Kirk remembered that day so vividly. Before he could surrender, the agents had him cuffed. They had seized the house, the car and all of his possessions in a matter of minutes.

After serving five years, losing his woman, and coming home to nothing, Kirk vowed never to get caught up again. He snapped back to the present as he thought of Devon.

He didn't care what happened to Devon at this point. But he knew he wasn't going down for nobody. *Especially his self-centered so-called boy,* he thought.

Leaving the room, Kirk carried all of his belongings to the grey Chevy he'd purchased a week ago. Opening the trunk in the underground parking lot, he loaded everything he owned and shut it. Kirk turned away and headed back through the lot to the front of the hotel. When he stepped outside, he searched the area.

Crossing the street Kirk headed toward a bike rack loaded with mountain and high performance bicycles. While he continued to watch his back he couldn't help but to drift into his thoughts again. He couldn't keep Carlie's face out of his mind. He'd wanted to check on her over the past few days, but he knew it would be playing it close.

Reaching down to work the combination, the lock popped. Kirk hopped on his newly purchased bike and headed toward route 1 near the meeting spot. Within minutes the 7Eleven was in clear view. But Tone was nowhere to be found.

Tone said he'd be in a beat up Thunderbird. Even though Kirk knew it would be hard for his salesman to spot him, it was fine. That was a part of the plan. Tone was the perfect person to unload the drugs Devon had gotten from Rico. He was new to the Washington D.C. area and not known by many. The best part about it was that he sold most of his product in his hometown near Norfolk, V.A.

Kirk remembered meeting Tone at his cousin's cookout. Although he dressed and drove a car that said 'I'm in the game', he never discussed his business. *Discreet* is probably his middle name. Even when his cousin tried to make the connection between the two of them Tone never admitted that he'd be interested in hearing about a good deal. Kirk's cousin assured him that Tone could be trusted. But at this point in the game no one could be trusted.

Kirk parked his bike across the street and watched Tone carefully. Several cars pulled in and out of parking spaces next to Tone. Horns beeped and cars rushed by as Kirk assessed the area.

About ten minutes had past when Kirk's phone rang. "Yeah," he answered.

"Man. I'm still sitting here. Where are you?"

"I'm two minutes away, partner." Kirk hung up quickly. After noticing that Tone didn't pick up his phone or do anything unusual, Kirk pedaled across the street.

Cycling up to the window gave Tone quite a shock. "What's up with you nigga," Tone asked confused.

"Just gettin' in some exercise."

Tone knew that wasn't true, but trusted him enough to go ahead and handle business. "You got that?" he asked.

"Right here," Kirk responded patting his backpack.

"I can't believe this is your last. This shit is sellin' like hot-cakes." Tone reached into his back seat. "It's all here. Now you sure you can't get yo hands on any more?"

"Naw…this was a two time deal. I'm done." Kirk's eyes surveyed the perimeter. "Don't send nobody my way either. I knew you were a good dude that's the only reason why we hooked up."

"Gotcha." Tone nodded and the switch was made.

Devon pedaled his way toward the parking lot of the Ritz Carlton. *Mission accomplished*, he thought. He felt good having sold the last batch of Devon's product. Especially to a guy who had no affiliation with their crew. It also didn't hurt to have a total of $400,000 in his possession.

Chapter 23

A Strange Visit

"I know you're pissed off, but I've been doing some soul searching," Carlie said into her cell phone.

"I'm sick of your excuses," Zarria snapped. "Excuses are tools of the weak and incompetent that are used to build monuments of nothingness. And those who use them usually amount to nothing at all."

There was a brief pause. Then suddenly both girls laughed.

Zarria always got a kick out of imitating the pledgees at Carlie's school. Although she had never been to college, she couldn't quite understand what would make a person go through hell and high water to be a member of a sorority or fraternity.

"It's so good to hear your voice," Carlie said as she breathed slightly. "I'm going through so much right now."

"Like what?" Zarria asked in a concerned voice.

"Well for starters, I'm on my way to the hospital to see Grandma." Carlie's demeanor instantly changed at the thought of her Grandmother being ill. "My aunt Angela said it's nothing major, but I can't help but to worry."

"Where are you?" Zarria asked quickly. "You need me to make you laugh," she said trying to cheer Carlie up a bit.

"I'm on my way to the hospital...."

"What hospital," Zarria asked cutting her off.

"Washington Hospital Center. But you don't have to come out. There will be plenty of people there. If there's one thing we've got, it's family support."

"Oh, no... that's what friends are for. I'm on my way. As a matter of fact I'll probably beat you there." Zarria checked the clock on her dashboard. "I'm just ten minutes away."

"If you insist," Carlie sung in a sweet voice.

"I do. What are you driving?" Zarria asked.

"My Dad got me a rental yesterday."

"That's so good. I knew you two would be cool again," Zarria said in the fakest voice she could muster. "I'm happy for you."

"Yeah, he came through, 'cause my car is done. But I'll tell you about that later. How about I meet you out front instead? I'm almost there."

"Bet."

Within minutes, Zarria waited at the front of the hospital for Carlie. Light blue pants and white button-ups were seen by the dozens. As people rushed in and out of the main doors, Zarria thought about what she'd say to Carlie. *Was she really going all the way with Devon's plan? All Devon wants to do is find out where she is. And gettin' paid in the process ain't hurting nobody*, she thought.

Carlie landed a huge hug around Zarria's neck. "Hey, girrrrr...l. I miss you," Carlie said with an oversized grin.

"Yeah, I can tell," Zarria said sarcastically. "Listen, can we talk just a second before we go in?"

"Sure," Carlie said sitting next to Zarria. At that moment, Carlie's eyes focused on a familiar car passing in front of the hospital. She couldn't place the car or the driver who paid close attention to her as his left arm hung from the window. Carlie wasn't sure if there was a need to be alarmed.

She jogged her memory in search of an answer. Between coming up with nothing and the car out of sight, Carlie's attention was re-focused back on Zarria.

"Girl, you might need some pills just to get yo mind straight. Zoning out and shit." Zarria mumbled as she rolled her eyes.

"I know it's Devon. I'm trying to get him out of my system. It's hard. Plus, I'm paranoid."

"Umm… that's that type of love that I'm trying to stay the hell away from." Zarria smacked her lips hard.

"Let's not confuse what he's offering as love," Carlie joked. *That's lockdown!* They laughed together like old times.

"Girrr…l, I don't know what kinda dick he got. But I wouldn't fuck him with somebody else's pussy."

Carlie was all laughs and thought it was the funniest thing she'd heard in a while. Zarria's entertaining thought ended when two men dressed in blue jeans and casual shirts approached the bench.

Instantly, Zarria could feel the guilt run through her body. Rather than fear, she was at a complete loss. By no means did she think she was in danger. It was Carlie they wanted. *Had Devon followed her that quickly with hopes that she'd see Carlie? It was all her fault,* she thought.

Carlie held the palm of her hand closely at her chest. She studied the badges before her. "DEA… DEA… DEA… ," she said softly to herself. Once again, visions popped in her head. The mole on one of the men's faces was familiar. It was difficult for Carlie to believe that a black guy wearing baggy pants would be a drug enforcement agent.

"Mam, I'm agent Willams and this is agent Meeks," he said pointing to his partner. We just need a moment of your time." "Alone," he added turning to Zarria.

"You don't have to tell me but once," Zarria said twisting her lips. "I'll be inside."

As soon as Zarria had completely entered the building agent Williams began. "We came to talk about Devon. Don't look shocked," he said. "It was just a matter of time before we came looking for you." Agent Williams stood with his hands in his front pockets and waited for a reaction or a response.

After not getting an answer, Agent Meeks was up to bat.

"Ms. Stewart it would be in your best interest to cooperate," he said in a harsh tone. "You could be on your way to jail on conspiracy charges."

"No…no…no. What he means is that if you decide not to help us, which I know you will, you'll be held accountable for what you've seen." Agent Williams possessed a mild mannered personality. His gentle way of dealing with Carlie settled her mind just a bit. "That would break my heart to have to lock you up."

"What exactly do you want from me?" she asked biting what was left of her stubby nails. "I don't know anything."

"Yeah, we know," Agent Meeks said in disbelief. "Devon has been under investigation for six months now. In the majority of the surveillance tapes you were there."

Carlie's mouth hung open. "I've gotta go," she said noticing a few people staring as they walked by. "I think it would be a good idea for me to get a lawyer."

"I'm sure Ricky will tell you the same thing we're telling you," said Williams. "Look Carlie, we don't want to see you in any trouble. You've been through enough."

Carlie held her head low and turned away.

"When Devon originally got locked up for assaulting you we found out about it. That incident actually messed up our investigation. We have enough information on him. We just need you to testify."

"Testify?" she said loudly.

Agent Meeks turned in a circle to watch for curious bystanders. Chiming in he said, "Devon murdered Junnie and had your own Father involved. He says he loves you and tries to buy you things to show you, but is that really caring about you?" His receding hair line seemed so familiar. And it wasn't difficult to remember a man with only a few strands of hair.

Carlie was shocked that the agents knew so much about their relationship. *How much did they really know?* she wondered. *Had they been listening when Devon cried on the phone months ago?*

"Listen, give me your information and I'll call you after I've consulted with my father."

"Williams handed Carlie a business card. He held onto her hand a few seconds longer than necessary. "I'll make sure we take care of you the right way. You've suffered enough," he nodded.

"Wait," Meeks interrupted. "Understand that Devon can't be held but for so long for Junnie's murder if he's not officially charged. He'll be out soon. Guess who he's gonna be lookin' for?"

"Don't mind him," agent Williams said pushing Meeks aside. "One more thing, Carlie. Do you know where he keeps his drugs or his money?" Williams whispered.

"Definitely not," Carlie answered quickly. She thought about the safe at Devon's place, but knew the time wasn't right to get back at him. Luckily, she didn't know where he kept his drugs and had no desire to find out. *Devon would get his one day*, she thought. *Even if I don't have the guts to do it.*

Carlie was on edge as she began to walk away. She backed away from the agents slowly as she asked her final question. "If I decide to give you information, I don't have to take the stand in front of him do I?"

"What stand?" Zarria asked holding the front door open for Carlie.

Carlie could tell by the water in Zarria's eyes and the look of terror on her face that something was wrong. "I think you'd better get up here. Grandma Jean isn't doing as well as you thought."

Carlie dashed through the door and past the elevator. Grandma Jean was the only mother figure that was constant in her life. After reaching the end of the hall she heard Zarria's voice. "This way," she called as she hit the up button.

Stepping into the elevator, Zarria wrapped her arm around Carlie's shoulder. Feeling like an emotional wreck, Carlie panicked. Backing up with a crazed look, she settled in the corner quietly while the elevator stopped at several floors. Without looking up she continued to squat ignoring the observers.

As soon as the doors opened Ricky was the first person Carlie laid eyes on. Their embrace was as tight as a father and daughter's could be. "Where were you?" he asked.

"Oh, making a phone call," she said giving Zarria the evil eye.

Zarria returned the look with her counterfeit smile.

"Sweetie, we need to talk," Ricky stated.

Carlie allowed her father to guide her step by step to a seat in the visiting area. She could tell from the grim looks of her cousins that something had gone seriously wrong. "What happened?" she blurted out.

"Mother had a heart attack," Angela said.

Carlie jumped up instantly feeling as if she needed to throw up. She coughed and gagged for several seconds until she felt Angela's palm touch her back.

"Let's stay calm," Angela said.

"*Calm.* You said it was nothing life threatening. I should've been here," Carlie yelled.

"There was nothing more you could have done. They're not letting us in the back yet," Angela said keeping her composure. "She's in intensive care."

Carlie really began to get troubled. Ricky knew his daughter well. He got up and held her arm as her tears began to flow. "Let's have a seat."

Carlie didn't resist. As soon as she sat down Angela moved in for what Carlie thought would be more lectures. Carlie could see the old mahogany box in Angela's hand, but had no idea what was going on.

"Carlie, Mother Jean had been trying to find the right time to give this to you. It's yours," she patted her on the wrist. "She collected the contents especially for you. It's not worth any money, but it's extremely valuable. Angela left the box sitting next to Carlie.

"What's in it?" Carlie asked looking at the box strangely.

"It would probably be better if you looked at it later," Angela said as if she were giving an order rather than a suggestion. "If you want, I'll take it to my house. Since you're staying with me you can open it there."

Carlie saw three doctors converse outside the double doors. She knew they were discussing her grandmother's condition by the way they pointed and scrutinized the family. "I'm gonna run to the rest room," Carlie said.

"I'll go with you." Zarria jumped to her feet.

"I'm okay. I need a minute to myself." Noticing that the doctors were gone Carlie was ready to proceed with her plan. Heading toward the double doors she could see a figure standing on the other side. Carlie leaned over the water fountain and drank with her eyes focused on the door. She knew intensive care was beyond those doors. And if no one was going to come out and give information, she was going in.

Suddenly the doors flung open. One of the doctors Carlie had seen earlier walked toward Ricky and Angela. Gathering the family in a huddle he began to speak. Carlie took advantage of the moment. She darted through the double doors in search of her grandmother. It was almost like a spirit guided her through the dim hallway.

Carlie followed the sound of the voices. Finally she stopped. Several doctors stood using medical codes and terminology that Carlie could not understand. However, she did know that there was a huge possibility that Grandma Jean was the person that they vigorously worked on.

"You have to go!" a short female doctor shouted. For the first time Carlie was noticed.

Numbness took over. The machine had flat-lined and

Carlie was in a zombie like state. An Indian doctor felt compelled to grab Carlie's arm and guide her to the waiting area. The tubes were being unhooked as Carlie was lead to her family. She could hear the wailing and crying several yards away. Carlie knew they had gotten the news.

As soon as the doors opened, Ricky and Angela embraced her. It was no doubt Carlie was the most fragile family member at the moment. From the group hugs to the *better place* speeches, Carlie was sure that nothing would help her recover from this.

Bruised

Chapter 24

Tell It All

As soon as Carlie raised from Angela's comfortable couch, a dent was detected in the seat. In a flash, wearing a multi-colored apron, Angela had come behind her to fluff the pillows just right. Ricky shook his head. *At a time like this she's still acting like Molly the Maid,* he thought.

The room had been relatively silent for the last few hours. No one knew what to say. Between the anticipation of the guests scheduled to arrive soon and the planning of Grandma Jean's funeral, they were all in a tizzy.

Most of Grandma Jean's descendents were holding up well. Angela had her moments when she broke down during brief crying spells. But between her *Bible* and the *How to cope with death books* that lined the coffee table, she was making it. Fortunately, Ricky and Carlie were staying with her so they could all comfort one another.

No one could relate to the way Carlie handled her grief. She hadn't dropped one tear since leaving the hospital. She sat dazed day after day without uttering a word. Most of her time was spent holding the box Grandma Jean had left for her. Ricky knew something wasn't right. So he continued to watch her like an orderly monitoring a psychotic patient.

Hour after hour Carlie hoped that she'd find out her grandmother's death was just another one of her bad dreams. She wasn't ready to accept her death or any troubles she had to face on her own. After taking a slow, smooth breath Carlie took a seat at the dining room table holding the mahogany box. Angela hoped that this would be the day Carlie would open it. She knew its contents but told Carlie she did not. Her response to Carlie was that Grandma Jean said she hoped it would be a mind changing experience for her when she opened it. Just like the contents of the box was a mystery for Carlie, figuring out why Carlie continued to move to different locations around the house was a mystery to Angela.

Carlie studied the box in such a daze that she failed to hear the door bell ring. Angela nodded to Ricky before rushing to open the door. The first visitor limped inside and shook Ricky's hand immediately. He then turned to greet Angela. "Thanks for having us," the second gentleman said.

At the sound of their voices, Carlie's face grew pale. Angela rushed to the dining room table and pulled her from the chair. She locked her arms through Carlie's without hesitation. "You will be fine," she assured Carlie. "Your father has this all under control."

"Listen, we just want to talk Carlie," Williams said. The agent smiled inside noticing the resemblance between his braids and Carlie's fresh set. He wanted to be able to relate to Carlie better. She was an important part of the puzzle needed to convict Devon.

"Carlie, remember what we talked about," Ricky interrupted. "This is not about you. All they want is Devon. Now you give them any information they need," he ordered.

Carlie nodded.

Agent Meeks limped toward Carlie at a snail's pace. "Our tapes show Devon purchasing high dollar items in your presence. He used cash on all occasions. Where did he get the money from?"

"I have no idea." Carlie trembled. She was determined not to look at Meeks.

"Ah… come on now," Meeks yelled. He looked toward Ricky. "I thought we came here because she was ready to cooperate."

"She is," Ricky said calmly as he looked at Carlie.

"Carlie we know he sells drugs," Williams intervened with his soothing voice. We watched him make several transactions. But once he got locked up it ruined our investigation. We need to know where he keeps his drugs or the money."

"I told you before I don't know." Carlie held her head even lower.

Williams looked at Ricky for approval. "All we need is for you to say you've seen the money and drugs at his house. We need to be able to get a search warrant."

"Why do you need me to say it?" Carlie asked in a child-like state. "Why not one of his friends?"

"Oh, they're going down too," Meeks said quickly. He ran his hand across his hair attempting to lay down the few strands. "That's right Ray-Ray, Kirk, Corrupt , Frank, Rico, Junnie…" He laughed. "Oh, I almost forgot, Junnie's dead."

Hearing the list of names concerned Carlie. She had to let Kirk know what was going on. *If the shoe was on the other foot, he'd do the same for her.* Although he had checked on her at the beginning of the week, she hadn't talked to him in a few days. Carlie knew she couldn't allow him to go down in Devon's mess.

"Are you okay," Ms. Stewart?" agent Williams asked observing the change in Carlie's demeanor.

"Yeah, I'm fine," she said staring at the mole on Williams' cheek.

Noticing her stare, he smiled slightly. For the first time since their arrival, she loosened up a bit. It was hard for her to visualize Williams as an agent. He resembled someone she would date or even someone who could be down with Devon. A frown appeared on her face. *What if Devon had sent him to get her?* Carlie quickly moved away from Angela and stood by Ricky's side. "I need to see some identification," she said.

"Sure," Williams said as he flashed his badge. He tried to hide his frustration. *Carlie was indeed a confused woman,* he thought.

"This is beginning to be a worthless meeting," Meeks moaned. "We showed you our badges four days ago. Why do we need to show them again?"

"Show her your badge," Williams said with raised voice.

"Okay, I'll show you my badge," he said flipping his wallet open. "But I need to know how many of those guys you know from the list of names I called off. And don't lie," Meeks said opening his eyes widely. "Because keep in mind we've been watching."

Rehearsed answers swam intensely in Carlie's head. *Had they seen her in the company of Corrupt or Ray-Ray? Had they tapped her phone to know she'd talked to Kirk?* When her father's hand touched the back of her shoulder she knew time had run out. "Yes, I know Kirk," she said calmly.

"What do you know about him?" Meeks asked sharply.

"He's Devon's friend," she answered.

"He's yours too," Meeks said sarcastically. "Remember, we've been monitoring all of their calls. He's said some things about you that Devon won't take too well. I hope we don't have to get to the point where we let Devon hear one of those conversations."

Ricky stood up at the frightened look on his daughter's face. "Look, we're here to help you put Devon away for good. Kirk's conversations about Carlie are irrelevant." Ricky walked around like Angela's living room was a courtroom. "Is there any one particular statement or action required on Carlie's part to keep Devon in?"

"We need that search warrant. The judge will grant it, if Carlie says she's been in the house and knows the stuff is there," Williams ended.

"No, I haven't seen anything," Carlie yelled. Although frustrated, she stood strong.

"I guess that's it," Meeks said heading toward the door. "Carlie, let me say this. We watched you wait for Devon in the car outside of an apartment building on Good Hope road. Not once, but on many occasions. You know exactly what he was doing inside those apartments while you waited in the car."

Meeks looked to see what type of response he was getting from Carlie. After seeing the blank look on her face, he continued. "The day that you give us the right information, he'll be in for good and you'll be set free. Otherwise, we'll have to take drastic measures." He stared at Carlie momentarily. "We might have to charge you with conspiracy."

"Let's step outside," Ricky said heading out in front of the two agents.

"Take care," Williams said over his shoulder. His wave was intended for Carlie who was already headed up the stairs. She never looked back.

"Take care," Angela responded as she fluffed the pillows and patted the couch. Although she thought deeply about Carlie, her first line of work was to sweep the areas where the agents had walked.

Outside Ricky assured the agents that Carlie would come around. He begged gracefully to exclude his daughter from any conspiracy charges. Although he didn't think conspiracy charges would stick, in the back of his mind he started putting his plan of defense in motion.

As soon as the officers pulled off, Ricky dialed Lisa's number.

"Lisa Duckett speaking, may I help you?"

"You sure can," Ricky said changing his tone. It's time to go to plan B."

"Gotcha boss." Lisa hung up and went to work.

Chapter 25

Not Another Death

Ricky rode in silence from the time he left Angela's place till now. He had been driving himself crazy lately. Between handling his mother's funeral, dealing with Carlie's issues, and watching his own back, he had another full time job. Luckily, Ricky had taken two weeks off to handle his personal business.

Making his way onto Kennedy Street, he tried to remember the request ·his siblings had made regarding Grandma Jean's funeral. It was difficult staying focused due to the hustle and bustle in the vicinity. Kennedy Street had become legendary for rowdy foot traffic and businesses that attracted drama. Over the years there had been talk about beefing up security on the busier end of the street, but from what Ricky could see, it wasn't happening.

Without an accurate count, he was willing to bet a barbershop and liquor store sat on every corner. Ricky still hadn't figured out why he was sent to finalize the arrangements, or why a funeral parlor in that area had been chosen. He was used to being more of a *'behind the scenes type of guy'*. But,

Angela wasn't having it. He remembered her saying, "You need to take some responsibility for this family." *So here I am,* he thought. *Amongst the ghetto superstars.*

Stopped at a light Ricky got a chance to see what its like to live on the rough side of town. Even though in his day work dragged him into the hoods, he figured it would be different if you had to live it every day. Several under aged boys crossed the street while Ricky waited. "Truancy officers, where are they when you need them?" he mumbled to himself. As soon as the light changed Ricky pressed on the pedal quickly only to slam on breaks. A metro bus sat with its backside in the middle of the street causing Ricky to miss the light. "Damn it." Ricky banged on the steering wheel.

Frustrated, Ricky waited at the long light again. This time he noticed an old Capri sitting three cars behind him. Having some reservations about the drivers sunk deep in their seats, he thought about making a u-turn. Before he could make a move, the light changed. Ricky made a sharp left into a parking lot. The Capri, containing three young men, passed by. Ricky couldn't make out their faces, but saw clearly that they weren't thinking about him. He sat up straight, breathed, and removed his hand from the gun strapped to his leg. *Maybe he had become paranoid just like the rest of his family. It was time to put those thoughts behind him. He had to be the strong one everyone would be counting on him.*

Ricky was attentive as he pulled back into traffic. With only several blocks to go before reaching Horton's Funeral Parlor, he checked his rear view mirror. *Good, everything is normal,* he thought to himself. *This was not the right time for foolishness.* After driving several more blocks less people were seen on foot. Ricky started to pass blocks that didn't seem like they belonged in the area. *Not that busy*, he thought. *No more Jamaicans hanging on corners and no more carry outs. Thank God.* As he pulled into the lot he felt good reading the address, "1450 Kennedy Street. Finally." He wasn't certain if they had opened yet. It seemed strange to see only one car in the area.

Ricky jumped from his Jaguar. As he approached the door he looked over his shoulder. *He wondered if his eyes had deceived him.* He thought he'd seen a Capri shoot past him and turn the corner. With one hand on the door Ricky looked back again. He shook his head and walked in. The sound of the hard wooden doors closing behind him triggered a weird feeling. He looked back.

Immediately, the eerie environment set off uneasy emotions. Ricky had been into silent business establishments before but this was too much. Ghostly thoughts crept through his veins, while the odd smell in the air caused his nostril to flare. Ricky waited patiently at the front wondering if anyone would be coming to assist him. He walked straight ahead several yards noticing a black chromed casket. Ricky backed up going 20 miles an hour. When his back felt the warmth of a body, Ricky's alarm went off!

Without turning around he quickly bent and reached toward his leg. "Oh! My goodness. Did I scare you?" the frail, male undertaker asked. In his high pitch voice and womanly stance, he stared at Ricky from top to bottom. "Honey this is a funeral parlor, but we won't kill you," he laughed.

Ricky took a moment to catch his breath. He surveyed the dimly lit room once more. "Where is everybody?" he asked unkindly. "I've been waiting several minutes for help."

"Well help is here," the undertaker said resting his palm

on his chest. "Besides, I'm the only one here." He rolled his eyes at Ricky and walked away. "Follow me," he said looking over his shoulder. "By the way, I'm Mr. Peaches."

Ricky followed hurriedly. *Mr. Peaches*, he thought. *Well at least he's dressed professionally and suited up like a man.* "I'm Ricky Stewart and. ..."

"Oh, I know exactly who you are," Mr. Peaches said interrupting. He spoke faster than an auctioneer at an auction. "Your sister has given me a research paper on you, *child*. I know everything you guys want and I know exactly what I'm supposed to do."

The two men stopped in front of Grandma Jean's casket. Mr. Peaches blocked Ricky's view. "Now, before you review the body let me say a few things." He stood with his hands on his small hips. "If there's anything you don't approve of, let us know. We can change her make-up and things of that sort, but your sister said *the clothes are staying*. Also. ..."

The sound of the wooden front doors caused both men to be a little apprehensive. "Was someone else coming with you," Mr. Peaches asked.

"No." Ricky answered quickly.

"I'm not expecting anyone. Hello," he yelled hoping the unannounced visitors could hear him. After not getting an answer Mr. Peaches walked a few feet closer to the entrance. "Hello," he yelled again.

Ricky knew exactly what was up. He listened for a noise, or even a footstep, but his sensors heard nothing. The sound of the velcro letting loose on Ricky's leg, startled Mr. Peaches. Before he could speak, Ricky had his nine millimeter in hand.

"What in God's name is going on?" Mr. Peaches

screamed. His hands smothered the side of his face.

Ricky was bent down low. He backed himself into a corner and signaled Mr. Peaches to take cover as well. He had to think quick. He knew his mother would not approve of shooting up a funeral home, but loosing his life was not on today's calendar. Ricky looked at Mr. Peaches who was now kneeling beside him. He focused back to allowing his eyes to circle the room.

"Is there another way outta here besides the front door?" Ricky whispered.

"Yeah. That way," Mr. Peaches pointed his finger crisply.

***

Crouched down behind the front desk, Ray-Ray signaled to another one of Devon's puppets hiding behind a door. Ray had no idea why the third member of their crew had not come in yet. He balled his fist at the thought of bringing a sixteen year old to do a man's job. Ray couldn't even think of a good reason for choosing such a jittery guy for this type of job. Nor had he realized why he'd allowed himself to boldly enter a funeral parlor.

Waiting in the still, barely lit area he started to have second thoughts. *He'd already been in the pen too many times. Devon was already locked up, facing multiple charges. And here he was prepared to kill Carlie's father and then make Carlie suffer a few days. Upon Devon's request, he was to beat some sense into her.* At the thought of his pay for such a task, he raised to his feet.

Ray whispered across the room to his young soldier. "You ready Dawg?"

The sound of the youngster's gun clicking was verification enough. "Yo, I'm always ready," the curly head youngster whispered. For a nineteen year old he used the strongest voice he could muster.

"Yeah. That's right. Me too," Ray-Ray mumbled hesitantly to himself. Ray had a bad feeling. He'd killed many times before, but today was different. Suddenly a door closed.

"It came from the back," the young bandit said with raised voice.

Within seconds, the missing member from Ray's crew opened the front door to the parlor. As the brightness zoomed in he yelled. "He's out here."

**

Running to his car from the back of the parlor, Ricky stopped short behind an oversized green trash can. He thought about jetting to his car several yards away, and escaping through the back of the lot. Then it hit him. *Devon's crew would eventually come after him again. He knew he could handle the heat, but what about Carlie?* He was willing not to disrespect his mother inside the parlor, but he had made up his mind. *Today, Devon's boys had to die.*

In an instant, Ricky made his position known. He held his hands in the air, and walked to the middle of the lot. The first shot rang out. At the same time he noticed Ray standing near the front of the lot with his Glock pointed directly at him. The bullet shot past Ricky's shoulder. Dodging the slug, he hit the ground, letting off two shots. Ricky could see the face of the timid 16 year old, but had lost track of Ray.

Three seconds later the curly head youngster stood above Ricky. His aim was precise, but his timing was off. Ricky pulled the trigger and within seconds the blood from the youngster's forehead had splattered the ground. Ricky breathed a short sigh of relief as he did a quick search for the other two hoodlums. He hated to be thrown back into murder mode, but it felt good. *It's either them, or me*, he thought.

Right away, Ricky spotted his paid executioner headed toward him. Ray had shortened their distance apart down to five yards when he came to a sudden stop. Both men thought about their plans as a few people walking by started to notice the drama. Quickly, they backed away straying from the gun battle. Ray had no intention on going back to jail; so he carefully slowed his steps. He checked to see who watched the action and what they could see.

Ricky continued to contemplate his next move. The intended shot was a long one, but he knew he could make it. His heart beat like a steel drum at the sight of a bystander pointing from across the street. Ricky searched for the third attacker. He was nowhere in sight. The thought of losing even one suspect was alarming.

Ricky sprinted across the lot, leaving Ray little time to react. As soon as he noticed a tiny movement, he lunged forward ready for attack. Ray ducked slightly as Ricky's slug hit him at full speed. The intended target was hit. Ray reached for his throat, but it was too late. His eyes rolled to the back of his head as he died instantly.

Ricky jetted to his car, hoping the bystanders could not make out his face from afar. He thought about Mr. Peaches as he hurried toward the back of the parking lot. Ricky knew that he'd have to slow down as soon as his car hit the side street. He would be in clear view for many people to see.

Ricky grabbed his phone to call his brother Charles. He needed someone to make sure Carlie was okay. His heart began to beat slower as he turned through an alley and ended up on 5th Street. Seeing that there weren't many people in the area, Ricky dialed the number. He waited for the light to change and hoped his brother would answer. Charles was beginning to be all talk in Ricky's opinion. He spoke about kicking Devon's ass often, but nearly pissed in his pants when it was time to act.

Ricky dropped the phone as the familiar face stood two feet from him. Staring into the barrel of the .357 his adrenaline surged. Without moving his head, Ricky's eyes shifted from right to left. Not a soul was in sight. A car flying by caught the attention of the young man. Ricky wasted no time. He grabbed his nine-millimeter off of the passenger seat, ready to unload. Unexpectedly, the gun jammed. Ricky panicked as he slid the shaft back.

Pow… Pow…, blood splattered the car.

Chapter 26

Missing You

It was nearly 12 p.m. when family and friends began to assemble at the New Samaritan Baptist Church. The small place of worship had been home to the late Ms. Stewart for over twenty-five years. Grandma Jean's body rested in a fine silver coffin near the pulpit, while her face bore a faint smile signaling her happiness. As each person passed the coffin to pay their respects, they stopped to give condolences to the children.

The wake was just what Grandma Jean would have wanted. Long extravagant roses had been sent to the church by the dozens from miles around. An enormous spray of flowers, and bright pink ribbons caught the attention of those nearby. Angela was the first child seated on the front row. Next to her sat her grieving two brothers Charles Luder and Calvin. Angela stood gracefully as she received embraces. She blotted her eyes several times after looking toward her mother and back at her brothers. "Where is Ricky?" Angela bent to ask Charles. She checked her watch for the third time. "The funeral starts at 12:30," she said.

Charles shrugged his shoulders. He had no idea where Ricky or Carlie were at that moment. All of the family had agreed to gather at Grandma Jean's earlier in the day so they could ride to the church together. Carlie wasn't ready to leave when everyone else headed to Grandma Jean's. Angela felt Carlie needed more time alone and assured her that she would send a car to pick her up.

Angela snapped from her thoughts when Charles jumped up throwing his arms in the air. Sweat dripped from the side of his face as he stood with his hands raised firmly. Angela moved closer to her brother. "They're waiting for us to come in the back, Charles," she whispered. There is a room prepared for us until the processional starts."

Charles stood still until his brother Calvin grabbed him by the arm and followed the funeral director. Angela nodded to the onlookers as she left the sanctuary. "He'll be fine," she said to an aunt passing by with a worried look. Angela looked around the room one more time in search of Ricky or Carlie. As she left the room she noticed Reverend Sharps approach the pulpit.

***

At the same time that Rev. Sharps reviewed the order of service for the funeral, Ricky was in the third chapter of his interrogation. Sitting in a small room at the 4th District Police Station, he tapped on the table irritated that his team of lawyers had not yet arrived. The scrawny investigator in charge drilled Ricky about the shoot-out that took place at the funeral home the day before.

"Listen, all we want to know from you is why you shot a 16 year old," the investigator said in a firm tone. He pushed a five by seven photo of the youngster in front of Ricky's face.

"He was trying to kill me!" Ricky shouted. "I was just protecting my damn self." Ricky boiled with anger. He couldn't believe his mother's funeral would be starting in thirty minutes and he was still being questioned. "What about him attempting to kill me along with those other hooligans?"

"Well we have a statement from Mr. Alphonzo Peaches clarifying that you shot two men on the property of the Hodges Funeral Home in self defense." The investigator scratched his head. "Your story collaborates with the funeral director. However, the problem is, no one can justify why you shot this 16 year old name Gary Bonds." He pointed to the picture again.

Ricky pushed the picture away. "I had the chance to make sure he didn't live. I had the perfect shot and I never miss." Ricky banged his fist on the table. "He tried to take me out and I spared his life. My mother would be pleased with me." Ricky was all choked up when the investigator prepared to leave the room.

As he opened the door the commander of the station waited outside the room along with Ricky's team of lawyers. After minutes of informal discussions, Ricky's head lawyer entered. He extended his hand toward Ricky.

"First, I want to offer my condolences," Mr. Turner stated. "Secondly, we need to get you to your mother's funeral as quickly as possible."

Inside, Ricky was delighted, but he could barely muster a smile. He never thought that he'd spend the day of his mother's funeral at a police station. "Let's go," he said tucking his shirt neatly into his pants. Ricky wanted badly to rush home for a quick shower but knew there was no time. Luckily for him, he was always dressed in his best attire. As Ricky exited the interrogation room, he noticed a petite woman coming his way.

With her hand extended she looked at Ricky strangely. "Thank you for saving my son," she said.

Ricky's brow crinkled. "And you are?" he asked.

"I'm Mrs. Bonds. My son told me everything. He said that he pulled a gun on you first." She paused trying to choose her words carefully. "He also told me that you could have easily killed him, but you choose not to. Even though you shot him, I thank you." She kissed Ricky's hand and followed the investigator.

Within minutes, Ricky had rushed out the front door of the police station and in the back seat of a Lincoln town car. Headed to the church he thought about the events the day before. He prayed that he had made his mother proud and that he and Carlie's safety would no longer be in danger.

***

"Ma'am, I think you should go in now," the tall limo driver said. It is a quarter after twelve and the funeral will be starting soon." He stared at Carlie through his rear view mirror. The driver couldn't understand why she had insisted on sitting outside the church for the last hour.

"I'll be ready in a moment," she said. "Whatever it cost for your time, my father will pay it."

"Oh, no… my intent is not to rush you. I just don't want you to miss the service."

Carlie seemed pre-occupied as the man spoke. When the driver turned his neck all the way around to make eye contact, he noticed her opening a small box that sat on her lap.

Carlie had promised herself she would become a stronger

woman in her grandmother's honor. For days she had wanted to open the box to see what her grandmother had left her but didn't want to cry anymore. She cried so many tears in her life for Devon, she felt it was now a sign of weakness. *Maybe the box contained pearls? Maybe family heirloom jewelry? What if it were some hidden information about her mother or father?*

Carlie decided not to wait any longer. She opened the box and pushed the articles aside. She searched diligently for tangible items, but felt nothing. The box only contained articles and a crinkled letter. The creases formed on Carlie's face explained her confusion. Grandma Jean's purpose wasn't clear until Carlie read the headline of the first article. She read the heading and caption silently to herself.

Dying for Love, *August 2003,*
Just outside East Point ,Ga., police responded to a domestic dispute and found the body of Freda Kennedy dead from multiple gunshot wounds.

Carlie was now even more confused. She knew she didn't know the woman mentioned in the article. She wondered if Grandma Jean even knew her. Then it hit her as she shuffled through the other titles. They all related to abuse, domestic violence, and death. Carlie paused thinking about her grandmother's intent. She knew she would eventually have to read each article in detail, but for now she'd read as much as she could. Carlie checked the time and began to scan each article.

January, 2004, Houston,Texas
Ronelle White was brutally killed outside her home yes-

terday, according to authorities, by a man she loved and trusted. Everyday in America, thousands of women are slapped, beaten, or threatened by the so-called love of their lives.

A Call for Help- New York, New York
A New York operator received a call from a woman desperately trying to get help. The frantic 911 call sent several officers to the scene. Unfortunately, when the police arrived twelve minutes later, the twenty-three year old female was found dead.

Interview on the Cycle of Violence, - Sarasota, Fl.
Sarasota Detective Charlie Vauss spent hours at County General Hospital, looking into the swollen eyes of a battered woman. He assured thirty-five year old Nancy Dean that help was there.

Nancy had married less than a year ago and had been beaten nearly twelve times since her nuptials. Early this morning her husband punched, choked and dragged her through their apartment. Nancy dialed 911 and fled the apartment in tears.

"Thank you, thank you, for lending your ear to me," she told Detective Vauss as he listened to her story.

She asked to keep a photo of her battered and bruised face. She wanted to look at it, to remember. "It'll keep me from softening up," she said.

"That's when I knew she'd change her mind," recalls officer Vauss.

Four days later, the woman stood on the steps of the county courthouse screaming at Detective Vauss. "Stay outta my life," he recalls her saying.

"Once you understand the cycle of violence, you won't be frustrated. This happens," Vauss said. "She really wants to believe things will change. But it probably won't. A man who beats a woman once will do it again and again. Study after study shows, it worsen each time."

Carlie breathed deeply. It was as if she looked at a mirror image of her own life. This is how she'd probably end up if she continued to deal with Devon. *Grandma Jean saw it all along*, she thought. Carlie sat in a daze. She then thought about the crinkled handwritten letter that her grandmother had written. Carlie began to read silently:

Carlie,

When you get this letter, I hope it finds you in good health. Let me start by saying how much I love you and what a blessing you've been to the Stewart family. Over the years I've watched you grow into a beautiful young woman. I try my best to stay out your business. But I can't stand by and watch Devon kill you slowly.

You don't know this, but I was abused too when I was young. It ain't fun either. Sometimes abused woman go the hospital, sometimes they go into hiding, and sometimes they die.

Carlie, don't make me go after Devon. 'Cause I'll whip him like he stole something. Leave him before it's too late.

Love,

Grandma Jean

Carlie smiled. She folded the letter and newspaper clippings with care, placing them neatly in the box. From the corner of her eye, she spotted her father strutting pass the limo. Carlie rushed to unlock her door, but opened it too late. The limo driver jumped out of the driver's seat and rushed to Carlie's aid.

"Thank you so much," Carlie said straightening the skirt to her black suit. She headed for the church at full speed. Carlie breathed when she reached the top of the stairs. She paused shortly before she flung the door open. Her heart came to a sudden stop as she began to have flashbacks. As soon as she entered, she saw Zarria walk away from the front of the church. Instantly, Carlie thought back to her dream. She remembered clearly seeing Zarria approach the casket. She watched her father crying and Angela standing proudly. It was just as she remembered.

Hearing the psalmist hit the first note sent pain surging through Carlie's veins. The church was immediately filled with the sound of grievers crying. Carlie walked straight down the center aisle. She felt the stares and heard the whispers. People were expecting her to fall out and do shows, but Carlie was on a mission to keep it cool. Besides, Grandma Jean was expecting her to be strong.

By the time she reached the front of the sanctuary, the casket was being closed. Reverend Sharps raised his hand requesting the attendants to stop as he laid eyes on Carlie. He nodded as she approached her grandmother. Carlie smiled as she ran her fingers over her grandmother's face. "You will truly be missed," she whispered. Within seconds, she had taken a seat directly next to her father.

Reverend Sharps began speaking at exactly 12:30. Carlie had prepared herself for the Eulogy and speeches about her grandmother. During the entire service she fought back the tears. Even with the whooping and hollering, she continued to stay strong. Near the end of the service Angela had passed her five tissues, all of which she never used.

Eventually the service was over and the family had begun

to exit. Carlie noticed a familiar face. She was pleased to see that Kirk had come to pay his respects. Kirk discreetly signaled for Carlie to follow him into the vestibule. She checked around her before moving. Carlie noticed her father standing slightly to her right enjoying the attention from both Courtney and Lisa Duckett. *How'd he pull that off,* she thought. She then checked over her left shoulder only to see her aunt watching her closely.

"You okay," Angela said pulling out a bottle of hand sanitizer.

"Yeah. I'll be right back."

"Where are you going?"

"To greet our guest," Carlie said backing away.

As Carlie got closer to Kirk, she was impressed with his attire. Well dressed in a custom made suit, he greeted Carlie with a hug. "You know I had to be here for you." Kirk smiled.

"Thanks. It means a lot," she said. "You look nice."

"You do to. How you holding up?"

"I'm okay." Carlie's cheeks reddened. She leaned close to whisper near his ear. "This is a bad time to tell you this, but the DEA agents have been asking about you." Carlie looked to make sure no one was near. "They're trying to get a search warrant for Devon's house. I'm not sure if they'll get it, but if there's anything in there to implicate you, then you're in trouble. They said they're gonna go after everybody in involved with Devon." Carlie had a worried look on her face.

"Oh, I'll be fine. I'm just worried about you," Kirk said. As he prepared to finish the conversation, he spotted Mike. "Carlie, who is he here with?"

Carlie followed Kirk's nod that led to Mike. "Oh, he's

here for me," she said.

Kirk's look showed disapproval. "Promise me you'll stay away from him."

Confused, Carlie waited before responding. "Yes," she finally said. "I promise." There was nothing else for her to say. She knew Kirk was going through emotional changes and didn't want to upset him.

Kirk watched Mike and Zarria squeeze their way through the crowd. He gave several fake smiles to members of the Stewart family as they passed. "I need you to call me tonight when you're by yourself," he said to Carlie. "I got a plan. It's important too. In the meantime, don't talk to anybody outside your family, somebody might be after you."

Kirk walked away before she had a chance to tell him that Ricky had straightened out everything. Before she knew it, Kirk had gone and Zarria and Mike were approaching.

"Was that Kirk?" Zarria asked with a stupid look spread over her face.

"Uh… Yeah," Carlie answered hesitantly.

"Ma, you cheating on me already," Mike said jokingly. He shook his head. "It's good to see you smiling."

"I'm trying," Carlie replied. "Are y'all coming to the repast?"

"Word, I thought you'd never ask."

Zarria stood in with her hands crossed over her chest. She had an attitude that shone brightly miles away.

"You okay?" Carlie asked headed toward her family?"

"Couldn't be better." Zarria lied. *I've been calling that damn Kirk for days. Something is not right. And I get the feeling that I'm the only one who doesn't know what it is,* she thought.

Chapter 27

Stranger in My House

Ricky frowned with disapproval when he saw Carlie combing her hair into place. He watched her head to answer the front door as she fixed her clothes and made sure she looked her best. He and his daughter had only been back in the comfort of their home for five days since Ricky's shooting spree had ended. He finally felt comfortable knowing that all of Devon's goons were either locked up or dead. Staying with Angela had been all right, but they were both glad to be back home.

Ricky kicked his frown up a notch when Mike stepped into the foyer. He couldn't accept the fact that Carlie was having male company, but admired Mike's crisp attire. *That was the way a young man should dress when showing up at his door*, he thought. Carlie shot her father a pitiful look as she introduced her guest. She hoped he wouldn't show off too bad. "Dad, you remember my friend Mike don't you?"

"Yeah, I remember him," he said. "I'm just not sure if we can call him a friend yet." With a toothpick straddled between his two front teeth, Ricky turned to walk away. "I'll be in my office if you need me."

Carlie tried to laugh off her father's comments. She hated the tone he used in front of Mike. It was down right embarrassing. But it wasn't the right time to start an argument. "He's still a little antsy," Carlie said to Mike.

It nearly killed Mike to muster up a fake smile. He didn't appreciate being treated like an intruder. *If I never see Mr. Stewart another day in my fuckin' life, it wouldn't make a difference, word* he thought. Carlie and Mike headed toward the great room.

As Mike followed, he watched her ass move like a 3-D movie in slow motion. The bulge that appeared in his pants moments ago hardened. Mid-way to the couch he grabbed Carlie before they had a chance to even sit down. He pulled her close and tight. Unfortunately for him, she yanked away from his embrace.

"Have a seat," Carlie offered feeling a bit uncomfortable.

"I was only trying to make you feel better," he said. Mike licked his full lips.

Carlie didn't know how to respond. Strangely, she wasn't attracted to Mike at the moment. She remembered being excited about his muscular build when she first laid eyes on him. But for some reason, he didn't have Devon's masculine ways, which had always turned her on instantly. The smell of his cologne was even starting to be a turn-off. Carlie moved away reaching for the remote as Mike moved closer. Quickly, she flipped through channels ignoring Mike in the process.

"Ma, if I didn't know better, I'd say you're running from me."

"No, really I'm not." Carlie shook her head several times. "I'm just not ready to be all lovey dovey."

"Word, I'm not sure what kind of relationship you had in the past, but I like to be affectionate with my women," Mike said with confidence.

"But that's just it," Carlie said softly. "I'm not your woman."

"Not yet, Ma," Mike said with a grin.

Carlie was somewhat relieved when she turned to *Making the Band*. She hoped that Mike's mind would be focused on the show. He had mentioned to her on several occasions that he never missed an episode. Within seconds Mike had sunk his body deep into the couch and appeared to be quite comfortable. Carlie's mind eased way too soon. She was shocked, when out of the blue Mike leaned closer and shot her a seductive look.

I'm not sure this was a good idea, Carlie thought. Even though she grew more and more bored by the day, Mike wasn't the right replacement for Devon. She was used to fine dining and shopping sprees. Not somebody who had an agenda to get into her panties. *I guess he does provide some company. Even if I have to fight him off of me.*

When Mike touched Carlie's hand gently, it caused her to wrap up her thoughts quickly. He was ready. "Don't run from me Carlie. I won't hurt you," he said in his sexiest voice.

Carlie grew more nervous. "Mike, I'm not ready. ..."

Before she knew it, his tongue was half-way down her throat. Carlie refrained from returning the kiss. Suddenly, Mike lifted his leg in an attempt to straddle Carlie. But as soon as she felt his hand palm her tits, she pushed him away. Carlie stood up and straightened her shirt.

"Mike, don't think I'm that green. I'm not some little freak!" She rolled her eyes and turned away. Bending down below the entertainment console she opened the door to Ricky's stash of alcohol. Shuffling through the Remy VSOP, Belvedere and Grand Mariner, Carlie spotted her favorite drink hidden in the rear. By the time she reached to the back and stood holding the bottle of Boones tightly, Mike looked her dead in the face.

He held her hand tightly. This time it wasn't a sex driven hold, it was a firm, controlling grip. "Ma, whatever your problems are, you can't erase them by drinking. Let me handle all of your problems," he said throwing the bottle into the trash. "You need to get your mind off the negative things in your life and focus on the positive, like going to school." He paused. "You are finishing?" He smiled.

Carlie's whole demeanor changed. She liked the way he had taken charge. There was something sexy about it. "Yeah, I'm finishing," she said wearing a grin that said *thanks for caring.*

"Let's go out for a while. Maybe grab something to eat."

"Umm… I've gotta tell my Dad. He hasn't been too happy about me leaving the house since all of the extra drama in my life has happened.

"Tell him you'll be with me. I give my word, nothing will happen to you, Ma." He winked assuring Carlie she'd be safe.

Mike licked his lips as she jetted out of the room. Within seconds he could hear the shouting match between Carlie and her father. All hopes of he and his *lady to be* leaving together were being washed away as he listened.

"Dad, I'm twenty-two."

"And I'm forty, damn it," he said. "You don't even know this guy."

"I do," Carlie shouted.

"How did you meet him?" Ricky asked suspiciously.

"Tamia met him at a club and they became good friends. Then, he came to my party. That's where I personally met him. So if he's cool with Tamia then he's cool with me."

"Carlie, if you had a brain you'd be dangerous. Tamia meeting him in the streets means you don't really know him. You're not going with him and I don't wanna see him over my house when I'm not home."

"Oh, so now I'm being treated like a teenager."

"You're acting like one," he shouted. "My word is final," he yelled as Carlie turned to walk away. Ricky continued shouting making sure she could still hear him. "You always seem to find a way to fuck our lives up. What will be next?" he said slamming the door to his office.

Mike gave Carlie a standing ovation as soon as she entered the room. His extended clapping act assured Carlie that he wasn't upset like she thought he'd be. Mike held his arms out for a hug. Surprisingly, Carlie dove in.

"I guess you won't need these," Mike said referring to the keys Carlie held in her hand. "Why do you have so many keys on one ring?" He waited for an answer.

"Umm...," "Carlie hesitated. She didn't think he really wanted the run down, until she noticed that he was concerned.

"Well, these are for my house, these are for Tamia's place, this one is for my old apartment, and...."

"So which one is for Devon's place?" Mike saw the anger building in Carlie, so he switched gears right away. "Does your father allow you to go places with other guys?"

"In case you haven't noticed, I'm not a little girl." Carlie posted her hands along side her hips. "He doesn't normally have control over where I go. He's just a little uneasy right now," Carlie smirked. "Trust me, I'm not always on lock-down."

"Word, I don't know what normally happens around here, but the sergeant ain't having it."

They both laughed walking towards the door. Carlie couldn't believe she'd spend another night cooped up in the house with Ricky. She was beginning to feel like a prisoner once again. When the door shut behind Mike, she thought about sneaking out anyway. Then her thoughts switched to Devon. *On second thought, I'll stay in.*

Before Carlie could make it to the top of the stairs the doorbell rang. She skipped one by one hoping it would be for her. Ricky cut her off after Carlie reached the bottom step. He looked through the side window and swung the door open.

"Hello Carlie," Lisa Duckett said as she entered.

"Hello, Ms. Duckett."

"Carlie, call me Lisa. Consider me a friend and soon a colleague."

Ricky held his hand out for Lisa to follow him into his office. Carlie missed her chance to find out what her comment was all about. Curious, Carlie listened outside the door. A Phd in mumbling was needed to decipher what the legal duo was up to. Carlie was well aware of Ricky and Courtney's sexscapades. She hoped that Lisa wasn't there for the same reason. Through the distorted chit chat, Carlie heard the name Devon. Her eyes opened widely. As soon as Carlie heard footsteps approaching the door, she darted up the stairs.

Chapter 28

Pay Back is a Bitch

Kirk walked backwards trying to keep the strong winds from hitting him in the face. Slowing his pace every now and then, he checked for any movement in the neighborhood. He had thought about hiring a look-out, but figured at three in the morning there would be no need. Although the urban neighborhood swarmed with people into the late evening, there was generally no one to be found after midnight.

Kirk allowed his hand to run across the top of his head. He played the plan he'd mapped out over and over again in his head. Even though his set up was concrete, he had started to become jittery. A pair of headlights between the fog caught his attention. In an instant he darted behind a brown Seville to watch the passing car carefully.

When the car stopped on the opposite side of the street, Kirk moved in for a closer look. Within seconds, the humming sound of the engine had stopped and the driver emerged carrying an oversized lavender duffel bag. Wearing his game face, Kirk rushed the driver.

"Boy, you scared me," Carlie whispered.

"What took you so long? You're fifteen minutes late," Kirk said slightly blushing. He removed the hoodie from his head and grabbed the duffel bag from Carlie.

"I'm nervous," Carlie said. On one hand she hoped that Kirk would feel sorry for her and offer to get back in their cars to leave. On the other hand, she wanted to stay.

Kirk tugged on Carlie's black baseball cap. "It's gonna be okay. Let's go."

As Carlie and Kirk climbed the stairs to Devon's apartment the wind blew harder. She wondered about what she was walking into. Carlie fumbled with the keys as an uneasy feeling continued to tingle through her body. Before sticking the key in the lock, she looked back over her shoulder.

"It's okay," Kirk whispered shaking his arms and fist speedily. He bounced around in the cool air like a boxer in training. In his mind, he had pumped himself up for what he had to do, or any drama he was faced to deal with. His intent was to feel no guilt and no shame.

When the sound of the last lock popped, Carlie's skin shivered. Once inside she stood by the doorway as if it were her first time in Devon's place. She felt her temperature rising, but refused to move.

Carlie looked around remembering the last time she was in the junky apartment. Clothes were scattered about giving the impression that Devon had run out in a hurry the last time he left home.

Carlie's eye's widened when Kirk approached her unzipping his jacket. "We're not staying," Carlie whispered. She looked back at the front door.

"Carlie, calm down. I'm just hot. Do you trust me?" he asked with a sincere look.

"It's not about trust. It's about whether or not we get caught."

Kirk shook his head. "First of all you don't have to whisper. Nobody can hear us. Secondly, if someone comes up in here, I've got my friend right here." Kirk raised his shirt to show off his 44 magnum. "Now, lets get busy."

Carlie eased up a bit. She thought about the gun and the two packages that peeked from Kirk's waist. As she followed him through the living room into the bedroom she had flashbacks of the good memories she and Devon shared. Walking down the dark hallway Carlie flipped the light switch on. Kirk quickly turned it off. "Remember the plan," Kirk said. He hoped Carlie wouldn't make too many mistakes. The team had to make sure all of the lights stayed off near the windows. Once in Devon's bedroom, Kirk kneeled to move the bags of new clothing from on top of the safe. He looked at Carlie, then back at the safe.

Carlie got down on her knees and squinted at the combination dial. She sat anxious as several numbers rolled around in her head. She had without a doubt remembered the correct combination days ago when she and Kirk concocted their plan. Kirk was shocked that Devon had even given Carlie the combination. But when he thought about Devon trying to make up for all of the beat downs, it made sense.

"You okay?" Kirk asked.

"I'm fine."

Kirk removed the two packages from his waist. While he searched for a good place to plant the drugs, Carlie turned the combination lock from right-to-left carefully. On her third turn, the clicking sound surprised them both. Carlie had done it.

"Grab the bag," Kirk said raising his voice.

Carlie turned slowly to watch him lift the front of the mattress with one hand. Using a handkerchief he placed the packages under the mattress. "Are we taking the loot or leaving it here?" he asked sarcastically.

Carlie snapped from her daze, crawled a few inches, and grabbed the duffel bag. When she opened the small door to the safe widely, the sight of the bundled bills made her smile inside.

"You're moving way too slow," Kirk said kneeling beside her. He pushed his hand toward the back of the safe and slid the money off the first shelf into the bag. When a stack of bills fell on Carlie's knee, she stared instead of throwing the bundle in the bag. Kirk knew he had to take over. "You still wanna go through with this, right?"

"Of course."

Kirk leaned toward Carlie with his lips ready for attack. Carlie turned away.

"It's okay," Kirk said. "I understand." Quickly he refocused on the plan. Kirk moved faster than ever. Grabbing armfuls of money at a time, he slid the bundles into the bag. Within minutes he had loaded the bag with nearly $400,000. When he raised to his feet, Carlie noticed him pushing something into his pocket. She wanted to trust Kirk, but knew no one could be trusted fully.

Kirk grabbed Carlie by the hand and led her out of the room. She moved slowly looking for anything that belonged to her. Reaching the front door, he pushed Carlie's hat lower on her head and pulled the hoodie over his. Together they crept back to Angela's car and pulled gradually out of the parking space.

"My car is 'bout three miles from here," Kirk said.

"How did you get here?" she asked driving at a snails pace.

"I walked."

"You're crazy," Carlie said.

"No, I'm crazy about you." Kirk's disposition changed. He stared at Carlie to see how she was handling what he'd just said. After noticing the blank look on her face, Kirk rubbed her left shoulder.

"Kirk, what are you doing?" Carlie asked.

"No need to get bent out of shape. I just thought I'd let you know how a brotha feel about you. I've always wanted the best for you. And that definitely ain't Devon."

Carlie's heart warmed. His touch sent chills down her spine. She kept her eyes on the road, but her heart was stuck on Kirk. She felt like dirt. *Was she catching feelings for Devon's boy? Would Grandma Jean consider that respectable?*

"Pull right here." Kirk pointed to a grey Chevy. Carlie breathed heavily feeling his stare. "Listen, I know this is strange, but it's real. Besides, I'm leaving town in a few weeks."

"Leaving. Going where?" Carlie asked.

"I'm not really sure yet. But you're definitely invited."

"Invited?"

"Bet. Just the two of us."

"I can't go," she said with frown. My father busted his ass to get my school to agree to our deal. All I have to do is make up my old work. And complete the rest of my classes online to graduate."

"Well come with me," Kirk smiled. "I'll buy you a computer." He shot Carlie a sad puppy dog look. "You can get the latest and the best money can buy."

"It's not that simple. I still have to go in from time to time and meet with my instructors." At that moment Carlie noticed the flawlessness in Kirk's skin. He wasn't as dark as she preferred; but the attraction was definitely there. She couldn't believe she was falling for Kirk. Whore's *burn in hell, grandma would say. Besides, Kirk may have been working towards being a retired thug, but could he really change?*

"Think about it," Kirk said leaning to kiss Carlie on the cheek. "Get up with me when you can." He rubbed his finger gently across the scar on her face before opening the door.

Carlie looked downward embarrassed by her war mark. "I'm marked for life, huh."

"You're still beautiful to me." He smiled. "I'm out, I'll check on you later."

"Wait," Carlie yelled. "Aren't you gonna take your half of the money?"

"Naw, you deserve it all. I've got what I need."

"No, you take it. I don't want it."

Kirk leaned in through the window. "Carlie, I wouldn't feel right taking from Devon. He's been fucked up toward you, but he hasn't done enough to me to justify robbing him." He watched for Carlie's reaction. He could tell she still didn't feel right about it. "I did this because he owes *you.* You know, for pain and suffering." Kirk smiled.

"I tell you what," she said. You keep it for now and I'll make arrangements to get the money from you later. You know my dad is a private investigator." Carlie joked about her father, but it was clear that if she walked in the house with a duffel bag, Ricky's senses would smell trouble.

Kirk reached into the car and grabbed the bag. "Stay up

and stay sweet." He walked toward his car. "Call me if you need me," he said sincerely. "Scream, if you want me." Kirk smiled and started his engine. As Carlie pulled off he followed her home safely.

Bruised

Chapter 29

Back Stabber

The rookie officer walked back and forth studying Devon while he slept. The tall pale guard with an enormous stomach and whiskers growing in place of a mustache would have been a good joke to Devon if he'd been awake. Instead, Devon lay tossing and turning obviously in the middle of a nightmare. Officer Berkley was already upset that he had to enter D block at 5 a.m. to check on the strange mumbles coming from his cell.

Berkley tapped on the iron gate lightly. "Wake up," he ordered.

Devon's breathing deepened. "No...No...," he yelled raising his voice.

"Hey, shut the fuck up!" Berkley paced back and forth. He knew he would eventually have to go in. *Just my luck,* he thought. *My shift is almost over and now I've got to listen to fuckin' Sleeping Beauty.* Berkley contemplated on getting another officer to assist him in whipping Devon's ass. *That'll wake him up,* he thought. Then, he decided to monitor Devon for a few minutes hoping he'd stop.

Meanwhile, Devon's moans grew stronger. "Run," he yelled. His mind focused on the loud footsteps coming his way. "It's six o'clock," he shouted to his sister. Her pig tails bounced as she ran to sit on the area rug.

"Daddy's coming Devon. Come on, I'm scared," she whined.

"I'll protect you," Devon said clearly. "He's a drunk."

"Are you up boy," Berkley yelled.

Devon spoke clearly as if he were carrying on a normal conversation. His hands were stationed in between his legs while his neck continued to twitch. The wild sleeping positions had caused the fitted sheet to come from under the mattress. Saliva dripped from his mouth slowly onto the bed.

Devon cried out. The first sign of sweat began to bead up on his forehead. 'Get off of her,' he wanted to yell, but nothing came out. When the first hit knocked his mother to the ground, tears welled in his eyes. He immediately ran toward the kitchen. He could hear his sister's voice crying behind him. "Don't leave me," she yelled.

By the time Devon grabbed the knife his father had kneeled before his mother's face. "I run this house damn it. Ain't no woman gonna ever disrespect me," Darnell McNeil shouted.

Devon now lay in a puddle of sweat. He raised his hand reaching for the knife that didn't exist. He knew he had to kill his father before he killed them. From the corner of his eye he watched his sister run towards him. With the strongest power a twelve year old could possess, Devon aimed nervously. Unaware that his sister had slipped through the space between his parents, he closed his eyes. He forced the knife deeply into what he thought was his father's back. When

Devon realized what he had done, his eyes stuck like glue on the knife lodged in his sister's back. Devon yelled out, while waking several inmates on his block.

Berkley decided not to wait for back-up. He had already made a mistake in letting it go this far. Before he could open the cell, Devon was hanging off the side of the bed crying. "I killed my baby sister," he hollered. She was tryna hug my momma."

Berkley developed a soft spot for Devon. He wasn't sure if it was still a dream or if he'd really killed his sister. By the time he entered the cell, Devon was making sense of what just happened. Berkley hated to see grown men shed tears. "Boy did you just confess to killing somebody?"

Although Devon wasn't completely focused, he was sharp enough not to confess to killing anyone. "It was a nightmare asshole," he said sarcastically.

Berkley wasted no time. He struggled to grab Devon as he pushed him against the wall. Realizing Devon's strength he slowed his moves a bit. "I've already wasted thirty minutes listening to your bullshit. Now, I'm ready to go the fuck home and I don't have time for your shit." Berkley breathed slowly. He didn't know if Devon would try to retaliate once he let him loose. "Do we understand each other?" he asked checking the opening to the cell.

"Man, I'm stressed out," Devon complained. He hated submitting to a white man, but he needed some assistance. Devon's conniving mind worked overtime. He had to think quick before other officers showed up on the block.

"I need a favor," Devon blurted out.

"What kinda favor?" Berkley asked with a crinkled brow.

"It's simple. You down?" Devon asked sitting on the bed.

Berkley stood nervously as he watched the entrance to the cell. He knew the favor came with a hefty payment. The idea of money was right on time, considering Berkley's measly salary. He was willing to help Devon depending on the severity of the wrong doing. Berkley knew it would be something illegal because Devon had only been in the possession of the Feds for a week, and was already a known trouble maker.

Devon quickly lifted his mattress in the air and pulled two C- notes from the hole he'd cut in his mattress. "I'm sure this will do," he said arrogantly. Devon waited patiently for Berkley to grab the two hundred dollar bills.

Berkley hesitated. As a neo to the game, he worried about accepting the money. Before he could finish thinking about the extra gas he could put in his ride, and the meals he could buy his lady friend, Devon had smashed the money into his chest.

"This is what I need," Devon said pounding his right fist into his other hand. "Get me a cell phone, fast!" Devon watched Berkley looking dumbfounded. He wondered if he had gotten the right guard. But at this point, he'd have to do. "And a nigga needs some supplies. I'll give you a list tomorrow. You aiight, dog," he asked.

Berkley nodded. "I'm cool."

"Bet, now work on that phone before daybreak," he ordered.

Berkley left the cell feeling like he just got pimped. He could tell Devon was a regular in the penal system. He could also, bet there would be trouble down the road in dealing with him. What he didn't know was where he'd get a cell phone from at 5:30 a.m., unless he used his own.

***

"Carlie," Devon yelled into Berkley's Nextel. "Did you come to your senses yet?" Devon paused while he waited for a response. "Do you hear me?" He looked at Berkley pretending there was wasn't a dial tone singing in his ear. "I'll call you later, baby." Devon hung up.

Berkley folded his arms outside the cell. He walked up and down the corridor acting as if he were monitoring the floor. "Hurry it up," he said slyly walking pass.

"Nigga, you owe me a refund then," Devon shot back in between phone calls.

Berkley frowned at the thought of being called a nigga. He twisted his lips and mumbled under his breath. "Cock sucker."

"Yo Zarria," Devon said into the receiver. Get yo ass up. We got work to do." Devon paced the floor listening to Zarria complain about the time of morning. "If you wasn't hanging out being a tramp all night you wouldn't be tired."

"Devon, I don't know who in the hell you think I am, but you forgot you need me." Zarria spoke like she had a cold. In between yarns she continued. "You want me to be at yo beck and call, but yo ass is broke. I haven't gotten paid one red cent," she yelled.

"Where the hell is Kirk?" Devon barked. "And where is my money from the shit he sold?"

Zarria's voice got louder as she talked. "I have been callin' that damn Kirk for days. He hasn't returned any of my calls. I thought the Feds had gotten him too, until I saw him at Carlie's grandmother's funeral."

At first there was no reaction from Devon. He held the phone like a zombie. "Kirk was where?" he asked.

"Duh…, at Carlie's grandmother's funeral," Zarria

repeated one word at a time.

"That nigga tryin' to get wit' my girl?"

"Look, I don't even care if he is," she said.

Zarria and Berkley were both growing impatient with Devon. Even though he was supposedly the money man, his financial future didn't look too good. "Two minutes," Berkley said, growing more irritated.

Devon shot him a look that said, *I'll shank you right here.* "Listen to me Zarria," he said as if he were instructing a toddler. "I want you to get in touch with Rico. Call Big Frank. ..."

Zarria breathed sarcastically. "I don't think that would be a good idea. The word is Rico ain't too happy about you right now. He wants his money," she ended with a slight attitude.

"Kirk never gave him any money?" Devon asked.

"Are you getting any of this?"

"Bitch, just answer the damn question," he shouted.

Zarria smacked her lips. "Le'me give you a quick recap. Kirk is ducking me, Carlie hates you, Ray-Ray is dead, and Rico wants his loot!" *It feels good telling Devon off. Thank God he's locked up*, she thought.

Devon banged his left hand against the hard wall as held the phone tightly with the other. With his head held low, he counted. He refused to shed a tear for Ray. "A weak soldier," he said to himself. Devon regrouped quickly. "This is the plan," he instructed. "Hire a locksmith and go to my house." He turned to check Berkley, but he was nowhere in sight. "See if the locksmith can crack the combination to my safe or get it open somehow. ... I don't give a fuck how you do it. Get it done!"

"Oh, you can't be serious," Zarria complained.

"Bitch, there's $400,000 dollars in there. Your broke ass

shouldn't complain."

Zarria's temperament changed instantly. "Now, who should I call?" she asked.

"Figure it out," Devon said in a nasty tone. Berkley was back in view. "Give $100,000 to Rico. Tell him I'll catch up as soon as I get out. It shouldn't be too much longer."

"Got it," Zarria said behaving like she was preparing for a 007 job.

"Oh, one last thing. Tell my secret weapon, to get ready and teach my girl a lesson. She'll come running back after this." Devon grinned wickedly as he handed Berkley his cell.

Berkley gave Devon a shyster's look as he reached for the phone. He nodded, "Keep this between us."

"No doubt," Devon said waiting for Berkley to return the pound.

As soon as Berkley's fist touched Devon's he felt what he assumed was paper on his skin. "Thanks," he said noticing the balled up hundred dollar bill. Berkley walked away with a smile.

Bruised

Chapter 30

A Nice Suprise

The plastic Glock had been concealed in Mike's glove compartment all day. Knowing that he was picking up Carlie at 2:00 p.m., he was prepared for drama. He was especially flattered when Ricky agreed to let him to drive Carlie back to her school. Carlie had already missed six weeks and arranged to return the first week in November.

Mike appeared to be happy about Carlie going back to school, but was even happier when she said he could spend the night. He had played the entire trip in his head over and over again. What he didn't think about was how to handle Tamia. She was cool, but Mike could sense that lately she wasn't really feeling he and Carlie together. When Mike first met Tamia, he had intentions on dating her, until he spotted Carlie at the party.

Mike's mind swarmed with *what if ideas* as he hurried down Route 301. With his brand new diamond Cartier watch, he checked the time. Being late was a sure way to piss Ricky off. He wanted to make sure nothing came up that would make him change his mind. *Mike had a plan.*

Once on Yorkshore Drive, Mike slowed the pace of his gold Yukon. He spotted Ms. Ellis checking his tag number as she watered the flowers in her front yard. Mike shook his head. He hated meddling neighbors. Before he could pull into the driveway, the screen door flew open and Ricky headed his way. He walked like a gang of soldiers in the army, except he was alone.

"This car isn't stolen is it?" Ricky questioned.

"No Sir," Mike responded quickly.

"Is it registered to you?"

"Yes Sir." Mike began to worry. *This is worse than dealing with the police*, he thought. He was starting to question whether or not Carlie was worth it.

When Carlie appeared from behind the door, Mike threw away his indecisive feelings. Her hair was pulled back into a wavy shoulder length ponytail. Dressed casually in a Roca Wear sweatsuit she waved like a school girl in Mike's direction. He all but drooled as he looked her up and down. At the same time Ricky had dissected his entire look. Ricky had always approved of Mike's attire and today was no exception. Sporting his gator boots, his long sleeve oxford lay tucked neatly in his pants. Although Mike always dressed like a respectable young man, Ricky still had his doubts.

Mike smiled like a forged signature when Carlie kissed her father on the cheek. "You got everything," Mike asked pretending to be extra concerned in front of Ricky. "What about your zillion keys?" he joked.

"I got everything." She smiled.

Carlie didn't lift a hand. Both men raced to load her five heavy bags into the trunk. As soon as Ricky finished stuffing blankets and a new dish set into the last empty space he could find, the truck pulled away. Ricky waved goodbye and so did Ms. Ellis. Carlie laughed at her neighbor as they turned the corner.

"It's good to see you laughing, Ma."

"Yeah, I'm glad," she said.

Mike pulled over into an apartment complex just past Bowie Town Center. The parking lot was full for a Monday afternoon. When he reached toward the back seat, Carlie checked her surroundings. "Who lives here?" she asked.

"Nobody. This is for you, Ma," he said pulling a three by six box from behind the seat.

Carlie's heart throbbed. "What is it?" *Now this is my idea of trying to get my attention,* she thought. *I'm not into receiving passion marks on my neck like Mike wants to give. I'm into receiving gifts.*

Mike held the box firmly on top of the middle console while Carlie untied the platinum colored bow. As soon as she opened the box, Mike anxiously pulled the coat from underneath the tissue paper. He held the three quarter length faux fur coat mid-way in the air. Surprised, Carlie stared blankly.

"Do you like it?" Mike asked.

"I love it," Carlie said like it had killed her to say those three words. Deep inside she felt it was a cheap replica of what Devon would have given her. "You didn't have to do this," she added.

"No doubt, but I wanted to," Mike said pulling back onto the main road. He examined Carlie's entire body in between stop lights. He thought about how much he'd spent for the coat that he knew Carlie hated. It was a small price to pay compared to what he could get for her jewelry. Silently, he calculated. *Roughly $5,000 for the tennis bracelet, $3,000* *for the diamond studs sparkling in her ear, and my fur of course. The stash at Devon's place-priceless.*

Mike grinned. He was so caught up into scheming that at first he failed to notice Carlie watching him. In a split second he turned the volume up bobbing his head to the sounds of the Legendary Whispers. Carlie couldn't relate. Besides she didn't have time for music; she watched her strange chauffer like a hawk.

While Mike drove way below the speed limit, Carlie couldn't figure out which route he had decided to take back to school. They traveled westbound headed back into the city. She wanted to ask if they were making a stop, but decided against it. After twenty more minutes passed she became somewhat suspicious, but didn't want to appear paranoid.

After observing her awkward behavior, Mike turned the music down. "Carlie, you're a mystery," he said.

"And why is that," she replied.

Mike shrugged his shoulders. He had become edgy within the last five minutes. "I'm trying to understand how you could be sooooo in love with a dude like Devon, but run away from a man like me."

"I'm not running from you." Irritated, Carlie said, "I'm with you now."

"Word," Mike agreed. "But that's because Devon is locked up."

Carlie started to think. She hadn't told Mike that Devon was locked up. *Well, maybe Zarria told him at the funeral?* Carlie tried to relax her mind, but riding close to Devon's neighborhood set off an alarm.

"Where are we going?" she asked sitting up close to the dashboard.

"I've gotta stop and see a friend."

"Who?" Carlie asked pulling her purse close. She checked the passenger door. It was locked.

"We're going somewhere real familiar to you," he said changing his mannerism. The old Mike had disappeared. His chocolate colored hands hit the steering wheel hard. "You let Devon come to your school, treat you like trash, whip your ass, but I can't even get a little tongue," he said half laughing.

'What do you want from me?" Carlie asked in a more serious tone.

"Something sweet." He licked his lips toward Carlie. "And if that won't work, the money in Devon's crib will." Mike took both hands off the wheel and navigated with his knee as he turned into Devon's lot. "Word, he owes me, Ma," he said looking toward Carlie.

After circling the neighborhood several times, Mike pulledtoward the rear in a secluded area of the L shaped parking lot. The setting surrounding the parking space had been bare on several occasions. Besides the broken beer bottles and piles of trash, no action was near the rear of the development. With no other cars in sight, Mike opened the glove box revealing his Glock. He watched Carlie from the corner of his eye removing his piece slowly.

Carlie's eyes widened. "What do I have to do with this?"

"Everything," he replied. "If Devon can't pay, *you will.*"

Carlie's expression tightened. "How can I pay?"

"Perhaps, with your jewels," he said touching her ear. "Your body, or even your mouth."

Carlie was on the verge of throwing up. Just when she thought her life was getting back to normal, another knife was being jammed into her back. *Was she a glutton for pun-*

ishment? Carlie thought about falling apart. She even considered jumping out of the truck and making a run for it. But she knew her best bet would be to outsmart her kidnapper. Carlie turned toward Mike with confidence. "How about I pay you to let me go?"

"With what?" Mike asked with a frown.

"I've got some cash at home."

"Bet, that would be nice. But for now we're going inside for Devon's money." *And then you'll never see me again,* he thought.

"How are we gonna get in?" Carlie asked nervously.

"Bitch don't play games. You got the key," he said reaching for her purse. Mike dumped the contents of Carlie's purse into his lap. Grabbing her key ring, he explained the plan in detail.

Carlie watched the Glock that sat in between his legs. She kept her cool and wondered what Devon would do in her situation. When Mike touched her shoulder a chill darted through her skin. Carlie didn't move at all.

"Lets go," he said opening his door. Mike got out and bent down slightly to observe Carlie. As he waited for her to follow instructions, he tucked his piece in the side of his pants. "Yo, don't make me have to come around there to get you," he said turning to watch his back.

Mike's back stared Carlie in the face. She eyed the gun peeking from his side. Carlie was prepared to go to jail if needed. While Mike's attention was focused on concealing his pistol, Carlie made her move. Before Mike could finish removing his shirt completely from his pants, Carlie had jumped across the seat and grabbed the gun. Her hands trembled while her grip tightened. She leaned back resting her back on the passenger door pointing directly at Mike's head. *It's either him or me*, she thought.

Carlie was startled when she heard heavy footsteps running her way. She figured the neighborhood boys had finally figured out that something was going on in their hood. It didn't matter, she was all set to blow Mike's head off if necessary. With her adrenaline at its highest point, she scooted off the seat a bit for a better view.

"Put the gun down," Carlie heard a voice say from behind. While the voice seemed familiar, it was soothing as well. Carlie wanted to turn around, but didn't budge. *If it was 5.0, they'd have to take her to central cell,* she thought.

Carlie breathed a sigh of relief when she spotted Ricky from the corner of her eye. He moved like a cast member from the matrix in her direction. With his favorite friend in hand, the nine millimeter had Mike's forehead in perfect range. When Ricky's hand caressed Carlie's wrist, she nearly melted. "Let it go, Carlie. Let me handle this." Ricky never let Mike out of his sight.

Mike stood proudly as if he'd done nothing. What he didn't know was that it was possibly his last day on earth. When Ricky chose to kill, it was done. Sadly, for Mike he wasn't willing to let another man or woman jeopardize Carlie's safety.

Ricky's light whistle confused Mike. He thought about making a run for it, but knew it was risky. The second whistle confused him even more until Kirk walked from behind the building wearing a bullet proof vest. Ricky took two steps backwards handing Kirk Mike's piece. "Wipe Carlie's prints," he ordered.

Carlie was stunned. First her father, and now Kirk. She

felt as if she was the only one in the blind. Carlie watched Kirk go to work. He wiped the prints clean and opened the back door of Mike's truck.

Carlie's expression changed when she saw Kirk throwing two guns into the backseat. The second gun may have been a mystery to Carlie, but Kirk knew exactly what he was doing.

"You're not as sharp as you think," Ricky boasted to Mike. "It's no coincidence that we're here." He shook his head shamefully. "Wanna-be gangsters don't make it in life. Besides, I can always spot a liar."

"Carlie, come with me," Kirk whispered. Dumbfounded, Carlie looked to her father for approval. If Mike was after her, then no one could be trusted.

Ricky nodded. Hearing the sounds of sirens excited Ricky.

"It's almost over," he said to Mike. His gun was still pointed firmly at the target.

"Why don't we both roll out of here, before we're all locked up," Mike pleaded.

"Nobody is going to jail, but you."

Mike frowned in disbelief. He had no idea he'd just been set up by Kirk. By the time the police arrived on the scene, Ricky had lowered his gun and motioned for Carlie to come near. By now a crowd had assembled as Mike was being handcuffed.

"Who made the call?" a tall officer asked pulling out his pad.

"I did officer," Kirk said emerging from afar.

"We'll need you to come down and tell us what you told us on the 9-1-1 call."

"Sure thing," Kirk responded. He turned to give Ricky a pound before leaving.

Carlie slumped down in her seat the entire ride to the police station. She couldn't believe she had to be rescued again. And now her father and Kirk were some kind of strange duo. She pondered different scenarios while she watched the cars roll by her window. Carlie sat there not wanting to think at all.

What she didn't realize was that Kirk had contacted Ricky telling him that Mike was sent by Devon months ago. His initial job was to entice Carlie to see if she'd cheat. Later, Mike's intent changed after Devon was locked up. Luckily Kirk had been watching Carlie like a guardian angel the entire time.

Bruised

Chapter 31

Sleeping with a Snitch

Ricky's Jaguar arrived on Federal grounds close to 8:45 a.m. The legal team felt relieved after spending close to an hour trying to locate the facility. As they approached the gate, Ricky slowed the vehicle scrutinizing the shabby looking guard. Before rolling down his window, he grabbed his business card to hand to the guard. "Good Morning Sir," Ricky said in his most professional voice. "We're headed to the District Attorney's office."

"Where's your summons?" the sixty something year old man asked rudely.

"I don't have one."

"Then, how do I know you're supposed to be here?" he snapped. His actions showed that he'd been on the job too many years.

"How about calling Marsha Vick's office," Ricky said sternly. He slid his business card on top of the ashtray.

The pot belly guard shot Ricky a nasty look and closed the door to the small booth as if he were on some secret task. After waiting several minutes for *Otis the security guard* to make his phone calls, the gate opened. He never opened the door to say proceed or anything.

"Retirement can't come quick enough, huh buddy." Ricky yelled just loud enough for the guard to hear. He drove through the gate irritated at what had happened. "Already these people are pissing me off. This better turn out to be a good day," he said turning to Lisa.

"Keep your cool. And let me do the talking," she said. "I think that would be best at the moment, right Carlie?" Lisa turned toward the back seat to watch Carlie's reaction. She hoped the amusing comment would loosen her up a bit.

Carlie didn't answer. She sat in the back in a frozen like position. Her mind focused on the undercover cars and lawyers with overstuffed briefcases walking toward the entrance. The whole idea of turning against Devon didn't sit well with her. Although he'd whipped her on several occasions, demolished her car, and caused her to struggle during her last semester of school; he still didn't deserve what she was about to do. Carlie prayed about it the night before. She even remembered talking to Grandma Jean in her sleep. "Let that hooligan grow old in jail," Grandma whispered. "Tell him, don't drop the soap."

Carlie messed up when she allowed a slight smile to seep through her lips. Her intention was to play the pitiful role as long as possible. Headed toward the entrance she breathed a heavy sigh. "I guess this it," she said softly.

"That a girl," Lisa said. She grabbed Carlie by the shoulders and pulled her close. "You'll look back on all of this twenty years from now and laugh." Lisa put her briefcase on the belt and passed through the metal detector.

As Ricky watched Lisa grab hold of her luggage he couldn't help but to think about all she had done for his family. She worked diligently with the Pennsylvania law enforcement agencies to make sure that once Devon had satisfied his federal charges, he'd be extradited to stand trial in Pennsylvania. "Oh and he will serve time," Ricky remembered her saying. She had even persuaded the defense to suggest a plea with Devon on the charge: taking property without permission. Even the judge thought that was bogus, but Lisa pulled it off.

Yes, he did offer her a job making a hefty salary; but she'd gone above and beyond the call of duty. Surely there was something more he could do for her. Maybe offer her a higher salary or even a *ring. Mrs. Lisa Duckett Stewart,* he thought. He chuckled inside thinking about how Courtney would devote her life to making them both miserable.

"We have five minutes to get upstairs," Lisa said hurrying through the lobby.

Ricky and Carlie followed along like school children. Carlie wanted badly to turn and go home. Guilt had taken over her spirit within the last hour. Reaching the top of the stairwell, her eyes widened. Agent Williams' mole brought back memories of her last interrogation.

"Good morning," he said cheerfully reaching for Carlie's hand.

Ricky interceded. He extended his hand. "Good morning to you."

"I believe they're ready for us," he said. Williams held the door open and waited for Lisa, Ricky, and Carlie to walk in. "You know Ms. Vick is always prompt."

Ass kisser, Ricky thought. "Have a seat Carlie," he said after realizing all of the seats were taken.

The room was small, but crowded. Carlie's eyeballs circled the room. She read the huge bronze lettering on the wall, *The United States District Attorney's Office.* She asked herself, *"What have I gotten myself into?"* While she watched the expression of those sitting next to her, her thoughts raced. *Are they here for Devon too? Why do they have summons in their hands? Where is their legal team? Am I in jeopardy of going to jail?*

Carlie snapped from daydreaming just in time to see Ms. Vick, a middle-aged white woman, waving her toward the wooden double doors. Actually seeing Ms. Vick in person stamped fear in Carlie's heart instantly. Days ago, Ms. Vick had appeared on Channel 7 news after the trial of a man who had killed three innocent people during a high speed police chase. Not only did he go down on three counts of manslaughter, but she's still diligently seeking the death penalty. *Whoa,* Carlie thought. *This woman is a hard-hitter and takes no prisoners.*

Ms. Vick's hand waited patiently for a shake from Carlie. "Hello, I'm Marsha Vick," she said proudly. "Lets talk in my office." She pointed to a door off to the right where Agent Williams had just entered.

Ms. Vick's attitude wasn't half as bad as Carlie had imagined. Most had painted her to be a brutal, aggressive slayer. Outside of being one of the country's most highly regarded district attorneys, she seemed down to earth for the moment.

With the door closed to Ms. Vick's massive office, Carlie and Lisa sat while Ricky stood. Ricky studied the room admiring the degrees and awards that lined the wall. He was especially interested in the photo and newspaper article displaying the headline *KingPin History.* Ricky remembered a few years ago when Ms. Vick tried legendary drug dealer Chop Chop Hudley on KingPin charges. Not only did she send him up the river for life plus 30 years, but every member of his crew received twenty years or more. Ricky really felt his daughter was in good hands.

"Ms. Duckett and Mr. Stewart, while you are here as Carlie Stewart's legal defense, you will not be allowed inside the grand jury," Ms. Vick preached. "If Ms. Stewart needs to leave the room to consult with you at any time, she has that right." Ms. Vick pulled Devon's files close. "This is not a case against her. We are simply trying to build the best case we can against Devon McNeil."

"We are clear on that," Lisa answered professionally.

Ms. Vick looked at Carlie ready for business. "All right Ms. Stewart, I'll make this short and sweet. Today the grand jury meets on the first floor for Devon McNeil's case. The purpose of the grand jury is to see if we have enough evidence to indict Mr. McNeil on several drug related counts. Agent Williams has already told me a little about what you know, or have seen first hand." Ms. Vick looked down and shuffled through a few papers, then raised her head. "The key is to tell the truth on the stand and don't purge yourself. Do we understand each other?"

Carlie nodded.

"Do we understand each other?" Ms. Vick asked again as if Carlie's nod wasn't good enough.

"Yes."

"Loosen up a bit. There's no need to worry," she said sharply. "I'll ask you a few questions about Devon, his lifestyle, and you of course."

"Me?" Carlie asked with her palm on her chest.

"Yes you. Now, my intention is not to file charges on you. However, you're not completely innocent in all of this." Ms.Vick looked at Carlie with a solid stare. "You did know he was a drug dealer, didn't you."

Carlie hesitated. She looked at Lisa, then toward Ricky. "Yes," she said softly.

"Well, it's time to pay the piper," Ms. Vick said standing. She handed agent Williams one stack of papers, while she carried the other. "Follow me," she said heading out of her office.

Within minutes, Carlie, Ricky, Lisa, Agent Williams and Ms. Vick stood outside the door to the grand jury. Ms. Vick walked in first to let them know Carlie was ready. When the door opened, Carlie attempted to get a sneak peak of the inside, but was unsuccessful. She bit her nails and prayed silently for guidance. "Okay, you're up," Ms. Vick said peeping around the door.

Carlie followed Ms. Vick as she was guided to her seat on the stand. Like a child at an amusement park, Carlie was amazed at the decor of the room. It resembled a normal courtroom, but fancier. After hearing the name grand jury she was expecting something different. Her brain worked overtime trying to count the number of jurors and do a quick zoom in on the judge. She was pleased to see an attractive female judge presiding. Carlie figured she was either in an abusive relationship now or had been at some point in her life. Sadly, Carlie thought that all women were subjected to a controlling man.

As she continued scanning, close to twenty jurors had been counted by the time Marsha Vick spoke. Carlie had so much on her mind that she missed the opening statement.

"This is Carlie Stewart in the case against Devon McNeil Jr.," Ms. Vick continued. After all of the introductions had been done the questioning began.

"Ms. Stewart, what is the relation between you and Mr. McNeil?"

"Boyfriend, girlfriend. I mean we used to be," Carlie said in embarrassment.

"Have you ever known Devon McNeil to have a job?" Ms. Vick asked with conviction.

Carlie hesitated. "No."

"Who purchased your 2005 Mercedes Benz?"

"Devon."

Ms. Vick checked her notes. " Have you ever seen him with a gun?"

"Ummmmm. Ummmmmm."

Ms. Vick gave Carlie the evil eye. "Have you ever seen Devon with a gun?"

"Yes," Carlie finally answered.

"I'm going to ask you about some of Devon's known drug associates. If you know them, or know that they solicited drugs then simply say yes," Ms. Vick instructed."

"Okay," Carlie answered.

"Rico Carerra."

"No."

"What about Big Frank?"

"No." Carlie couldn't understand why she felt so guilty. She really hadn't heard those names before.

The speed of Marsha Vick's questions grew faster and her voice hardened. "What about Kenneth Chavis?"

Carlie frowned. "No."

"So, are you telling me you never had dinner with

Kenneth Chavis, also known as Corrupt?"

Carlie tried to look cool. She knew the people on the jury were watching her every move. Up to this point, none of the jurors had spoken. Some made notes and others just stared. Suddenly Carlie burst into a loud coughing spell.

Ms. Vick grew impatient. "Would you like some water?" she asked unbothered by Carlie's more intense cough. "If not, I need to know if you remember meeting Corrupt."

"Yes I remember meeting him," Carlie said. "Uh... But I don't know. ..."

"Answer the questions with a yes or no answer!"

This woman has turned into a vicious snake, Carlie thought. *She was much nicer in her office. I guess this is what it takes to be a famed district attorney.* Carlie looked toward the door she had entered, with hope that someone would put an end to the interrogation. *Where is Lisa when I need her?* Carlie breathed slowly and turned toward the judge. She wanted to see if she had it in for her like Ms. Vick.

Judge Baker was the name displayed on the copper name plate. In the midst of all of the questioning, for the most part she paid Carlie no mind. Judge Baker was only interested in the facts.

"Have you ever heard Devon talk about murdering any-one?" Ms. Vick asked.

"No," Carlie answered in a frustrating tone.

"Did you ever ride with Devon during a drug transaction?" Ms. Vick crossed her arms and puckered her lips. Her stance said *if you lie you'll be in lockdown by noon.*

"I've waited in the car with Devon on several occasions. I don't know what he did once he got out of the car."

Ms. Vick walked closer to Carlie. "Now you consider

yourself a pretty smart woman don't you?"

Carlie felt like a crab in a pot waiting to be cooked. "I guess." She shrugged her shoulders.

"Now I find it hard to believe that you dated a guy for over three years, knew he didn't work, rode with him to inconspicuous places, and didn't know what was going on." Marsha Vick was now two inches from Carlie's face. She looked as if she were ready to draw blood. "Now we already know what you know. Remember Devon has been under investigation for quite some time and keep in mind you are under oath. "Do you believe Devon is a drug dealer and has sold drugs when you were around."

Carlie wasn't willing to commit perjury, or be locked up for conspiracy. She had heard stories about females who were charged for simply being present during drug deals. In addition, she had touched Devon's money several times in the past, and even put items in her name for him. Both Lisa and Ricky had pleaded with Carlie during their numerous pep talks to tell all that she knew. They assured her that she wouldn't be charged if she came clean.

"Yes, I think Devon is a drug dealer," she finally said. I've driven with him to a place called '*the hole*' on several occasions."

"Did you see him take anything inside?"
"Yes."
"Did he ever take unknown packages from his house?"
"Yes."
Ms. Vick smiled victoriously. "Have you ever seen him with large sums of money?"
"Yes." Carlie felt relieved.
"Did you ever purchase high dollar items in your name

for him?"

"Yes," she answered quickly.

"Ms. Stewart, considering you don't have a job and he doesn't either, would you consider the funds used for purchases, drug money?"

"Probably so."

"I have one last question." Ms. Vick walked toward her papers. She checked her list. "Do you know someone by the name Kirk?"

"Yes."

"Do you know him as an employee of Devon's?" Ms. Vick asked with a smirk.

"Uhhhhhh…, I think they were more like friends," she said hesitantly.

"He has been photographed with Devon on more than a few occasions. Do you think he has sold drugs too?"

Carlie thought about the penalties for lying on the stand. She thought about the times she and Kirk could have been photographed together. She even wondered if her phone was tapped at some point. After all, she had called Kirk several times over the last few days, but hadn't gotten an answer. Carlie knew all about loyalty and believed in it strongly. She just didn't know if her loyalty would take her down in the end.She looked at Ms. Vick out of the corner of her eye. Then she took a sneak peak at the jurors.

"I've had many conversations with Kirk," she finally said. Although he hung with Devon I'm almost positive he doesn't sell drugs because he never has any money," she ended.

"Ahh… ha," Ms. Vick said skeptically. She wanted Kirk's name to appear in the paper with the list of defendants who would be indicted along with Devon, but at the moment she was satisfied with the information Carlie had given. Besides, Lisa Duckett had already put in a good word for Kirk and Ms. Vick had already summoned residents of 'the hole', along with Junnie's brother. With all of the testimonies combined, Ms. Vick was sure she had enough evidence.

"Well, I'm finished," Ms. Vick said taking a deep breath. She turned to the jurors. "Do any of you have questions for Ms. Stewart?" Before giving them a chance to speak she added, "Most likely not since I've covered everything that's necessary."

Even if a juror wanted to raise a hand, it didn't take a rocket scientist to understand that she didn't need to hear anymore. It was now mid-morning and the torture was over. As Carlie was excused from the stand and the jurors took a short break, she noticed Ms. Vick calling agent Williams from the back of the room. She whispered just loud enough for Carlie to hear, "Prepare the search warrant request," she said to Williams. "Contact Judge Kenny," he'll be the best man for the job," she grinned devilishly.

Carlie bolted out of the courtroom just in time to see the next person waiting to be questioned. Big Frank stood with no shame next to his lawyer waiting to snitch on everyone he knew. He smiled slightly at Carlie. She continued to walk as she pulled out her cell phone. She thought, *who the hell is that big dude.* Carlie dialed Kirk's number. Again, no answer. At that point she decided he was probably pretending to care just to get Devon's money. Carlie knew she'd never see her half of the money, or Kirk again. Once more, someone came into her life, pretended to care, and left her *bruised.*

Chapter 32

Untouchable

Six months later Devon sat slumped in a courtroom chair awaiting his fate. He had been trying to find himself lately, and decided on a new look. He and his fellow inmates talked so much about black pride that he decided to dump the usual Michael Jordan look. With hopes of growing twists, his frizzy miniature bush made the prosecution frown on him even more.

The trial was over and today was the sentencing. Ironically, it was the same day as Carlie's college graduation. While Devon sat dumbfounded and looked as if he'd just robbed a convenience store hours away Carlie walked proudly across the stage to receive her degree. As she shook the President of Lincoln University's hand, she breathed a sigh of victory. A slight thought of Devon popped into her mind. *If only he had changed, he could've been here,* she thought.

In the courtroom, Devon sat thinking about Carlie as well. He wanted to be there for her. For some crazy reason, he thought he had earned the degree along with her. He considered the money, gifts, and financial supplements as an investment in her education. Although Devon hadn't talked to Carlie, he squirmed in his seat at the thought of another man sharing *this day* with *his woman.*

The judge presiding over Devon's case shook his head at his slouched position. Most could tell he felt no remorse for the crimes he'd committed. In fact, his attitude toward life hadn't changed at all; however, his lack of freedom was about to. Devon's plan on being released would come to a crashing end when the judge decided to read the sentencing.

For most, Devon's future was a no brainer. Many folks had turned against him. One by one, throughout the proceedings, seven people he knew looked him in the face, and testified against him. Luckily for Carlie, she never had to appear in front of Devon. Although she gave information and confirmed events, she missed being with Devon. Even the flashbacks of his mistreatment wasn't enough for her to want him jailed for life. Unfortunately for Devon, the testimonies of others, was more than enough for a conviction. Thanks to Marsha Vick, the trial had been moved up on the docket and all charges stuck like glue.

After Carlie's testimony during the grand jury, and the statements from others, a search warrant for Devon's place was granted. The two keys of cocaine found under the mattress didn't help his case at all. Besides, Devon's court appointed lawyer was no match for Ms. Vick.

At first, Devon figured he'd try a few pay-offs and have his folks handle any one who needed to be done. But it didn't take long for him to realize that nobody was left in his corner, nor did he have any money to pay for those kinds of services. Devon assumed that the money in his apartment had been taken by the police, and he took it as a temporary loss. But never in a million years did he think he'd do serious time.

When the judge cleared his throat, the chatter in the room ceased. "Devon McNeil, do you have anything to say before sentencing?" Judge Thomas asked.

Devon shrugged his shoulders and slouched deeper into the seat. He looked toward the incompetent lawyer on his right. He figured it would be a waste of time to seek advice. "Nah," he finally said. Devon had a blank look as he listened to Judge Thomas' words.

"Devon McNeil on the count of murder in the first degree you have been sentenced to thirty-seven years to life. On the count of drug conspiracy you have been sentenced to one life sentence."

Devon sat in disbelief with his head held low. For the first time in his life, he realized there was no such thing as being *untouchable*. If he had things his way, his lawyer would be in a choke hold position. Instead, Devon was handcuffed and sent back to prison.

Before long, he arrived back on cell block D. Devon had already made a name for himself over the past few months while awaiting trial. Even though he had nobody looking out for him on the streets, he owned the guards and inmates on his block. Devon figured it was his new life, and he had to make ends meet. He assumed Carlie would eventually come to her senses and stack his commissary with the finest things prison had to offer. In his opinion, that was the least she could do. Quite frankly, he was tired of relying on Zarria. He needed Carlie more than ever before, and would do anything in his power to get her back.

Devon tried to call Carlie on several occasions, but never

got an answer. Once he even left a message asking her to pay him a visit. He even threw in what he thought would be an enticement. "I got something for you," he remembered saying. But nothing seemed to work. Carlie never showed up.

Before long, Devon couldn't take it anymore. He contacted Berkley and arranged a call to Carlie. He was sick of thinking of her and needed to unload his frustration about his sentencing. When Carlie heard her cell ring, her face showed uncertainty at the unfamiliar number. She contemplated on not answering, but decided to pick up.

"Hello," she said into the phone.

Grinning he said "Hello."

Carlie's heart rate tripled. She hadn't heard Devon's voice in over eight months. The uneasiness she felt inside had her confused. Devon was like a magnet. Just hearing his voice brought back memories, *good and bad.* Even though Ricky warned her that it was too dangerous to ever talk to Devon again, fear never entered her mind. She knew Devon had no idea that she'd given up information that helped to indict him. Thank God, she never had to testify in front of him like some of the others. Devon had done some bad things to her in the past. But Carlie felt that no man deserved to do twenty seven years without the support of family and friends.

"Congratulations," Devon said cheerfully.

"Thanks," she responded dryly. Carlie got up from the table. Her family had all gathered at the Cheesecake Factory for her graduation celebration. As she walked toward the bathroom she checked her surroundings to make sure nobody had come behind her, especially Ricky.

"So we made it, huh?"

"We?" Carlie responded. "I'm the one who graduated." It

ceased to amaze her how he could turn his *sweet guy role* on and off. Carlie knew she was a fool for even being on the phone with him, but she couldn't resist.

"How was the graduation?"

Carlie hesitated when the bathroom door swung open. She peeped from the stall for a closer view. "It was fine," she stated after realizing it was no one from her party. Carlie remained jittery as she spoke. "I'm at a restaurant with my family, so we'll have to talk later."

"When?" he asked catching her off guard.

"I'm not sure."

"Carlie, I gotta tell you what happened in court. You know they tryna ruin a nigga's life. Come see me tomorrow."

"I don't. ..."

"Pleaseeeeeee," Devon interjected. "Baby, you my queen and you know I love you. You don't have to be wit' me, I just need you to hear a brotha out."

The words '*you my queen*' gave Carlie flashbacks from when she was in the hospital. Those were the exact words Devon had said when he wanted to make up. But just like the sun is sure to rise in the morning, Devon was sure to mess up again. Carlie was determined not to give him another chance. It was hard, but she decided to think with her mind and not her heart. She was a different woman now. A strong, black sistah with enough common sense to get off the phone.

"I gotta go," she said.

"Wait!" Carlie, you comin' tomorrow?" Devon put it on thick. "You know I love you. Don't you love me?" He was sure that if he had a few more minutes to work on her, she'd say it.

Carlie wanted to say it too. Her heart beat fast. She paced

the bathroom floor as she spoke into the phone. She hesitated, "I'll think about coming tomorrow, but not as your girlfriend. That part of our relationship is over."

As soon as Carlie hung up, she breathed like she'd over-
come a major task. When her cell phone rang again, she was
speechless. *He won't give up*, she thought. Carlie answered
with the intention of letting Devon know that she wasn't
going to say I love you too. She pumped herself before
answering, and armed her voice with major attitude.

"Hello," she barked. Shocked, Carlie snatched the phone
from her ear and checked the number. It said unknown, but
the voice was way too memorable.

"You're just like your damn father," Courtney shouted
into the phone. "Huh, and he says ya'll have nothing in
common." Loud sounds could be heard in Courtney's phone.
Carlie squirmed at the thought of Courtney following them
to the restaurant. "That's funny," she continued. "Two turn-
coats from the same family. How in the hell can you just forget about me?" she screamed.

"Huh?" Carlie asked.

"You couldn't invite me to your lil' graduation, but you
got that bitch Lisa there!"

"Courtney, that's between you and my father," Carlie said
calmly. She opened the bathroom door and checked the
restaurant carefully as she headed toward the table. Carlie
wondered how Courtney knew that Lisa was there.

"No!" Courtney screamed like a stubborn toddler. "It's
between all of us. We were supposed to be a family."

Carlie was taken aback. She never expected Courtney to
behave this way. As far as she knew, Ricky and Courtney
ended on a positive note. *This was right in line with fatal*

attraction, she thought.

"Courtney, I'll tell you what, let me have my dad call you," she said after reaching the table. Carlie wasn't about to let Ricky's old fling stress her out too. The men in her life had done enough already.

"Oh, don't bother," Courtney said in a treacherous tone. "You'll see me around." Click.

Bruised

Chapter 33

Caught Up

The next day, Zarria parked outside the federal facility for nearly three hours waiting for the signal. Officer Berkley rang her cell phone as soon as his people were in place. Zarria sprang from her car quickly realizing that visiting hours would be ending soon. As she switched across the parking lot, the cocaine packs in her vagina tingled.

Devon anxiously anticipated her visit. He spent the whole night thinking about his sentencing and his fate. He needed to make money fast! The word was out that Rico didn't accept losses. It didn't matter that Devon had gotten locked up, or that he didn't have anyone on the outside to handle his debt. He owed Rico, and the bill was expected to be paid.

Devon understood Rico's position. He respected the man and would have handled it the same way. It was all considered business, but the contract put on Devon's life had him stressed. Rico offered $10,000 for the man who could take Devon out. Death was the criteria for getting paid. The fee was nothing to a free man, but behind bars it was Hollywood money.

Zarria had more than a half ounce of cocaine stored in the tampon she wore. Along with the ounce stuffed in her rigged sanitary napkin, Devon stood to make over $5,000. Although not enough to cover Rico's bill, it could be added to the pot. Zarria had visited nearly twenty times over the last two months. Between Berkley and the other officers paid to help her get in, she had become a necessity to the operation.

While her pay wasn't even close to what she thought she'd get out of Devon, it was all she could look forward to. On average, he would slip her two hundred dollar bills on every visit. An extra hundred would be given if they were cleared for a blow-job. It didn't take Zarria long to realize she'd been spoon-fed bullshit all along. She often thought about reasons why she got herself involved with Devon. The word *greed* was a big part of the problem, but she never reaped the rewards. Zarria attempted to erase Carlie from her mind. But the memories stayed deep within. The two had not spoken since Mike's plot to rob Devon. Zarria knew that Carlie was on to her, and couldn't cope with facing her.

As Zarria approached the counter in the visiting center, she handed the male guard her license. Scrutinizing her picture, he looked at Zarria, then back at the photo. She breathed heavily. *Now, he's seen me a million fuckin' times*, she thought. Slowly, the guard handed her the I.D., and pointed to the gate. "Thanks," she said sarcastically.

"Sure thing," he said shaking his head at her skimpy attire.

Zarria rolled her eyes as she turned to see a familiar face. She felt right at home seeing the skinny, female white officer who had watched her back on many occasions. She knew with Devon's girl, Officer Lacey on the scene, today's visit would be a breeze. Zarria pranced toward the gate arrogantly and removed her shoes. When Officer Lacey waved her through the metal detector, she shot the other male guard on post a nasty look.

He stopped her with his wand as if there was a problem. "I didn't say go," he said pretending to be in charge.

"Do I go through?" Zarria asked looking toward Officer Lasey. She was almost positive everything was arranged as usual. *After all, that's what the bitch is paid for*, she thought.

Unknown to Zarria, a lot of information about Devon's drug activities in jail were revealed during his trial. Everyone was on edge and needed to take things slowly. Lacey waved her through once again. This time no one stopped her.

"Whew," Zarria sighed. "Now that's the kinda service we pay for," she boasted under her breath.

As she followed Officer Lacey down an unoccupied corridor, Zarria grinned at the royal treatment she was receiving. While others had to wait in line to visit in a crowded area, she was given a personal escort to a private room. When they stopped in front of a staff only restroom, Lacey nodded for Zarria to enter. "Make it snappy, Devon is waiting in a room next door."

Inside, Zarria quickly squatted and removed the tampon. Dollar signs flashed in her head as she dumped the contents into a bag given to her by Lacey. As she prepared to package the drugs the way Devon ordered, a loud thump knocked at the door. Zarria didn't answer. A knock wasn't part of the plan. Assuming that she was taking too long, she ripped the sanitary napkin from her panties in order to empty the remaining cocaine.

"Stay here, I've got an unexpected call," Officer Lacey whispered through the door.

"What the hell do you mean?"

"You heard me. Don't move! I'll send Berkley to take you to Devon."

Five minutes later another fist knocked at the door. "It's me," Berkley called out. Zarria was pissed, but figured everything would be okay. Unbeknownst to her, she was being watched from the bathroom ceiling.

Zarria opened the door wearing a frown. "What kinda games are y'all playin'," she asked following Berkley to a secluded room off the corridor. The fussing ended as soon as Berkley opened the door. Immediately, Devon focused on the rayon skirt that clung to Zarria's hips. He welcomed her in with a grin.

***

Back in the front, Officer Lacey stood at the visitor's desk with a crazed look on her face. She studied Carlie's I.D. over and over again. "So, Devon is expecting you," she said.

"Yes, he is." Although irritated, Carlie leaned slightly on the desk and waited patiently. She didn't understand what the problem was, or why Officer Lacey had to be radioed when she came in.

Lacey looked Carlie up and down. She scanned the loose fitting denim dress that she wore, wondering how many ounces of drugs she carried. In her opinion, Carlie didn't seem like the smuggling type, but figured there was no other reason she'd be there. Maybe Devon had forgotten to let them know that this was a part of the plan.

"Listen, I'm on his list and he's expecting me. What's the problem?" Carlie asked. She shot Lacey a look that was misinterpreted.

"Come this way," Lacey said. She didn't want to mess up and not get paid. The extra cash coming to her from Devon came in handy.

After making it through the gates, Carlie followed Lacey down the same path Zarria had taken twenty minutes earlier. She took lengthy steps trying to keep up with Lacey as they hurried down the same deserted hall. Carlie became skeptical after realizing this wasn't the same route that she normally took to the visiting room. Noticing Lacey's abrupt stop in front of a staff only restroom, Carlie's brow puckered.

"I don't need to use the restroom," she said firmly.

"Yeah, you do." *What a rookie*, Lacey thought.

"Take me to Devon. Or, maybe I should leave." Carlie stood in front of Lacey with her arms folded. Strangely, she wasn't intimidated.

Lacey huffed. She was more than irritated with the way things were going. She nodded for Carlie to follow her. "Somebody has some explaining to do," she said using her key to unlock the door several yards away. "Y'all can figure this mess out on your own."

The door squeaked when it opened, and Carlie's jaw dropped several inches. Her vision became blurred at the sight before her. She just knew she'd faint. Devon wasn't hers anymore, but never did she expect this. Devon sat posted in a chair, while an unidentified woman with her back to Carlie, rode him like a horse. Although his face was blocked by the woman, she recognized his legs that were visible several inches away from his pants that hung below his knees.

When Lacey cleared her throat, Devon peeked around the woman's body. Instantly, he released the grip he held on her ankles. Instead of slowing his stroke, he pulled out instantly, causing Zarria to turn around.

Devon pushed Zarria immediately. But before he could shove her completely from his lap, Carlie was deep in her face. With a handful of her hair locked tight in her grip, Carlie pulled Zarria's head in perfect range. The glob of spit landed precisely where Carlie intended. Zarria wiped her lips in disgust, but said nothing in retaliation.

"I knew it," Carlie said. "I knew it all along. I just didn't think you'd go this far." Carlie shot Devon a look that said '*don't say a word*'.

Little did she know, Devon had nothing to say. He gave Lacey an evil eye as he slowly bent to pull up his pants. He made sure to keep an eye on Carlie. Not clear about how she'd play things, he told Zarria to leave. Zarria retaliated in silence. She snatched the bag of cocaine in defense, and was sure not to make eye contact with Carlie.

"No, she doesn't need to leave," Carlie shouted. She moved her head back and forth and raised her voice even louder. "You two are made for each other." Carlie balled her fist and held them in the air. "Here I am thinking you needed some moral support, and you're in here screwing someone who used to be my girl!" She lunged at Devon as if she were going to hit him. Devon didn't move. He'd never seen Carlie like this before. It was a first, and he was starting to enjoy it. *At least she's fighting for her man*, he thought.

When Carlie looked over her shoulder ready to blast Zarria with another wicked look, Berkley entered the room with a worried glare on his face. "Devon, we need to figure some things out! Fast," he said.

Devon was so into Carlie that he ignored Berkley's words.

"Devon, whatever you've got going on here, count me out," she said pointing her finger. "I never should've considered coming here!"

"I think we should lower our voices," Berkley interrupted. He walked in Devon's direction with a hurried pace like he had something urgent to say.

"Lower our voices for what," Carlie shouted. "Everybody is on his fucking payroll!" Carlie shocked herself when she thought about what she'd said. She knew that she was now totally out of character. Walking around the small room like a mad woman she continued. "The problem is, I don't know why these people are catering to you." She looked at Lacey and Berkley. "He has no more money. Kirk and I took all of it!" Carlie watched Devon closely. She wanted to hurt him as much as she could. "That's right!" she said to Devon.

Devon raised from his seat in anger. His face began to change colors as Berkley laid a hand on his shoulder. "It's important," Berkley whispered.

Trouble was near, but Carlie didn't care. "I'm not scared of you anymore, Devon." She took several steps backward as Devon rushed her way. She stood still and closed her eyes ready for the blow. All at once, several investigators burst through the door. The loud noise caused Carlie to open her eyes. Instantly, the room was filled with close to twenty people. In the midst of it all, Carlie tried to make sense of everything. What was evident, were the handcuffs being put on Zarria.

"Keep the two of them here," the head investigator said. "I'm taking this one out."

"Why do I have to stay here?" Carlie asked.

Neither of the two officers remaining in the room had an

answer. The mood changed instantly. The once chaotic room was now silent. Devon rotated hitting one fist into the other. Thoughts of Rico's face were plastered in his mind. He had to make some money someway, somehow. His life depended on it!

Although Carlie had caught him with Zarria, he had to work things out. She was his last resort. Devon knew that many prisoners would jump at the opportunity to do him for $10,000; so he quickly concocted a plan. The idea was to apologize, sweet talk Carlie, and cry with her as they'd done together many times before, even if it had to be done in front of the two officers. He'd tell her he loved her, with hopes of hearing her say *I love you too.*

As Devon prepared to speak, he briefly thought about Zarria, who was now on her own. *Those are the risks you take*, he thought. *She's too disloyal to be on my team anyway. Look how she betrayed Carlie.*

"Carlie," he called out.

Carlie waited close by the door. She knew that as soon as it opened, she was out. Hearing Devon call her name caused her to scoot even closer and turn her back toward him.

"Carlie, I know you hear me baby," he said louder. "I'm so sorry for all the shit I did. I know I was an asshole, but le'me make it up to you." Carlie's faint sniffles had Devon going. He grinned slightly knowing this was how it always worked between them. All he could think about was making up with her. He knew it wouldn't be long before he convinced her to smuggle his drugs into the facility. At least he would be able to pay down his debt with Rico and live. Jail was already rough enough without having a contract on your head. "Don't you love me anymore," he said in a fake, heart-breaking tone.

Devon was devastated when the door opened. Not only was *his woman* leaving, but he watched Berkley approach him with investigators. "Carlie, I never meant to betray you," he yelled.

"Yeah, I'm sorry that I betrayed you too. Now I'm sure that I did the right thing when I snitched on you." She opened the door. "Oh, and I fucked Kirk too." Carlie was gone. *Gone for good.*

Devon folded his hands together, pretending that he wasn't having a panic attack. Instantly, he had thoughts of Rico with his arms around Carlie as they both grinned over his grave. He hoped that prayer would keep him alive.

Bruised

Chapter 34

Something in Common

Carlie opened the Louis Vutton luggage that lay on her bed. Each garment placed inside had been perfectly folded compliments of her Aunt Angela. With Angela's help, everything had been gathered and ironed the night before. Carlie had mixed feelings about leaving. A part of her wanted to stay under the reign of Ricky. She knew she'd be more focused on her career, and well taken care of. Another part of her grew excited about the opportunity to attend Harvard.

Harvard law school was well renown world wide, and Ricky's alma mater. Carlie busted her butt in the last semester to bring up her grades. She studied hard and stayed up many nights making up work. After all, getting into a top notch school wouldn't be easy. In the end, she graduated with a 3.0. It wasn't her best, or an impressive grade point average in the eyes of the Harvard board. However, between Ricky's huge donations to the school, and the recommendation letter received by high-profile attorney Marsha Vick, Carlie was accepted.

"You are moving way too slow," Angela said bursting into

the room. Your father will be ready shortly." She rushed to Carlie's side making sure she had maintained her army style folding. Carlie smiled at her aunt. *You gotta love her*, she thought.

Angela and Carlie grew close over the last few months. When Angela realized that her niece needed a mother figure in her life, she clung to her as much as she could. Although her intent wasn't to replace Carlie's biological mother, or Grandma Jean, Angela gave her all the love and guidance she could. Ricky was so thankful. He loved Carlie dearly, but couldn't fill that motherly void the way Angela did. Besides, Ricky's chances of snagging a step-mother for Carlie were slim.

Two weeks ago he got busted by Courtney Cox. He tried to play things off as Courtney shouted and banged obsceni-ties outside his front door. Ricky contemplated on going to the door, but decided against it after seeing the fright in Lisa's eyes. When Courtney shouted, "I'll be out here all damn night if need be," Ricky called the police and held Lisa tight-ly. For the first time in months, he slept like a baby. He knew Courtney had been following him for weeks, and really did-n't care. Ricky wanted a woman who he could respect and Lisa was that woman.

"Carlie, I've got a question for you," Angela said folding back the comforter. She sat on Carlie's bed baffled at her niece's expression. "You don't appear to be happy about going off to law school. Is there something wrong?" Angela asked in a concerned tone.

"I'm fine. It's just strange."

"What's strange?"

"The fact that I'm leaving the only family I have." Carlie

looked at Angela sadly.

"You'll be fine. And you know we'll be coming to Massachusetts to visit quite frequently," Angela said. "Brighten up. How many students do you know who go off to school, and their father opens a law firm for them to head in the same town?"

Carlie started to speak. "Well. ..."

"None," Angela ended.

"I don't even have a man," Carlie said half whining.

"Honey, let me let you in on a little secret." Angela crossed her legs and interacted with Carlie like long time girl-friends. "Don't be so pressed to get a man. Most that you come in contact with ain't worth a damn, 'cause all the good ones are taken and at home where they should be. And another thing," she said switching positions. "You are a woman of the 2000's. You're headed to law school and you don't need a man for shit." Angela grabbed Carlie by the shoulders. "Don't you remember what your Grandma Jean always said?"

"She said a lot." Carlie smiled slightly.

Angela chuckled before even getting her words out. "She'd say, *I don't need a man but for one thing, and now with those machines, I can do that my damn self.*"

Both ladies fell out laughing until Ricky walked into the room. "All set," he asked.

"Sure am," Carlie said.

"Just these three bags?"

"Yep."

Ricky grunted as he grabbed the bags. "You got a dead body in here?" he asked jokingly. Ricky spotted Carlie's cell phone on the dresser as he left the room. "Don't forget your phone," he yelled.

Carlie smiled. What Ricky didn't know was that she'd turned her phone off days ago. She wanted all possible connections to Devon cut off. Carlie closed the door to her room and followed Ricky and Angela down the stairs and out the front door. A funny feeling ignited inside. She turned back to glance at the house that held her memories. Water built up in her eyes, but did not fall. Carlie was a new woman, a woman of the new millennium. A woman who stood strong, and a child of the most high God. She strutted down the driveway toward Ricky who waited patiently in the silver convertible Benz. He ordered it just for Carlie as a graduation present. Ricky had plans on shipping the vehicle in the next few days, but for now he'd drive his daughter to the airport. By the time Carlie got a few days to settle in Massachusetts, the car would be arriving.

***

Fifty minutes later, Carlie and Ricky walked toward gate #16 at the Baltimore International Airport. Carlie dashed inside the restroom for a quick bathroom break before boarding. She marveled in the mirror momentarily at her new flattering hairstyle. She felt good about herself and her new life ahead.

Upon exiting the bathroom, Carlie was shocked at what she saw. She watched her father and Lisa Duckett engaged in a long and passionate kiss. Now Carlie knew that Ricky had hired Lisa to open the new office in Massachusetts. She also knew that the two had been seeing each other regularly. What she didn't know was that things had gotten serious enough for them to be slobbing each other down in the middle of the airport.

Lisa turned when she noticed Carlie watching. "Hello Carlie." She wrapped her arm around Ricky's waist. "I have a great surprise."

"What?" Carlie asked unbothered.

"Guess who's here?"

"Who?" Carlie had already been surprised by her father's teenage-like behavior. *What would be next?*

Lisa pointed over Carlie's shoulder. "A friend ," she said.

Carlie's mouth dropped. The brown-skinned brother with naturally curly hair stood at a distance. He held two carry-on bags and a boarding pass in hand. "What are you doing here?" Carlie asked.

"I wanted to surprise you," Kirk said.

"Well that you did. I've been calling you."

"I know. But I've had my folks checking on you." He looked slyly in Ricky's direction.

"I thought I'd never see you again."

"You thought wrong." He smiled.

"So, why are you here?" Carlie asked suspiciously. She hoped like crazy he'd say that he was boarding her flight and leaving with her. After all, Grandma Jean had told her one night in her dreams that some day she'd settle down and find herself a good man. *Kirk could definitely be that man*, she thought. But then again, Grandma Jean would say, "*that's just plain trashy.*"

Carlie smiled inside at the thought of her grandmother and felt good about her future. Even though she figured the chance of finding someone who really loved her was slim, she was satisfied.

"That's us," Kirk said at the sound of the first boarding call.

"Us?" Carlie questioned.

"Yeah, us. You wouldn't come with me, so now I'm going with you." He kissed Carlie on the cheek. "That's if you'll have me."

Carlie's heart melted. "Sure," she said.

Ricky handed Carlie an envelope diverting her attention off of Kirk. "Well, I'm not sure how or why this happened. But $200,000 has been wired to your account young lady." Ricky smiled. "Here's the receipt."

"We're now boarding first class customers for flight #7677," a stewardess said over the loud speaker.

"That's us," Lisa said signaling Kirk, and grabbing Carlie by the arm.

Ricky felt good inside. As he watched his favorite two girls head through the gate, he smiled. Noticeably, Kirk followed behind them as if he were a bodyguard protecting a celebrity. At that moment, Ricky knew in his heart that Kirk would take good care of his daughter. For the first time in years, he and Carlie had something in common. He was happy and Carlie was too.

Words from the Author

Greetings Readers,

I hope you enjoyed **Bruised**. Some people will say, "I used to be like that" or, "I know someone like that." However, the intent is to recognize that physical and mental abuse against women does exist and that it is not that easy to escape. This novel does not promote domestic violence at all, the purpose is to acknowledge that there is a problem. Although domestic violence deals with women of all descents, **Bruised** focuses particularly on the African American community.

Despite any circumstance or what you've seen in the past, a strong woman can rebound from an abusive relationship. Black women are naturally strong. Think of those you know who can work a full time job, raise several children, and still have time for her man. Think of woman who works six days a week, going from the corporate office to a part time job, and still sit in church on Sunday. Think of all the women you know who make everyday struggles look easy. It can be done. It's evident in the lives of females all across the country. If all of this can be done, why can't we get a better hold on domestic violence? We can! If you or someone that you know is in an abusive relationship, stop it now. Contact the following agencies for help: The National Violence Hotline @1-800-799-SAFE, The National Resource Center on Domestic Violence, www.pcadv.org, National Center on Domestic and Sexual Violence, www.ncdsv.org, or Institute on Domestic

Violence in the African American community, 1-877-643-8222.

As the author, I'd love to hear your comments about this book. Order an autographed copy from our website at www.lifechangingbooks.net. and post your comments on our guestbook. Tell others to pick up their own copy, not yours!

If you love Urban Fiction and have teenagers in your home, purchase a copy of Teenage Bluez for your teen. It's G rated and full of life lessons.

Life Changing Books Order Form

A Life to Remember	Double Life	New! Bruised by Azárel

 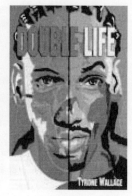 

Add $3.95 for shipping. Total of $18.95 per book. For orders being shipped directly to prisons Life Changing Books deducts 25%. <u>Cost are as follows,</u> $11.25 plus shipping for a total of $15.20.

Make money order payable to <u>Life Changing Books</u>. Only certified or government issued checks.

Send to:
Life Changing Books/Orders P.O. Box 423
Brandywine, MD 20613

Purchaser Information

Name _____

Register #_____
      (Applies if incarcerated)

Address_____

City_____

State/Zip_____

Which Books _____

# of books _____

Total enclosed $_____

Nvision Publishing Order Form

Don't Ever Wonder *the sequel to* BILG
Available June 28

Add $3.95 for shipping via U.S. Priority Mail. Total of $18.95 per book. For orders being shipped directly to prisons, Nvision Publishing deducts 25%. <u>Cost are as follows,</u> $11.25 plus shipping for a total of $15.20.

Make money order payable to <u>Nvision Publishing</u>. Only certified or government issued checks.

Send to:
Nvision Publishing/Order P.O. Box 274
Lanham Severn Road, Lanham, MD 20703

Purchaser Information

Name _____

Register #_____
       (Applies if incarcerated)

Address_____

City_____

State/Zip_____

Which Books _____

# of books _____

Total enclosed $_____